B'racha For a .38 Special
A Guide for the Perplexed

a novel by
Tanya Coovadia

BROKE DOWN PRESS
St. Petersburg, Florida

PUBLISHED BY BROKE DOWN PRESS

ISBN 978-0615779652

Acknowledgements

Many thanks to Hilary Flower, literary midwife, for careful reading, ongoing encouragement and gracious example. Many thanks to David Pinto, for excellent notes and steadfast suspension of disbelief. Thank you, Tracy Lee Bird, good friend, gifted writer and editor extraordinaire. Thanks, Dee Gill, for inspiring talks and judicious use of literary beer goggles. Thanks also, to my willing, indispensible readers Lois Buxbaum and dear friend Donna Westbrook. Thank you, John Bruce, for telling me I should. Thanks to Lee Irby, for having my back. Thank you, Adam Coovadia, for making sure I was fed and clothed throughout the process. And thank you, Jackie Cappiello, for everything else. You are *not* Bubbie. Everyone is.

B'racha / brah'-khah / n. *Hebrew.* The *b'racha*, or *berakhah*, is a Jewish blessing recited in Hebrew at prescribed moments in a ceremony, or as part of a daily activity such as the breaking of bread or washing of hands. The function of a *b'racha* is to acknowledge God as the source of all blessing.

"This day's black fate on more days doth depend:
This but begins the woe others must end."

Prologue

The sensation of his cheek gently burning in a pool of his own vomit was not unfamiliar to Aubrey. But the cat—calmly lapping at the half-digested remains of whatever the fuck he'd consumed in what must have been an unprecedented après-show rampage the night before—was a most incongruent element in his rise to awareness. A foot from Aubrey's bristled pallor, an equally bedraggled orange tabby regarded him with the demeanor of one reading the paper over breakfast on a rather slow news day. Aubrey closed his eyes and the cat disappeared.

He was hazily aware of his side pressing cold concrete, the quiet ache radiating from the ground like a plant taking root in his bones. The vivid images skipping across his mind were more immediate: The garden of the first house royalties bought, lushly overgrown for his benefit alone. A decrepit football he'd found as a child, its black and white hexagons fitting together in odd symmetry. A fast car, burning in slow motion. An elderly woman murmuring to her little dog, lifting her eyes to his, recognition twisting her face from sweetness to contempt.

His father's face, pulling into itself in the months leading up to his mother's death. A corpse on the floor of a seedy Balkan hotel; a lunatic of his passing acquaintance finally succumbing to habitual overdose.

The chorus of a trite, momentarily popular song rotated in the background of Aubrey's mind, relentless, pulsing with the agony of heartbeat in his temples. His fickle morning erection surged half-heartedly as memories of his first orgy flitted past.

Disparate memories of *her*: sunny, studious, orgasming.

Waves of pain rose and dissipated in sluggish retreat, surging in and out of his awareness, returning, subsiding. Nauseating, slow. To the same rhythm, a hospital room, softened by gauze, moved in and out of focus, then gently slipped away.

Superimposed on the images flitting behind Aubrey's eyes, the cat hunched itself against the backdrop of a quiet street, a busy city humming somewhere in the distance. Another anomaly: When the ruins of a tastefully appointed hotel room should have formed the backdrop of the headache thundering through the front of Aubrey's head. It seemed heavy-handed, his evening joie de vivre humbled by this degree of suffering.

Aubrey had waged this battle with reality many times before, and reality had each time emerged with him in tow. For now, he would continue to fight its pull. Groaning, he wrapped his arms around his aching head and allowed his consciousness to descend to the level of stupefaction at which he spent most of his mornings-after. The cat ran off

Chapter 1

On screen, there'd been nothing to indicate *Dini in the Evening!* was filmed in the tidy metropolis of Toronto. Salla imagined the designers had been aiming for the ambiance of an antebellum drawing room—Tara 2010, *sans* fourth wall and Confederate angst. Between the velvet settee, the curving desk and *Dini!* herself, the studio seemed intent on obscuring the tall, shining city outside its brocade facade.

Salla's presence in this improbable sitting room, on the tenth floor of a steel and glass skyscraper, was a consequence of years of scholarship on writings that originated in an ancient country six-thousand miles away. A county wedged between sea and desert and crumbling mountains as Toronto was, between Great Lake and subdivisions.

These juxtapositions didn't trouble Salla. She, herself, was an odd collection of opposing purposes and strengths, anachronisms and cutting edges, dried clay and molded steel.

She pulled her eyes from the gold and ivory rotary phone on Dini's desk just as the cameras began to lunge. A trio of one-eyed robots surrounded them like a firing squad. One turned its glassy stare on Dini and the floor director began the countdown.

"Five... four..." He signaled three, two, one, silently, and Salla gulped in a breath, staring into the eye that had fixed her in its sights.

"Hi, and welcome back to *Dini in the Evening!*" In person, the joy with which Dini delivered this line bordered on hysteria. It struck Salla as funny and disturbing in equal measure. "I'm joined tonight by Dr. Salla Kahn," Dini told the camera, sincerity squeezed through the wind in her voice and amplified out the tilt of her head, "...a Jewish Studies fellow at the University of Toronto. In light of the latest bombings in the West Bank, we thought we'd bring her in to talk about a rather controversial paper she published. In it, Dr. Kahn claims to prove that the Palestinian Israeli conflict violates Jewish Law."

Salla, watching Dini's intro, felt as though she'd fallen all the way through the looking glass, and was watching herself from the other side. Startled, she realized Dini had fallen silent and was motioning, with raised eyebrows, for her to speak.

"Oh! Yes. Thanks for having me on your show." Salla aimed for a conversational tone. She'd agreed to do this, and here she was, so she straightened her spine and smiled into Dini's eyes. "But please, call me Salla. Doctors heal the sick. I just scrutinize ancient texts in obsessive detail."

Dini's chuckle was as warm as a photograph of fire.

"Salla, then," she said. "Am I correct in saying you think Jewish law demands a peaceful solution to Israel's—ah—relationship—with the Palestinians?"

"Well, yes, that's *one* implication of my work. Although many would, and do, disagree. One thing I should make clear: I'm not yet a member of the rabbinate, so I don't have a formal voice in the debate."

"Yes. Well, please go on." Dini's gesture was that of an impatient traffic cop.

Salla paused, nonplussed. She was accustomed to making methodical arguments to an audience of nodding students. She drew a breath to push herself along.

"As part of my study of the *Mishnah*, I started exploring the doctrinal basis of the principle known as *Pikuach Nefesh*."

Dini nodded rapidly.

"So," Salla responded to Dini's impatience by talking faster, "there's been a lot of scholarly back and forth on the implications of *Pikuach Nefesh*. From the Hebrew, it translates roughly as 'The Saving of Human Life', and it states—more or less—that biblically mandated laws can and must be ignored, if necessary to save someone's life."

"Oh." Dini waited.

"Most Orthodox Jews consider Zionism a divine commandment, you see. Zionism meaning the movement to resettle the Jewish people in the holy land."

"Ah, yes," Dini gestured at Salla as though waving her more quickly to the point, "So Jewish law *supports* the conflict in Israel, no?"

"Well, in my reading, *Pikuach Nefesh* means you must disobey a commandment, when necessary, to protect human life."

Dini tilted her head. "You're saying, then, that a Jewish person *must* break Jewish law to protect Palestinians from the war they're having with each other?"

"Well, it's not quite that simple, sadly. The chief rabbinate of Israel ruled, in explicit terms, that *Pikuach Nefesh* describes *any* human life, Jewish or otherwise. It's based on a passage in the *Talmud* which reads 'Who says that your blood is redder? Maybe your neighbor's blood is redder.'" Salla hesitated.

"But that passage could also be interpreted to mean the life of a Jew, only. In which case, you could not break, for example, the laws of the Sabbath to save the life of a gentile."

"Laws of the Sabbath?" Dini prompted.

"So, driving on the Sabbath is prohibited, you see."

A skilled interviewer knows when to apply silence. Salla stared at Dini, and Dini, for what seemed an eternity, looked back, her eyebrows lifted, the corners of her mouth curled.

Salla took a breath and continued.

"On the Sabbath, they'd say, you must not drive a non-Jew to the hospital, even to save his life."

Dini sat, leaning forward, looking at Salla. She waited.

And thus goaded by silence, Salla uttered the words that she would immediately wish to retract.

"A Jew's blood is redder," She said.

Dini nodded, smiling.

"Very interesting. Well, thanks for joining us, Doctor Salla," she said, turning to the camera, "And that does it for us, folks—thanks for watching *Dini in the Evening!* We'll see you tomorrow, when we discuss the latest trend in hair color—and what it's doing to your kids!"

Salla, poised to quote an Orthodox Israeli paramedic who'd said the shade of one's blood was determined by oxygen content alone, sat forward in her chair, her mouth agape.

"A Jew's blood is redder" would be her last words on the subject.

As Salla sputtered and tried to explain, Dini reached over and squeezed her arm, waiting for the credits to finish rolling and the phones to start ringing. And the virtual Rube Goldberg machine—since antiquity the primary engine of human society—melted the ice that cocked the hammer that hit the nail that caught on the string of unintended consequences that would change the course of several lives.

5

Twenty-six people called the small local station that evening. Five callers stated unequivocally that Salla was correct, and that all Palestinians should be exterminated. Six were just as insistent that Salla was correct, and that Jews, and Judaism itself, were evil. Fourteen others said it was irresponsible to broach the subject of the Palestinian-Israeli conflict at all.

One called to notify Dini that God had commanded him to masturbate on his television.

Twenty-three composed emails that were variations on the sentiments above.

As the phones rang, a dozen people switched off their TVs as though nothing at all had happened. Three nodded off in their chairs at the reruns that followed. Seventeen people prepared a snack. One called his rabbi for clarification. Seven said a prayer for the world.

One elderly woman, sitting on a worn sofa, announced "that's my girl!" to her empty living room. She smiled at the credits scrolling up the screen of her late-model television.

A majestically bearded man, in the full dignity of his late middle age, turned down the sound, tucked his white prayer curls behind his ears, and sat at his desk to prepare a sermon on the dangers of hubris in women.

Two rapidly-aging men, with five piercings and forty tattoos between them, drank and argued about how it all fit into their opposing world views.

Three young men in a wood-paneled basement took turns yelling at the television and each other in angry camaraderie. They vowed to do something about it. And so they would.

Chapter 2

Blessed are You, LORD, our G-d,
King of the universe, Who has created the fruit of the vine.
~The Berakhah for Wine

Ian Al Habib, Aubrey's Bishop's friend, manager and general factotum scowled into his Guinness. The spider tattoo on the knuckle of his ring finger jumped as he tapped his glass. Aubrey, watching for this sign that his argument was getting under Ian's newfound certainty, smiled. He tipped back the last of his fourth scotch and motioned for another. Ian looked away from Aubrey's smirk, intent on keeping his voice a semitone down from shrill.

"Right, but that doggah on the telly *did* say Jews are better than Palestinians. Their blood is redder, yeah?" His voice was quiet with anger. He took a deep swallow of his beer. "Justified decades of Palestinian apartheid with that rot."

"But surely you see my point," Aubrey said, certain—they were both aware—of the sanctity of his every thought. "The thrust of *every* religious tome on the planet *is* that *your* ideas, *your* god, *you*—are superior to the other bloke. Muslims think Jews are godless heathens, and god knows—"

"Wait! That's not true then, is it? According to the Holy Qur'an—" Ignoring Aubrey's expression at the word "Holy", Ian dug in the messenger bag slung on the back of his bar stool. He glanced quickly around the pub before pushing reading glasses onto his face, and flipped open the leather case of his electronic Qur'an. A search for "Jews" and "Marriage" yielded several results right away.

Ian nodded. "Right then, here it is. Islam says all religions that read the same—'scripture' they call it here—are people of the book. It's just that we had Mohamed who wrote the final, correct version."

Ignoring Aubrey's sigh, Ian held the Qur'an at arm's length and read aloud.

"The food of those who were given the Scripture is lawful for you and your food is lawful for them.' Yeah? By that it means Christians and Jews. Who were given the scripture first."

At Aubrey's snort, Ian moved the Qur'an to his left hand and gave him a quick shove, harder then he'd meant to. Aubrey shoved him back to show no harm had been done. Ian found his place and read on.

"And here, too—'lawful in marriage are chaste women from among the believers and chaste women from among those *who were given the Scripture before you*'." Ian closed the book, nodding in satisfaction. "So there you are, mate. According to the *Holy* Qur'an, Jews—*and* Christians for that matter—are all people of the book. We're even allowed to marry them."

At this, Aubrey laughed, a gust of non-verbal sarcasm.

"Well isn't that brilliant! How generous—how magnanimous! Muslims, allowed to marry the dirty *Yahudi*[1]."

Ian, glaring, glanced once again around the bar. The other patrons, sporting a motley mix of tattoos and piercings and hair cut in irregular patterns, were now staring openly. Glances were traded. Elbows were nudged into ribs. A few moved closer to the pair, in hopes of overhearing what was certain to be a newsworthy exchange.

"Ah, sod off, then, Aubrey!" Ian hissed. "I told you, *Yahudi* is *not* derogatory." At Aubrey's expression, as often happened, his anger broke into a laugh.

"I know. Just *sounds* derogatory, eh?"

Aubrey chuckled, swallowed three more fingers of Glenlivet, and waved at the bartender again. She'd been watching him, ever ready with the bottle, and poured three and a half. He tipped his plaid fedora at her, admiring the contrasting purple and green stripes in her hair and the flock of swallows tattooed around her bared torso. Looking into her eyes, he captured her hand and smeared his lips across her wrist, breathing in the

---

[1]*Yahudi* / yah-hU'dE / n. *Arabic.* Jew.

metallic scent of her hand. She smiled.

"Later, yeah?" he said.

She smiled and nodded. "Sure, okay. I'm done around two."

Ian rolled his own eyes at this exchange, but straightened his back as Aubrey turned to him. Aubrey's eyes, bleary from the Scotch but self-righteous as ever, forced themselves onto his.

"It's just such a load of cack, though Ian. I can't believe you're buying into that Mohamed shite now, after all we've been through."

"Hold it there, mate." Ian stood. "Watch what you say about the Prophet. I won't stand for it. I mean it, Aubrey."

Aubrey stood as well, his face too close to Ian's. When he spoke, he did so quietly.

"What the fuck are *you* going to do, my little Mohamed lover? You should tell the all-powerful Allah to fight his own battles. Come on then—smite me now, motherfucker!"

Aubrey was shaking his fist at the ceiling and laughing when Ian's fist caught him right at the spot where his jaw met his neck.

Aubrey went down gracefully and bounced up just as quickly. His eyes were unfocused but his mouth was undeterred.

"Come on, you bleeding ruthless bastard! Come and get me!" Still directing his ire at the ceiling, Aubrey hardly seemed to notice as Ian tossed a one-hundred dollar bill on the bar, tucked his neck under Aubrey's arm, and half carried him out to the car.

Chapter 3

Salla Kahn placed her prayer book on the table and took her guitar from its stand. She played, on and on, until the calluses on her fingertips chafed. She stopped to perform a well-rehearsed series of finger stretching exercises, sighed, then picked up the guitar and played a half - hour more. When her hands had lost their accuracy, she placed the guitar carefully back on its stand and lay on her back on her crinkled couch.

Are you there, G-d? It's me, Salla

When she noticed herself praying like this, she felt silly. The dignity of formal prayer was in sharp contrast to her intimate, chatty tone, as though the *Sh'ma*[2] was directed at a greater, grander deity. In more reflective times, she worried she spoke to a made up G-d when she prayed like this, an idol she'd carved in her own, irreverent, temple. But she'd been making this sort of addendum to her formal prayers since she was twelve and the habit was too firmly implanted to break. Besides, it made her feel as though she was actually moving forward, while in the daily ritual of prayer it seemed she was merely keeping pace.

Are you there G-d? It's me, Salla. I wish... I want... I'm sorry to bother you. Never mind. Amen.

Salla knew from experience that it was useless to pray for things, for events, for people, as though they were prizes you couldn't win if you failed to enter the contest. But sometimes a vague longing in her made

---

[2] *Sh'ma* / shmah' / n. *Hebrew.* A reference to prayer, from the Hebrew words Shema Yisrael; literally, "Hear, O Israel."

her try.

Dear G-d. I don't want to be alone. I want to feel... I want... I want to do something. To... laugh.

Her head on the seat of her battered red couch, her long legs draped over its armrest, Salla covered her face with both palms and smoothed her eyebrows with her fingertips, trying to figure out what exactly she *was* wanting. A man? She knew no specific man whose presence made her want anything but to be left alone. A pursuit? She was engaged in the most important one of her life. An event? She'd already been given so many. What she wanted, probably, was to be involved in something important, something outside of her small world. Rabbinical school would be that for her. She just needed to be patient.

Thank you G-d. Amen.

She chuckled self-consciously, pushed herself off the couch and went to the front door to retrieve the morning paper.

The eye-watering aroma of whiskey and vomit slapped her face before her brain could process the information from her eyes. There on the concrete steps lay Aubrey Bishop, the man himself, curled up and clutching his head like a fetus with a migraine. Momentarily, Salla wondered if she'd conjured him from his own bed—wherever that might be—her obsessive practice of his difficult guitar piece having unwittingly triggered some musical spell that transferred its creator to the player's front porch.

Overwhelmed by this vision, the newspaper she'd meant to retrieve forgotten, Salla sat down hard beside him, wobbling at this new proximity to the odor.

There they stayed, for the better part of an hour, Salla rehearsing each exchange one might have on such an occasion, Aubrey fighting to stay as far below consciousness as consciously possible.

As astonished as she was by his presence, in time Salla's shock faded enough to allow her to pity him, this talented man whose audacity had been both the life and death of his career. Too young to be so careworn, too old to start fresh, Aubrey Bishop's life was a cautionary tale on sharing incendiary thoughts in a culturally popular way. He'd attracted the attention of the wrong kinds of fans and they'd devoured him.

By the time Salla had grown bored with her thoughts, Aubrey had begun to stir. Slowly, tenderly, he allowed himself to rise, crawling to a sitting position on the step next to her. He groaned.

"Hello," she said, all her carefully crafted conversational gambits tangled in her throat.

"Ugh," he replied.

So they continued to sit there, Salla opening and closing her mouth, Aubrey rubbing and re-rubbing his face as if to wipe away the hangover he found himself coated in.

"Is it true you're really Jewish? I mean, it's not that I don't believe it. I loved your song about how the desert doesn't care," Salla blurted, immediately aghast at the jumble of phrases that seemed to have fallen out of her mouth. She stared into his blue eyes which were clogged with bloody veins.

"What?" Aubrey felt like a hairball the size of his fist was wedged in his throat. He took in the lanky, plainly-dressed young woman sitting on the steps beside him. Her pale skin glowed against her dark hair. A quirky, shy smile played about her mouth. He was never at his best in the morning, but this morning, for this woman, he'd rouse himself.

"Jewish? Oh. I guess. Emphasis on the 'ish'. If whiskey and cocaine are Kosher, right?" He laughed, then winced and held his face in his hands.

"What are you doing here?" she said. "I mean, I was just playing your song! And…"

"Oh? Playing my song? Which one?" Aubrey squinted at Salla and smiled politely, as though she'd just introduced herself at a cocktail party.

"I'm trying to learn the solo in *How the West was Run*. It's so complicated! My fingers are practically bleeding, to tell the truth." Salla held up her callused fingers, and he took them in his hand, running his own fingers across their roughened tips. She suppressed a shudder.

"Oh, you mean *play*ing my song. You must be quite the guitarist— I'm not sure I could pull that one off myself right now."

"Oh, I didn't say I was playing it—I said I was trying." Salla gently pulled her fingers from his. "Not quite there yet!" She was breathless, and chagrined at the chirpy tone she'd adopted. She must sound positively asinine. Salla turned the spotlight back on Aubrey, where it belonged.

"So, how *did* you end up here?"

"Ah. Not sure, really." Aubrey spoke from behind his hands, which he'd placed over his face again. "Did I have a show nearby last night? I think... It's hard to remember. I must be on some kind of tour—"

"I'd assumed you were on tour, but what are you doing here," she pointed down, "on my step". No happier with this turn of the conversation, she gave herself a mental shove. "Not that I'm saying you should leave. Please, make yourself comfortable".

Aubrey laughed, and winced, then looked over at her. Salla laughed, too, relaxing into the incongruity of the moment.

"Well you look familiar, now. Have we met before?" He asked.

"Definitely not," she said. "I'm sure I would remember."

They smiled at each other, until Salla looked away.

"Ach." Aubrey finally decided. "I think I should call some people." He rummaged in his leather jacket, checked both of his socks and then, somewhat furtively—glancing sidelong at Salla—he stood and searched inside the front, then the back, of his pants. Sighing, he gave up. "Do you have a phone?"

"Yes." Salla said, too loudly, standing too quickly. "Please, come in Mr... Aubrey. I should have invited you sooner. Can I get you a cup of tea?"

He followed her inside, to a tiny apartment decorated fitfully with framed leaf pressings, bright, abstract oil paintings, and multi-hued glass bottles. It was scrupulously tidy, other than the books scattered everywhere, each one placed as though it had just been set down.

Salla gestured to a crackled, red leather couch, crowded against a wooden crate that served as a coffee table. Aubrey thanked her and sat, examining the corner of her apartment that served as a living room. Dominating the wall opposite the couch, a photograph of a stained glass window glowed in brilliant reds and greens and yellows and blues. At least seven feet tall, judging by the woman standing beside it, the perfectly circular piece leaned against floor-to-ceiling factory windows. It bore the image of a stylized tree, its canopy mirroring its root system, its branches loaded with varied, fantastical fruits and flowers. It burned in contrast to the matt grey of the surrounding factory walls.

Aubrey glanced at Salla in time to see a pensive frown disappear from her face as she turned her eyes from the photograph to him. Then she rose and retrieved a late-model cell phone from the top of another crate, this one serving as a bookshelf and side table.

As she turned to hand the phone to Aubrey, Salla caught him looking at her legs as her skirt whirled up around them. She smiled a tilting smile which he acknowledged with a shrug and a wink as he accepted the phone. He gazed bemusedly at the device in his shaking hand.

"Well, then, I'm not sure whom to call. Usually Ian handles all that. And my numbers are in my phone. Damn." Aubrey's voice was little more than a croak. He sat looking at Salla, defeated for a moment, then tilted his head, smiled, and sat forward.

"Please excuse me. I've been terribly remiss: Aubrey Bishop."

13

Standing, he reached his hand to Salla's.

"Oh. Yes, well. I'm Salla. Kahn. It's nice to meet you." After a single, perfunctory shake, Salla struggled to not wipe her hand on her skirt. His hand was sticky in a way that invited unpleasant speculation.

"I hope you know I'm not in the habit of this sort of…"Aubrey's gaze did not quite meet hers. He stopped and swept his eyes around the room. "Excuse me, but would you mind if I visited the loo?"

"Absolutely! Of course." Salla pointed across the living room. It wasn't difficult to find the amenities in her tiny apartment. She could see every inch of it from where she stood.

Aubrey squeezed himself between sink and toilet of the interesting woman's comically small bathroom and pulled the door closed. He washed his hands, rinsed his mouth and splashed his face, then assessed himself in the decaying mirror over the sink. He'd looked worse. Really, the ravages of alcohol had nothing on the effects of aging. He regarded the mottled skin of his neck. Yes, that *was* a wattle. It wasn't just the harsh light in his hotel suite, sadly. He hadn't realized that it would bother him, getting old, until it did. The tattoo on his arms were starting to looked as though they'd been printed on parchment. He sighed.

Opening the medicine cabinet, Aubrey smiled. The sparsity of its contents was almost a political statement. A generic bottle of Ibuprofen, a tube of toothpaste and a bottle of mouthwash: the absolute essentials, sir, nothing more. On the edge of a bathtub a razor, a sponge, soap and shampoo. Nothing more. It was obvious the lovely, yet scrupulously plain woman whose doorstep he'd landed on was disdainful of the usual embellishments. Perhaps she was some kind of religious nut. A shame. He was particularly drawn to long-limbed women with milk-fed skin and serious eyes. But he had no time for fools.

Either way, her medicine cabinet was not the place to root for hair products or recreational drugs. He molded his hair into some semblance of his usual style and squeezed his way back out the door.

As Aubrey busied himself in her "loo," Salla ducked quickly into her narrow kitchen, filled a kettle and placed it on her rickety stove, then busied herself tidying her already tidy apartment. Aubrey emerged several minutes later, less malodorous but still a pallid version of his glamorous public self. She saw his eyes fix on her ostensibly unassuming guitar, propped on a stand in the midst of a carefully arranged shrine in the corner of the living room.

"Wait, is that a Herman Hauser"? Aubrey approached the corner with awe. "It is! My God. What year?" In palatable reverence, he left the guitar in its place, kneeling to peer in the sound hole. "I can't believe it. 1938. And it's signed! Incredible. Are you a classical player, then?"

Salla laughed. "Well, sometimes, but nothing in the spirit of that guitar. You know, mostly Aubrey Bishop tunes." They laughed, Aubrey perhaps a trifle nervously. Salla's smile crept further up her right cheek.

"Kidding!" She laughed. "Let's see. I play quite a few Israeli folk songs... some Neil Young, of course—I *am* Canadian. Um. A lot of Nirvana tunes move really well on a classical guitar. I worked out an interesting riff for 'Come as You Are' on it." She shrugged self-consciously as she traced the guitar's headstock with her fingers. "I'm sure Segovia would consider my treatment of it a special kind of sacrilege."

"I'm sure he'd be impressed with your ingenuity," Aubrey said. He waved his hands at the guitar, yearning but reluctant to touch it.

Salla took it from the plain metal stand and offered it to him.

"Go ahead. It's meant to be played."

"Oh, no. I can't really. Not like this." He looked down at his spattered jeans, pulled at the sleeves of his leather jacket. "God knows what I'd get on it. Why don't you play me something? You said you were working on *How the West Was Run*? Go on, then. Maybe I could give you a bit of a lesson, yeah?"

"Well, yes, I suppose."

He sat back on the couch and watched her place the guitar strap over her well-formed shoulder. Eyes down, she picked out the opening notes, approaching the song in a leisurely way that Aubrey had never tried. In a husky, sweet soprano, she sang each word shyly, her leisurely tempo changing the song from rock anthem to blues lament.

Aubrey joined in at the chorus, having found a new harmony in this unusual take on his old song. They sang it to the end, which Salla played with a flourish of Spanish strumming. They laughed, as though they'd laughed together for years. Then silence. Salla shrugged, and put the guitar back on its stand.

"Well, that certainly worked," Aubrey said. "Thanks for teaching me my song."

"I didn't mean to change it." Salla turned to look at him. "But I had to slow it down for my voice to make sense of it."

"I'm thrilled you did. It's always flattering when a serious musician takes your work to a new level. Thank you."

15

Salla looked at his face, then looked down, as if to hide her crooked smile. Aubrey was charmed.

"The Hauser's an incredible instrument, though—probably worth as much as my car," he said. "Where on earth did you get it?"

She looked up, searching for something in his eyes.

"It was my father's," she said. "He told me he'd stumbled across it in some antiques stall at Kensington Market. He always said it cost him a fortune—probably a fraction of what it's worth today. It was something he treasured." Her tone was oddly neutral.

"Wait. I'm sorry?" Aubrey stared at her, a vein in his temple pulsing. "Did you say Kensington Market? What city is this, please?"

"City? Oh! Um. Toronto. You know, Ontario."

"Toronto! Canada." Aubrey cogitated on this information, the methodical firing of his synapses all but audible. "Oh my God… now I remember. Oh God. Oh shit! What was his name? What was his name?" He held his temples, as if to squeeze the information loose. "Oh. Shit. Shit. Jerry…Jerry... Jerry... Shit!"

"Jerry? I'm sorry. What are you talking about?"

"I'm not here on tour at all! I came to act in a film!"

"I'm sorry?" A dim memory was surfacing in Salla.

"I'm hammering the last nails in the coffin of my putrefying career. As I speak. Fuck me."

"Um," Salla prompted.

"We're supposed to be filming, right now. They're shooting my death scene. Without me! Shit. Jerry... Jerry... Jerry Something. Ugh. I've got to call him."

"Oh. I *had* heard something about you doing a movie, come to think of it. Did you want me to—?"

"Yes, please—call the studio. That's where Jerry would be. It's called something with an R. Or an S. Maybe R.S. Studio something. Jerry Something's an important type, there."

"Absolutely, I'm on it." Salla slid across the room to her laptop.

"Brilliant." Aubrey slumped back on her couch. "I'm glad someone is."

Twenty minutes later, hands still shaking, smelling faintly of vomit, soured Scotch and what may have been tomcat spray, Aubrey crawled into the back seat of a dented black Cadillac Escalade. Waving weakly at Salla on her porch, he was driven off.

She watched him leave, feeling inexplicably wistful. The vehicle stopped, the window crawled down, and Aubrey Bishop's head appeared.

He smiled and waved, then disappeared inside the car once more. She held up a hand and froze, wondering what she could do to make him stay, and, also, why she would want him to. The window rose, and the car drove away.

Ten minutes later, Salla was immersed in a quickly improvised *mikvah*[3]. While she was reluctant to consult the Rabbi on the finer points in this particular instance, she was certain some form of ritual purification was called for. So she filled her rust-tinged tub close to the brim and climbed in, lying on her back, her long legs drawn up in a lotus position to keep every part of her submerged. As she stared upward through the skin of the water, bubbles rising from the hair swimming languidly around her face, she said a prayer and tried to think of anything but Aubrey. She couldn't.

---

[3] *mikvah* / mik'-vey / n. *Hebrew*. A purification ritual requiring full immersion in water obtained from natural sources.

Chapter 4

*R. Hisda said: "The soul of a man mourns for him
the first seven days after his death.
That is based upon an analogy of expression; viz.:
It is written [Genesis l. 10]: 'And he made for his father a
mourning of seven days'; and the verse in Job previously quoted
also contains the word 'mourn,' hence the analogy."*
~ The Babylonian Talmud,
Book 1: Tract Sabbath

When Aubrey appeared at the abandoned hangar where they were
staging the shoot, the crew leapt to their feet as if released from
suspended animation. He felt a familiar surge of guilt.

Jerry Edwards—writer, producer, editor, light designer, occasional
camera operator and his own best boy for "This Night, Mine"—ran
toward Aubrey, recoiling when he got close. The arm he'd been ready to
throw across Aubrey's shoulders was retracted, mid-air. Instead, he
pulled his reading glasses from the top of his head and pushed them over
his nose, the better to examine Aubrey's haggard face.

"You look awesome," Jerry said. "What's with the rancid cologne?"

Chuckling politely, not ready with an answer, Aubrey allowed Jerry
to grab him gingerly by the sleeve and march him to the set, bypassing
the makeup artist.

"Well, man," Jerry said, "I'm glad you came in costume. Looks like
you've been living in it a few weeks, though, eh?" If he was angry with

Aubrey, he wasn't saying so, but he wasn't as jovial as he'd been in the past.

When Aubrey had first heard of the script for "This Night, Mine," he'd been unimpressed. All accounts, however positive, gave the impression it was a campy horror flick, a blackly comedic interpretation of a macabre Dr. Doolittle. This turned out to be close to the truth, but when he had the script in hand he found that the writing achieved a poignancy—on themes such as bestiality and cannibalism—that spoke to Aubrey on a level he himself had never plumbed. As he'd read the script, his excitement grew. It seemed he'd accidentally found something worth doing for the first time in a decade. By the time he'd reached the oddly moving ending, he would have taken the part for free.

Surprising himself, as well as everyone who knew him—a man of considerable notoriety who'd made a very public journey to his forties never betraying a hint of guile—Aubrey was a very good actor. Memorizing lines, delivering each phrase as though it originated in his own mind, immersing himself in the improbable character, inhabiting the same plane as the other, equally improbable characters; these abilities seemed like muscles he'd simply never flexed. Once flexed, he marveled at their strength. He was, he noted, very good at professional make-believe.

Jerry kept his own excitement in check as he watched the dailies from Aubrey's scenes, enjoying the dawning realization on the faces of his crew. Courting Bishop had been a difficult and expensive process. It had also been risky. While the movie's success did not ride on Bishop's acting ability, the reputations of everyone involved did. None of them were in this for the money; they were here because they'd read the script and they believed in Jerry. As for Bishop's infamy, well, he *was* playing a monster. It couldn't have been more fitting.

"Places!" Jerry yelled, projecting his voice across the cavernous room. "Let's get this together, now!" The other actors positioned themselves around a dinner table. They were filming the movie out of chronological sequence, and this was to be the ending. The scene was a last supper, of sorts. For supper was none other than the infamous Aubrey Bishop.

Aubrey climbed onto the table, festooned with black flowers and rotting fruits, and arranged himself as the centerpiece. He closed his eyes and played dead.

After shooting his scene in a set of long takes, most of which he slept through, Aubrey returned to his hotel, still weak from whatever had led to his morning on Salla's porch. The cast had repeatedly referred his to his "method" approach to the role, and he was pondering the meaning of this redundancy when he heard Ian's call. Bounding across the opulent lobby on a course to intercept him, Ian was like a child reunited with a missing pet.

"Oi! Aubrey. There you are—there you are, mate!" Ian jumped at Aubrey and threw an arm around him.

"*Salaam Aleichem* to you, too, you crazy bastard." Aubrey stood with his arms at his sides. He wasn't in the mood to entertain Ian's innocent approach.

"Ach, do you have to use blasphemy, for God's sake? Look mate, I'm really sorry. I couldn't remember where I'd dropped you last night. I spent the day freaking out, didn't I?" Ian's eyes, enormous and bloodshot, supported this.

Aubrey was having none of it. "Right. No wonder I'm such a balls-up. I rely on you to keep me together and you're at an absolute loss when it comes to such challenging tasks as chewing your own food. Not to mention you just toss me out of the car when you've decided to win a round."

Ian continued to hug him, vigorously clapping his back, releasing him when the embrace began to feel more like affection than a greeting. He put his hands on Aubrey's shoulders.

"Stupid cunt." He smiled at Aubrey, his face inches away.

"Fucking arsehole!" Aubrey pulled himself away. "The last thing I remember was your cell phone bouncing off the side of my head. What in hell were you thinking, mate?"

"Aw, come *on*, Aubrey. You were a ruddy blighter last night. Right back to your old preachy two-shoes, you were. I guess I thought a talking to from that Rabbi lady was in order, yeah? " It was obvious that, while Ian may have been worried about misplacing his employer, he was unrepentant.

"Brilliant. What Rabbi lady?" Aubrey knew this could mean any one of a dozen combinations to Ian, none of which would have been apparent to anyone else.

"You remember, Salla Kahn, sounds like Chaka Khan? That preachy Jew lady from telly, last night, yeah? She's listed in Google—address and all." Ian shook his head in distaste. "These people live in the dark ages. Anyway, after listening to her going off about how Jews are better than us lot, I figured you needed a dose of her yourself. Yanking on me about

Islam all the time."

"So that's why I thought I'd seen her before. She looks very different on television. But what are you talking about, Jews are better? She said nothing of the sort. She was talking about blood types or some such." Aubrey looked off into the distance. Ian turned his head to follow Aubrey's eyes, and frowned.

"Whatever, Aubrey. You're always being led around by the bell end. I didn't expect you to give a toss, but that's all right."

"So, what do you know about the little Rabbi, anyway? She seemed a bit of alright, to me." Aubrey's memory worked only sporadically, but unusual women reserved a special place in his mind. He smiled, musing. "She's actually quite the fit one, in a Canadian Mother Theresa way."

"Oh fuck off, then—listen to you. She's a complete Doris and you're still up for a shag." Ian's laugh was like the crust on old snow.

"She's not flashy, like those silicone-based life forms you gawk at, but she's got amazing legs. Any idiot can see she's a stunner. She plays, too—did you know that? Classical, flamenco—serious chops. And her voice has incredible tone—like Pink raised on the Delta Blues."

"Go on then Aubrey—listen to yourself jabber. You've turned into a schoolboy over some Jew lady."

"You know, you'd quite like her if you gave her a chance. Dresses like a granny, but she's quite funny, really. She had me laughing right over my own pounding head."

"Yeah, right. You'd laugh at your own shite if it talked back to you."

"I have no idea what that means." Aubrey paused, waiting for Ian to look at him. "She's obviously an expert on world religions, though. I bet she knows more about Mohamed than you, Haji-man."

"Ach, would you just shut up now, Aubrey? You're starting to dodder." Ian's anger showed itself only in the way his shoulders stiffened. Others would have missed it. Aubrey ignored it.

"I'm sorry old son, but it's just the truth. Anyway, you do see the irony in you accusing someone else of being preachy, yeah?"

"Sod *off* now, Aubrey. I'll bloody drop you off on her doorstep right this minute if you like—I won't wait until you're too blotto to know better."

Aubrey laughed. It was likely he *had* been insufferable last night. Blind faith drove him absolutely round the bend, and Ian's recent conversion to Islam was particularly galling. Aubrey was more zealous in his atheism than most believers were in their religions. He'd only gotten worse over the last ten years. And when he got into his cups, well, all restraints were off. Still, he couldn't allow an incident like this to be repeated. He caught Ian by the arm, squeezed it for emphasis.

"Listen Ian, a joke's one thing, but this was different. What if one of my rabid fans had found me? It's not like you never get an address wrong, yeah?"

"What, are you having me on? You're forgetting this is Toronto. Safe as kittens, yeah? Not like those knob jockeys in Japan." They laughed together; Aubrey, they were both aware, with some embarrassment.

Years before, Ian had deposited him at a Buddhist monastery in Kyoto, Japan, in much the same manner. When Aubrey awoke the next day, he'd found he'd been bathed and changed into a simple grey robe, he was startled to find he wore nothing beneath. He jumped at the sight of a slim young acolyte standing at the doorway. The small monk, his face delicate to the point of prettiness, was dressed in a robe identical to the one Aubrey wore. He spoke in soft Japanese accompanied by hand gestures that suggested an offering of either sexual services or breakfast; Aubrey's grasp of Japanese wasn't sufficient to determine which. He didn't stay to figure it out. Ian caught up with Aubrey hours later, wandering the grounds of the monastery, barefoot, compulsively clasping the thin robe to himself.

They both smiled, remembering. This story never failed to entertain them.

"I never did get my boots back, either, mate. Tony Lamas, they were," Aubrey said. "Cost me a thousand pounds, that little escapade of yours."

Ian nodded, chuckling. "But it wasn't me having the little escapade now, was it?"

Aubrey laughed heartily. Ian was the only one he could expect to hear the truth from, however distorted the delivery. While millions of people were fascinated by Aubrey, Ian knew him in every way that seemed to matter, more than anyone ever would again.

As far as Ian could tell, fame had not changed one iota of Aubrey Bishop, himself. He'd always been loud, opinionated, and loquacious. Fame had, however, distorted the lens through which people saw him. Total strangers treated Aubrey with either a contempt or a reverence he had done nothing, as far as he could remember, to earn. Almost every person he'd met over the last two decades assumed they knew all there was to know about Aubrey Bishop, and in his every word, his every act, they saw confirmation of their beliefs. It was lonely and pointless to continually explain who he truly was, and, after a while, he'd stopped trying. But Ian had always been there, it seemed, treating Aubrey with the same mixture of admiration and irritation that he always had.

With Ian, he'd already been himself for a decade before the fame occurred, and he simply continued to be.

To Ian, Aubrey offered meaning and means, and the kind of vicarious joy gleaned from proximity to fame without its suffocation. He'd been Aubrey's guitar tech for two years before Aubrey's band, the BishoPrics, could afford to hire a professional. At that time, he'd taken over as Aubrey's assistant and became the reluctant yet ready enabler of Aubrey's habitual self-medication for lifelong angst.

And, ostensibly, angst was something Aubrey had in abundance. He and the BishoPrics had gained notoriety over a decade ago with their concept album *Your God's a Prick*, a collection of songs featuring caustic observations on organized religion. It was intended, in Aubrey's oft-reported words, to "take the piss out of the ones who've been pissing on everyone else."

In its day, *Your God's a Prick* prompted everyone from the Anti-Defamation League to the Supreme Leaders of Iran to call for boycott of the band. Within a week of its release, Baptists held ritual burnings, Shias declared fahtwas; even a few Buddhist monks waded in, taking umbrage to a song entitled *Saving Siddhārtha the Trouble*. To the shock of everyone who had ever had anything to do with Buddhism, Aubrey had the hitherto unimaginable temerity to suggest that the Supreme Buddha was a "self-righteous bore" who had "wasted his life / in suspended suicide" and directed his followers to do the same.

Catholicism took a lot of hits, with everything from the Spanish Inquisition—"get behind me, Satan / I keep my cat o' nines in front"—to the Holocaust "look the other way / look the other way / don't jump into the fray / until the victors walk away"—to a jig about pedophilic priests, lusting after Mary's eternal virginity.

While Judaism remained relatively unscathed—more astute critics said Aubrey didn't know enough about it to pen a meaningful critique—*Your God's a Prick* was considered especially antagonistic to Israel. His songs about Israel, according to the punditry, were the most egregious assaults since the Yom Kippur war, when a coalition of Arab states had launched its surprise attack on the holiest day of the Jewish calendar. Titles like *Fascists in Prayer Curls* got millions of backs up, while *Kicking the Fuhrer's Dog*—which suggested Israel was punishing Palestine for Hitler's sins—confirmed Aubrey as a new kind of Holocaust denier in the minds of many. And the title *Kill the Jew*—an angry, neo-punk piece written from the perspective of a suicide bomber—served to alienate both sides of the Israeli-Palestinian conflict.

While initially the BishoPrics' fan base loved the furor—merchandise sales were unprecedented—for several years after no large venue in any major city would risk the blowback that would result from allowing the band to play. Over time, language ratings kept most of the songs off the radio, and the ready availability of the BishoPrics' catalogue on file-sharing sites kept their media sales down. The band's revenues shrunk to a thin trickle that barely covered their bar tabs.

Although the furor died down—the more incendiary lyrics, in a more incendiary age, were relatively less fiery—the effects were permanent. None of the few record companies still afloat in the wake of the peer-to-peer tsunami that destroyed their revenue model would touch the BishoPrics or Aubrey. The other members of the band, estranged before the record had dropped, took turns publically condemning Aubrey for abusing his platform.

The BishoPrics had brought him perhaps eight-million pounds over the course of Aubrey's career. He'd squandered most of that on great parties and bad investments. Living off the remaining proceeds from the sale of an estate in France, he was thinking of selling his share in the BishoPrics catalogue to the highest bidder just to hold on to his last remaining residence, a small London brownstone. His compensation for the role in "This Night, Mine"—unless it was a massive hit—would barely cover his taxes on the property.

This state of affairs, however, made barely a ripple on the glassy surface of Aubrey's habitual equanimity. A bon-vivant of the old school, he simply didn't see—and wouldn't have been greatly concerned by—the fact that his life made him profoundly unhappy.

"C'mon, let's go then," Aubrey said, giving Ian a shove. "I'm going to shower and change and then we will hit the town with some prime totty I snatched up on the set."

"Right oh, mate." Ian's tone was subdued. "Though I don't expect we'll be welcome back at the Kings Arms right away."

Aubrey turned to stare at Ian. "Oh. So, what hijinks did you get up to whilst I enjoyed my punishment?" His tone wasn't as casual as his words.

"Went right back to the pub, then, I did. Worked up a little argy-bargy with that mong who called me a fascist. Fuckin' cunt for a brain!"

"Argy-bargy, was it?" This wasn't a question. Aubrey's face was grim. He remembered the 'mong' in question. The kid's primary offense had seemed his assumption that Ian would return his romantic advances.

"What exactly did this 'argy-bargy' entail? Did the poor bloke leave on his own legs?"

"Yeah, mate. I'm not a complete div. His friends pulled me off him before I broke anything important."

Aubrey shook his head, then caught Ian's eye and held it. "Ian, you've got to stop with the fists, yeah? Or it's back to the anger management for you. They have no tolerance for punch-ups, here. They'll send you to jail for something like that. And when—*if*—they let you go, it's straight back to dear *old blighty*[4] for you. You want to spend the winter in London, yeah?"

"What? Of course I do. Anyway, it would have been worth it. You should have seen the look on that poof's face as my fist was coming toward it." Ian punched his hand, laughing, then paused and looked at Aubrey. "Why take his side, though? You're supposed to be *my* mate."

"Yeah, well if I'd been there, it would have been *me* pulling you off him."

"But not before he jimmied himself." Ian was smirking.

"Jimmied himself? Really?"

"Yeah, mate. Mong piddled his kecks out of sheer terror—inspired by yours truly! Facking little ponce—see how many fascists he greets after that, right?"

"You're telling me you hurt that poor sot so much that he urinated on himself?"

"So I did, old boy. So I did." Ian's smile was defiant.

"What could you have been thinking! Are you completely barking? Fuck, Ian. Fuck! Did you think I was running out of people to hate me?"

Ian ducked his head, glaring sidelong at Aubrey.

"Why the fuck is everything always about you, Aubrey?" he said quietly. "Fucking princess."

"Ian, Ian." Aubrey sighed, and put his hands on Ian's shoulders. "So he was prattling on a bit. Poor bastard." Aubrey's eyes were sad. "He couldn't have been older than twenty. You said a stupid thing or two in your twenties, yeah? No need to leap right to bodily harm and public humiliation just because he's at the age to challenge authority."

Ian was, finally, subdued. It had never occurred to him that he might have been mistaken for someone in authority. "All right. I suppose I'll keep it in check, next time."

"Brilliant." Aubrey sighed. "Right then."

---

[4] *old Blighty* / old bly-tee / *English*. British slang for the city of London.

They cast their eyes around the over-decorated lobby, searching for something other than each other to rest them on. Aubrey cleared his throat.

"Well then. I'm off. I need a shower and my bed."

Ian watched Aubrey's back as he strode off.

"Hey—what about our little outing to the pub?" Ian's voice filled the lobby. Aubrey, at the elevator, pressed the button.

"Just have them send a bottle to my room. And ring up those girls from last week—the ones who wore matching dresses to that party? Have them drop by in about three hours."

"So I guess we're to stay in tonight?"

"Do as you will—I'm staying in. Perhaps you'll find some twelve-year old to beat the piss out of."

"Yeah, well fuck you, anyway," Ian said quietly.

"I heard that." Aubrey entered the elevator. The doors closed between them.

Chapter 5

*Honor your father and your mother, as the
LORD your God has commanded you,
so that you may live long and that it may
go well with you in the land the
LORD your God is giving you.*
~Deuteronomy 5:16
The Holy Bible

Salla closed her laptop on *iFrumish.com* and leaned back in her
battered desk chair. Touted as "The Dating Service of Choice for Modern
Orthodox Machmirs" and "the place for Orthodox Jewish Singles to find
their basherts," iFrumish stocked thousands of thoroughly vetted
potential mates. And yet Salla sighed. Today, none of her erstwhile
perfect matches measured up to one morbidly alcoholic Englishman with
a rich, three-octave range and a penchant for alienating three quarters of
the known world.

She was bursting to relive the experience of her morning, so she did
the one thing that never failed to complicate matters: She made the short
walk to her Bubbie Adira's house.

Sitting at her grandmother's chipped Formica table, Salla watched as
Bubbie bustled angrily about her tidy kitchen, preparing the mandatory
snack tradition dictated she force on Salla. Bubbie delivered the
lecture—one Salla should have been expecting—at a volume sufficient
to drown out the ever-present background of Fox news on the living

room TV.

"Ach, I can't believe you allowed yourself to speak to that *mishuginauggener*[5] bastard! Him and his *fercockt*[6] music. Do you cozy up to every anti-Semite you meet, or do they have to be world famous first?" Bubbie threw some crackers to the plate of cheese she'd placed on the worn countertop, and turned to the sink to wash a cluster of green grapes.

"Bubbie! Stop that. Aubrey Bishop is *not* an anti-Semite. I assume he's not terribly fond of Israel's domestic policies, but he seems to be a decent person. I think he might even be Jewish."

At Bubbie's dark look, Salla went for broke. "Besides, I'm not even hungry!"

"*A chorbn*[7] Salla! What am I to do with you? Have you forgotten that evil song he wrote? What was it? Oh yes! '*Kill the Jew*'! Kill the Jew, for God's sake! Salla! What in the world are you thinking? And you need to eat! You're as thin as a toothpick."

"Bubbie, Bubbie." Salla took a deep breath. "That song wasn't meant to incite anti-Semitic violence." Her tone was calm, but inside she was wincing with chagrin. She'd forgotten that Aubrey Bishop's notoriety had worked its way into such remote corners of the world as Bubbie's bridge club.

"In fact, if you'd listened to the words, you'd know it was actually a lament on the Israeli-Palestinian conflict. He called it a blood feud between brothers with different names for God."

"Brothers! And you don't think that's ridiculous!" Bubbie shook her head once, then again, as though shaking away the thought itself.

"It isn't, Bubbie. I think it's rather insightful, myself. They have both experienced a Diaspora, in their own way. They both have lived through persecution."

"That's outrageous. Diaspora!—the Palestinians abandoned Israel so the Arabs could finish us off without harming their own. How is that the same as being driven from your home?" Bubbie was not to be deflected. "Anyway, I don't know how you could stand to be in his company, even. What's your next plan? Have me sit *shiva*[8] while you two run off to push Israel into the sea?" Bubbie placed the cluster of grapes she'd washed on the plate.

---

[5] *mishugina* / me-shug'gen-ner / adj. *Yiddish*. Crazy; senseless. n. One who is crazy.

[6] *fercockt* / fer-cokt' / adj. *Yiddish*. All screwed up. *Vulgar*.

[7] *a chorbn* / a-'khor-bin /phrase. *Yiddish*. "What a disaster!"

[8] *shiva* / shiv'-ah / n. *Hebrew*. A ritualized grieving, observed after the death of a loved one.

Salla took a deep breath but Bubbie wasn't finished. Taking a deep breath of her own she continued, steel in her voice, "I know what you're thinking—you think I can't see right through that big glass head of yours? You're thinking I see danger behind every rock! That it's my imagination the temple has to hire security guards because the Rabbi's gotten another death threat. That the Palestinian cancer is just an ugly little mole. You, my little *Bubbeleh*[9], don't see hatred when it's actually there. Never forget, my darling: Innocence in a woman isn't endearing. It's endangering."

Pleased with this turn of phrase, Bubbie nodded and handed the plate of grapes and cheese to Salla. Salla took the plate from her and set it down, where it would remain untouched until after Salla left, when Bubbie would return the crackers to the bag, sealing it shut with an old clothes pin, and return the grapes and cheese to the fridge.

Salla shook her head. "Bubbie! Surely you know I'm not naive. I just prefer to give people the benefit of the doubt. That never hurt Daddy, did it? Remember? He used to say that he always looked for the best in people and he never failed to find it?"

"Yes, well, he'd been lucky. That's all I'll say." Bubbie knew she had to step back now. Salla was only just arriving at the point where she could even talk about her beloved father—may he rest in peace—in a happy voice. After they'd buried the esteemed Rabbi Yosef Avi Kahn, Salla had observed *shiva*, the week-long ritual mourning period required in Judaism, a full three months. Today, ten years later, it seemed her grief was not yet fully slaked. Adira, while she had loved her son-in-law, did not feel the adoration for the man that everyone else who encountered him had seemed to share. For one, she knew more about his politics than most. Very few in his congregation would have approved of his giving money to organizations serving impoverished Palestinians. The older people would have considered it nothing less than an act of terrorism.

"Well, regardless, I can assure you that Aubrey Bishop doesn't have a truly hateful bone in his body," Salla said, locking eyes with her grandmother.

"Who do you mean Salla? They call him 'Mel-with-a-Gibson' for God's sake! Of course he's hateful. How could you not know? He made a whole record that was hateful."

---

[9] *bubbeleh* / bU' beh-lah / n. *Yiddish*. Literally, "little grandmother." A term of endearment for women of any age.

"It wasn't hateful, Bubbie, and it isn't as if you're up on your indie rock lyrics. If you knew the words—other than the three reported in the tabloids—you'd know that. He was singing about all the bad things religion has wrought. He wasn't even saying that religion, itself, is evil." Although Salla did assume Aubrey believed religion itself was evil, she didn't feel the need to share her every assumption with Bubbie.

"Actually," Salla added quietly, "his quarrel with Israel is similar to mine."

Bubbie was shocked into silence. For a moment.

"Aach! I'll never understand you, Salla! Sometimes I think you're trying to drive me right up a wall! I can't believe it: How can you, a Talmudic scholar, be against Israel? I get so angry at you when you talk like that."

"Bubbie. I am not—I repeat, *not*—against Israel. I just think its policies are bad for the Palestinians, bad for the Middle East and—most especially—bad for Jews. What I don't understand is why you continue to support a Jewish state when you don't even *go* to temple. I mean, most days you don't actually seem to believe."

"Wait one minute! I never said what I do or don't believe. Whether I go to temple on Yom Kippur or not, I'll always be a Jew, no matter what those Orthodox think. Which reminds me: Do you think you are bettering yourself, spending all your time at that Orthodox temple? Those people must live in the Dark Ages, with their *mishegoss*[10]."

"As a matter of fact, I *am* bettering myself. Bubbie, you know how committed I am to *halaka*[11]."

Bubbie shook her head, disapproval pinching her mouth. "Oh you're committed—no lie. Those people will never accept you, you know."

"They're the most observant group in the city. I'm there to learn. They have a lot to teach." Salla steeled herself. In this particular argument, her own ambivalence gave Bubbie the upper hand.

"Yes, well I don't know what you think they're observing. Women shouldn't go up on the *bihmah*[12]?—it's craziness. Do they think women are too weak to pray? And women can't form a *minyan*[13]? Why do you

---

[10] *mishegoss* / mish'-ah-goss / n. *Yiddish*. Crazy or senseless activity or behavior; craziness.
[11] *halaka* / ha-la'kah / n. *Hebrew*. Talmudic literature that deals with law and with the interpretation of the laws in the Hebrew Scriptures.
[12] *bihmah* / bE'mah. / n. *Hebrew*. A raised platform in a synagogue from which the Torah is read.
[13] *minyan* / min'yan / n. *Hebrew*. The quorum required for Jewish communal worship that consists of ten male adults in Orthodox Judaism and ten adults of either sex in Conservative

think that is? I'll tell you! It's because they think a hundred women can't add up to ten men!"

"Bubbie, you know I agree with you about that. And I'm just one person; I can't change their views by myself. But what if my presence there changed the thoughts of just one little girl? What are you worried about, anyway? When was the last time you went to *shul*? Was it even this decade?"

"The last time I went was Yom Kippur, the year your father—God rest his soul—became ill. Would I go back after that? Why?" They were silent at this, for a moment.

"Anyway, Bubbie, you can't very well argue against the Orthodox for denying you a right you're disinclined to exercise."

"Hmm," Bubbie replied. Her face tightened as she turned to the fridge to put away the grapes.

"Yigal's coming," she said, her back to Salla.

"I'm sorry, what?" Salla was hoping she'd misheard.

"Yigal? Your cousin? You have forgotten little Yigala?"

"*Little* Yigala. Bubbie, what are you thinking? He wasn't little even when he was ten! As if you don't you have enough to worry about. I can't imagine what kind of handful he'll be at nineteen! Besides—doesn't he have to finish his stint in the army?"

Bubbie, staring into the fridge, shrugged. Salla waited.

"You want me to ask? If Ava says he can come, he can come. All he does is play video games and sleep! It's not healthy."

"And how healthy will it be for you to look after him, Bubbie?"

"Salla," Bubbie sighed. "Always so quick to argue, *nu*."

"Hmm, yes. And where, do you suppose, I get that particular trait?"

Bubbie closed the fridge door, and turned to look at her beautiful, intractable granddaughter. In spite of herself, she returned Salla's smile.

"Ach Bubbeleh," she said, sitting down, taking Salla's slim hand in both of her own. "It's just that I worry. I worry! How is that such a crime?"

"It's not a crime. I know. I worry about you, too."

There they sat, enjoying the moment of silence, each holding the other's hand as though understanding could be forced through touch.

Emily, Salla's friend since childhood, banged impatiently on Salla's door, careful to avoid the areas where the paint was flaking off.

---

and Reform Judaism.

"Okay Asperger-girl, I know you're in there," she shouted at the door. "Crawl out of your Torah study with your hands up." Emily scanned the porch, waving at her pert nose to dispel the malodorous fumes rising in the unseasonal heat. Leaning off the side of the porch to peer into the living room window, she shouted triumphantly, "Salla! You know I can see you on the couch, right? I can practically hear you breathing. Open the door! It stinks out here."

Salla, who'd been willing herself to perfect stillness in the gloom of her living room, sighed, pushed herself off the couch and dragged her feet to the door. She loved Emily the way a mother loves a wayward child. She wasn't always happy to see her.

Salla unlocked the heavy wooden door and Emily pushed past her into the living room, a sweet gust of expensive perfume billowing behind her. Whirling, she grabbed Salla's jaw in her hand, and smacked a wet kiss on each cheek. Squeezing Salla's cheeks, forming Salla's lips into a fish-like pucker, she examined her face from all angles. "You're looking as gorgeous as ever for someone who absolutely cannot be bothered."

Emily wore sparse makeup, the season's perfect sweater, meticulously careless hair; sensible boots handmade in Italy. Over her shoulder hung a slouchy, colorful handbag, likely made real from the pages of Vogue Paris.

"You might want to have your steps hosed off," Emily said. "I think some homeless guy threw up out there."

Salla raised her eyebrows. "Oh yes, I'll have that looked after right away. You know how the help loves to wield a hose." They laughed together, Emily somewhat ruefully. Remembering the source of the odor, Salla quickly closed the door. Emily whirled to face her.

"Okay, so, your Bubbie told me all about it. Give it up, kiddo. Aubrey Bishop, for heaven's sake? I mean, really? Aubrey "*Kill the Jew*" Bishop?"

Salla shook her head. Put like that, it did sound outlandish. It *was* outlandish. But Emily was just warming up.

"I can't believe you didn't call me with a play by play, *while* it was happening! Did you forget how much trouble I got into that time I snuck out to see his show? Remember how *you* bailed at the last minute, leaving me to face the wrath alone?"

"I know, I know Em. You're right. I'm so sorry." Salla shrugged her shoulders, honestly contrite. "But, I don't know. He seems to be... oh, I don't know. Kind. Decent. Real. It just doesn't feel right to turn him into some gossip column. I never made a conscious effort to keep it a secret, though. If I had, it would have lasted exactly thirty seconds." Salla shook her head. "I don't know what I was thinking, running off to Bubbie."

"Yes, well, she was livid. More so than usual. You'd think he was the leader of Hamas, or something." Emily touched Salla's arm gently. "The fact that she called me at all, when I know she considers me a complete miscreant."

"Oh Ems, that's not true, she's just—"

"Oh, I know exactly what she's just. She's just jealous of anyone who gets between her and her precious Bubbeleh, especially if they aren't giant suck ups. She knows you love me, and that makes me a threat."

Emily's voice trailed off as she stepped into Salla's kitchen to make herself a tea. She peeked out the doorway, yelling over the sound of running water.

"But I'm still expecting a detailed description of your morning, *mon petite* Rabbi!"

Minutes later, Emily handed Salla a cup of tea prepared to Salla's standards—half a teaspoon raw sugar, two splashes almond milk—and settled beside Salla into the faded couch, pinning her there with a stare.

"So. Kind and decent, eh? Those are not adjectives you typically hear bandied about with regard to Aubrey Bishop. Speak, girl. Speak!"

Salla, returning Emily's look, accepted the tea, took a few slow sips, and placed it carefully on the table before she began.

"Okay. Well, I found him when I went to grab the paper this morning." At Emily's frozen smile, Salla couldn't suppress a chuckle.

"Yes. On my front porch. He was absolutely wasted. Smelled faintly of vomit." She paused after this white lie; Aubrey's odor could hardly be described as "faint." She couldn't help but try to clean things up for Emily, who'd loved Aubrey Bishop passionately throughout his career burnout.

"Wait, what? He was in your house?" Emily paused, her jaw unhinged. "Funny you didn't mention that to Bubbie." She shook her head and laughed. "Guess it was difficult enough to convince her that the infamous Jew killer was allowed in the country. Much less on your doorstep."

"Well of course," Salla said. "I may as well tell her I invited him in to deny the Holocaust over a cup of tea."

They laughed at this and fell quiet, contemplative.

"I mean, he obviously *was* trying to piss people off, but once he got your attention, the message was rather positive." The wistful tone in Emily's voice had been there, quiet but steadfast, for years. Emily had worn her beloved BishoPrics t-shirts almost daily until the controversy itself made it a symbol for neo-Nazism.

"I know. I remember." Salla leaned back on the couch, an arm behind her head, her eyes pointed at the ceiling, reflecting on something beyond. "I may not have leapt into the mosh pit with gleeful abandon, but I never understood the reaction. I think it's because he'd gotten more mainstream. His newer fans felt betrayed."

"Yeah. You're probably right." They sat for another quiet moment, remembering.

"Anyway!" Emily sat up. "Back to your story. So, there he was, lying in his own puke—so totally *not* hot, by the way—and Rabbi Salla Kahn comes sweeping in to his rescue. Carry on."

Salla laughed ruefully. "Yes, well. Something like that..." she started.

When the story had been told, Salla crossed her arms and slumped further back on the couch. First one then the other, she clunked her feet on the wooden crate *cum* coffee table. Emily looked up at Salla from where she'd settled on the floor.

"Wow. I can't believe you had a jam session with Aubrey Bishop. Right here. It just defies belief," she said, shaking her head. Then she pointed a sly smile Salla's way. "Something like that would never have happened if you were in Israel."

"Well, I didn't make it up, obviously."

"Obviously, Salla! Stop being so defensive."

"I'm not defensive, Em. I'm just not in the mood to be nagged, and I know that's why you're really here."

"Come *on* Salla! As if I *didn't* want to hear that story. You're so touchy, sometimes."

"Emily Sloane. Tell me you're not here to try to talk me out of Rabbinical school, *again*. You were talking to Bubbie, for heaven's sake. I can see right through you guys."

"Well, we did have a chat about you, of course," Emily allowed. She paused until Salla's stare forced her to speak. "We're worried you're committing yourself to something that you'll regret later."

"You see, that's where you guys lose me. It seems you're basing that scenario on the imaginary Salla in your heads. What could I possibly have to regret?"

"Salla, come *on*. Since when have you wanted to be a rabbi? You have to admit this wasn't exactly your life plan."

"Maybe it wasn't *your* life plan for me, but it's been at the back of my mind for several years now. Why do you think I changed my discipline?

You don't pursue a graduate degree in something you don't plan to use in life."

Emily returned Salla's stare until Salla shifted her eyes away.

"What do you think, I think? The Toronto Symphony was a sure thing—you'd been heading there for a solid decade!"

Salla's silence would pass for admission.

"Salla, you can't pick up where he left off. Your father lived for other people. You, well, you simply *don't*. Nothing wrong with that, but come *on*. You don't even answer your phone half the time."

Salla stood quickly. "Why do you think that is? When it's usually you, calling to talk me out of abandoning you guys for Israel—and that's exactly how Bubbie phrased it —come on your*self*!"

Emily's head was bowed. For a moment, silence sat between them.

"I'm sorry," Emily murmured. "I shouldn't have brought it up. I didn't mean to upset you."

"Look Em... I'm sorry too. You know I love you, and I appreciate that you care about my happiness. But you're wrong about my motives for becoming a rabbi. I promise you. Okay?"

Emily nodded, her eyes on Salla's.

"And you know I'll be a good one, right?"

Emily nodded again, firmly.

"I feel happy whenever I think about it," Salla said. "Happy! Okay?"

"Okay." They smiled at each other.

"So, were you attracted to him?"

"Who, Aubrey, Lionel, Bishop? Himself? What do you think? Despite the odor. I bet he cleans up good."

They laughed.

"He's got such a great speaking voice, Em. Deep, in that manly way some guys have, you know? And he has lovely manners."

"Uh huh." Emily was deadpan."Too bad you weren't in Israel already. You could have avoided meeting him altogether."

"Emily! Shut the fuck *up*!" Salla's exasperation was not forced.

"Okay! Okay. Shutting up." Emily paused, smiling sidelong at her friend. "It's just that we'd miss you."

"Aach, you're such a *nudge*[14]! You drive me right up a wall!" Salla's imitation of her grandmother made them both laugh.

---

[14] *Nudge* / nUdj / n. *Yiddish*: Affectionate term for a nag or pest.

Chapter 6

Kiss me with the kisses of your mouth
for your love is more delightful than wine.
Pleasing is the fragrance of your perfumes;
your name is like perfume poured out.

~K'tuvim
Song of Songs 1:2

Once again conjured to Salla's porch, freshly bathed, clean shaven
and well—albeit uniquely—dressed, Aubrey Bishop now looked every
bit the rock star people expected him to be.

"Hiya, Rabbi Kahn," he offered, with a carefree smile and a shallow
bow. As Salla stared, he tipped his plaid fedora to reveal thick graying
hair shaped into a modest point. His crinkled blue eyes suggested he was
enjoying the impact of his presence on Salla's equanimity. "I don't
suppose you could spare us another cup of tea?"

Salla beamed, unable to dim the joy she felt upon seeing this newly
minted face. She'd expected never to see him again in person—had, in
fact, been preparing herself for chance encounters via television or the
Internet by forcing herself to think about radishes whenever he entered
her thoughts. Radishes, because they seemed the most pointless of foods:
crispy, granted, but with an unpleasant spiciness as inappropriate as it
was unexpected. To Salla, radishes were the sour note in a salad; one that
declared its birthplace in a truck stop or a bar. Perhaps a lunch counter in
a department store. A handful of iceberg, two wedges of tomato and the

omnipresent slivers of radish. Edible strictly for purposes of thoroughness and nothing else. Gradually, Salla, her coping mechanism succeeding, allowed her eyes to return to Aubrey's polite, slightly puzzled gaze.

"Certainly. Please do come in," she murmured distractedly, turning to hide a blush.

"Are you sure? I hope I'm not interrupting?" Aubrey's gaze ran along her right arm, stopped at her forehead. "Is that some sort of bondage gear you're wearing?"

A little-dog-bark of a laugh leapt from Salla. "I'm sorry? What did you say? Bondage gear?" She waved Aubrey through the living room to sit at her tiny kitchen table. "No! I've just finished my morning *Shema*— the daily blessing. These are *Tefillin*[15]."

The black leather strapping that wrapped around her forearm, the black boxes on her forehead and right bicep—she must indeed look odd to him. Salla thought of the airline passenger who'd caused an international incident by laying his own Tefillin on after the in-flight meal was served. The crew had panicked and returned the plane to its departure point, certain this young man was engaged in a confusing sort of terrorist act requiring electrical tape. They'd probably assumed the black box, protruding from his forehead like a miner's light, was a homemade bomb.

"Just Tefillin," Salla soldiered on. "They contain passages from the Torah and, uh, please excuse me while I put them away." She hurried to her bedroom, leaving Aubrey to hover inside the front door. The moment she'd spied him through the window beside her door, she'd forgotten everything and run at a gallop to let him in. She was upset with herself for failing to treat her phylactery with the proper respect. Thinking about radishes and babbling about nothing—she'd broken at least half of the commandments that prescribed their use. Bondage gear! Oh G-d. After she'd kissed each one and deposited it gently in the special box she'd ordered from Israel for this purpose, she pulled a hair brush through her already smooth hair and called out, "If you'd like a cup of tea you could put the kettle on."

Aubrey floundered to the kitchen. He'd been unacquainted with the use of a kettle for many years. Ordinarily, he took his meals at the

---

[15] *tefillin* / tih-fil'-lin / *Hebrew*. Two, small, black leather boxes, containing biblical passages, worn on the left arm and on the forehead during the weekday morning prayer. Traditionally worn only by Jewish males past the age of 13, the practice is increasing amongst observant Jewish women.

nearest restaurant that had alcohol on the menu. He bravely took up the challenge of tea making, but forgot to add water. The kettle, still hot from Salla's first cup, whistled out its high-pitched shriek the moment he plugged it in. In response, Aubrey emitted a small, involuntary shriek himself.

As Salla hurried to rescue him, it occurred to her that his helplessness was a dangerously endearing quality. His striking, perfectly aging looks, his incredible voice—he would have made a superlative cantor—even his infamy attracted mobs, but for Salla at least some of his allure lay in the fact these assets were useless to the everyday world in which everyone else was forced to dwell. What kind of malady was this, to find appeal in another's disability?

She poured tea and settled Aubrey in her living room, his knees wedged between her coffee table and the couch, and looked at him expectantly.

"Right. You're wondering what I'm doing here," he said. "Well the thing is, I thought I'd ask if you minded teaching me a bit about Judaism." The surprise on Salla's face spurred Aubrey to continue at a faster pace. "You see, my mate, Ian, he just converted to Islam, yeah? And he's on my back about me finding God, myself. Now, don't get me wrong. I keep asking him where he found Allah—under the cushions along with the change, was he? Ian doesn't find that as amusing as I do." Aubrey looked at Salla for a response but she was carefully expressionless.

"Anyway, I'm not interested in some kind of late life conversion, but I want to be fully prepared when he comes at me next. You know? My mother was a Jew, and all, which I assume—in accordance with the matrilineal thing—makes me one as well, yeah?"

Salla took all this in with a blink.

"So, let's make sure we understand each other, Aubrey." This was the second time she'd said his name aloud and she found it peculiarly exhilarating. "You do know I'm not a rabbi?" Aubrey nodded "But I am preparing for Rabbinical studies in the fall, so you can imagine I take this subject very seriously. I mean, I'm happy to teach you about Judaism as I experience it, but you must approach the subject—and me—with respect. Is that clear?"

"Brilliant, yes! Just because I think religion is asinine, doesn't mean I think its practitioners are, right?"

This wasn't quite the tone Salla had been working toward, but it would do, for now. As she poured the tea, she considered the alternative.

What was she to do, throw him back on the porch? He'd probably dwell there until someone showed up to rescue him. Besides, he smelled heavenly today.

"One more thing, Aubrey," she said, forcing herself to concentrate, "some people—and you are certainly among them—should not use the word 'Jew' in conversation. Say, instead 'Jewish' as in 'He is a Jewish person'. Never 'He's a Jew'. Okay?"

Aubrey dropped his head, chagrined.

"Got it. But tell me: Am I a Jew? Ish, I mean? Am I a Jewish person? It's something I've always wondered. Because my mother was Jew-ish, but my father wasn't. They never did anything religious. You know? A Christmas tree, when I was little, but nothing else."

Salla thought this through. "Well, I'm afraid the jury's still out on that one. It really depends on whom you ask. Like most reform Jews, my father would have said you're Jewish, simply because your mother was— and you're right, it's a matrilineal thing. Also, because my dad cared so deeply about knowledge, he would consider your study of Judaism confirmation of your Jewishness. My current Rebbe, however, would say you are absolutely not a Jew, since you have no learning, and you don't practice."

"See, that's what I mean, about religion. I never understood the whole practicing thing. It's not like your belief system's a guitar you have to tune, right? If it's reality, why do you have to practice believing it?"

"Well, that's what I've been trying to say. If you want me to debate the underpinnings of theology, I'll consider it, perhaps, but you told me you hoped to learn about Judaism. Which I'm much more qualified to teach. Okay?"

"Okay."

Salla paused, searching his eyes for sincerity. Satisfied, the teacher in her took over."I have to say, your analogy about tuning a guitar is really apt. It *is* something like that, for me. Every time I have a new challenge, I take it to the Talmud for interpretation. That's how I fine tune my own spirituality."

"Ah. So, your father was a Rabbi, was he?"

"What?" For a moment, Salla was startled to know that Aubrey found her interesting enough to have learned this about her. Then, at the thought of discussing her father with this man, her head shook of its own volition.

"Oh! No! I mean, Aubrey, that's another subject I'm really not ready for." She lowered her voice and concluded on a gentle tone. "Okay?"

"All right then." Aubrey was silent. He looked around the little apartment, then his eyes settled on the photograph of the stained glass tree. "I was wondering if you took that picture," he said, waving at the wall behind her.

"Oh!" Salla, turning, marveled at his ability to hit every single one of her sore points without knowing anything about her. "Yes, I did, actually." Her eyes were on her hands, which were engaged in absent-minded stretching exercises. "My father commissioned that window for his synagogue."

"It's beautiful. Really stunning."

Salla turned her face to him.

"Yes, I think so too," she said, her calm eyes resting on his.

"Right. You don't want to talk about it. But. Do you think it would be acceptable if I played your father's guitar?"

She flashed her crooked smile. "I was hoping you'd ask. After the indignities I've visited on it, I'm sure it's in need of some decent playing."

So play it he did, and Salla learned that the rumors were true: Aubrey was a gifted classical guitarist. He also had an uninhibited wit which had them both laughing to the point of painful gasping, Salla begging him to stop, and then setting him up again. It was a refreshing change to be around a man who was so attractive, as well as interesting and funny. Freshly scrubbed, he smelled fantastic, even from the distance at which she kept him. Salla politely forced him out, a full two hours after she'd decided it was prudent to do so.

For his part, Aubrey learned everything there was to know about *Tefillin* and their use, and also that the future Rabbi Salla Kahn knew every word to Nirvana's 'Smells like Teen Spirit'. And that, if he didn't have her soon, he might never get a chance.

The next day, pacing back and forth past the dusty beige speakerphone on the scratched Formica of her kitchen counter, Bubbie Adira was agitated. Her arms punctuated her words as though she was conducting a Stravinsky composition in double time. In Israel, on the other end of the conversation, her nephew Yigal held his own phone six inches from his ear, his replies drowned under her ongoing crescendos.

"Can you believe it? And now he just stops by whenever he feels like it, pretending to be a student of *Kabbalah*[16], or something—you know

---

[16] *Kabbalah* / kah-bahl'-lah / n. *Hebrew*. The study of Jewish mysticism, traditionally taught only to those over forty years old, who were thoroughly versed in Torah and Talmud.

how those celebrity types are—and she lets him in!" Adira glared at the phone, as if it were Aubrey Bishop himself. "She says he wants to learn about Torah, for God's sake! He's probably using her so he can write more of those evil songs. And she's just naive enough to help him!" Adira paced back and forth in front of the speakerphone, floorboards creaking in her wake. After a loud, mournful sigh, she resumed.

"She didn't call me all day yesterday, and when she finally called, this is what I get! She's going to the movies again with him tomorrow, now. I tell you, he's going to break her heart, and all I'll be able to say is 'I told you so'. That's what I'll say! Because there's nothing else, to say, right? That's all there is to say." She paused, her voice ragged, even to her own ears. "Yigal? Say something already."

"I can't believe Salla would do such a thing. With such a man. What more is there to say?" Yigal's flat voice was tinny, issuing from the old speaker phone. "It's disgusting. And rather out of character, I would have thought."

"Well, it's not really disgusting so much as, well, I don't know. But it has to end, sometime. I told her that! She's a good girl, she'll listen, eventually. She'd better! Before she gets her life ruined." Adira shook her head, temporarily resigned.

When she remembered to whom she was talking, she rubbed her eyes and took a deep breath, in preparation for her next question.

"Well then, *Bubbiela*, why did you call?" She knew it was something—with this one, it was always something. Yigal managed to drive her poor sister completely up and down the wall every day of his life, and now, from almost ten-thousand kilometers away, was starting in with Adira. But he *was* a good listener, at least.

"Actually, Doda, I called to ask you if you would mind a visitor sooner than we discussed. Meaning next week."

Adira stopped and stared at her phone, surprised. "You're coming to Canada next week? But what about your service? You've only been enlisted a year. You'll lose your citizenship!" Having a nephew in the Israeli Defense Forces had been a source of pride to Adira, as long as she didn't think too much about this specific nephew.

"A year and a half, but I'm going to be leaving anyway. They insisted on putting me in with the Jobnicks." Yigal's habitual terseness was sharp as a knife. "What am I supposed to do—become a plumber? I was born for combat."

"But you *can't* just leave. You'll go to jail. You want me to harbor a fugitive?" Adira was shrill. "I can't do such a thing!"

41

"Well, don't worry. It's even worse than that. I've been discharged. Unfairly."

"What, unfairly?" Adira, prepared with a tirade, instead threw both hands in the air. "What does that mean? Dishonorably?"

"Well, yes, I guess so, only because my commander disagreed with my politics. Stupid lesbian bitch!"

"Yigal!" Adira switched the speaker off and put the phone to her ear. She pulled out a chair, its aluminum feet scraping against the linoleum, and sat heavily, clutching her forehead, her elbows on the kitchen table.

"I'm sorry," he said, his voice deeper, quieter than she remembered it. "I don't mean to snap. It's been a difficult few weeks. They made me speak to a psychiatrist, just so my stupid commander didn't have to deal with me." He paused but Adira had no response.

"They forced a Profile 21 on me, Doda! A Profile 21. My life here is ruined." Yigal's voice creaked, quieted. "The IDF cares more about the Palestinians than they do about their own soldiers."

"Oh!" Adira paused, her nerves jumping. "Yigala. I'm so sorry." She pushed the unwelcome sense of foreboding down deep within her. She didn't want to know the details. "Of course you can come stay with your Doda. I have plenty of room, and it will be nice to have the company. Besides, your cousin Salla may need you too."

"Thank you, Doda. I knew you would make things turn out for me."

"Of course dear. Is Ava there? Can I talk to her? How long has it been since I've had a chance to talk with my baby sister?"

Yigal put his mother on the phone and the arrangements were made. When all was set, Adira slumped, elbows on the table, forehead in her hands, and tried to imagine how she would tell Salla about this turn of events. It would not go well.

Chapter 7

*And call ye on the name of your gods, and I will call on the name
of the Lord: and the God that answereth by fire, let him be God.
And all the people answered and said, It is well spoken.*
~Kings 18:24
Holy Bible

For the five-hundredth time—an event which passed without fanfare
since she'd never counted—Salla's Bubbie Adira transferred her cane to
the crook of her elbow and pulled open the glass doors of the Lake Hill
Revolver club. She walked down the main hall, smiling in anticipation.

The shooting range was an unassuming yellow brick building
directly beside the Forest Hill fire station. The owners didn't believe in
signage—prudent in gun-averse Toronto--and thanks to state of the art
sound proofing, most people had no idea the gun club was there.

"Good morning Mrs. Cohen. How are you today?"

"I'm well, thank you Bill. It's been quite temperate, for fall." Adira
hooked her cane on the counter and studied the inventory, smiling.

"I'll take the Speer Lawman please," she said, pointing at the wall of
ammunition behind him.

"For your LCR?"

"Yes, the 158 grain, please. I was very happy with it last week. I
appreciate the recommendation."

"Anytime. Glad to hear you liked it." Bill smiled. "We 'aim' to
please," he said, pointing to the sign beside him which echoed his words.

Adira smiled, unable to pretend she hadn't heard that one close to five-hundred times before.

"And you're sure you don't want to give the Lasergrip 'a shot', Mrs Cohen?"

"Positive. I'll just stick to using my eyes, thanks. Uh, I don't have my seniors' discount card here today. Can you just look me up, please?"

"Sure—every cent counts, right?"

Adira didn't answer. Silently, she paid for her purchase and, nodding, turned toward the bank of lockers at the end of the long hall. Glancing around, she slipped a small revolver from her handbag and tucked it under her arm. Strictly speaking, she wasn't permitted to ferry a gun between her house and the club. But licenses to carry a firearm were rarely issued and she could only afford a single gun. She wasn't about to be without it in her own home.

Placing her handbag and cane carefully in her locker, she entered the range and headed toward her favorite bay. It was empty. Adira suppressed a girlish shiver of delight.

"Hello dear," she said to the blonde lady loading a pistol in the bay next to her.

"Adira. It's good to see you! How's that pretty granddaughter of yours? I saw her on the Dini show the other day! She's a smart one."

"Thank you. Yes, she's a good girl. How's your tendonitis, Debbie? Affecting your aim?"

"Nah, not too bad today. It's warming up a bit, eh? I think we're going to get an Indian Summer this year. Say—did you watch Hannity last night?"

"Of course!" Bubbie smiled coyly. "Sean's my favorite imaginary boyfriend, you know." They laughed.

"He really put that Senator in his place, didn't he?"

"He always does." Niceties dispensed, Debbie pushed her earmuffs into place, and Bubbie did the same. Each turned to her target.

Adira loaded her Ruger LCR, skipping the third chamber from the barrel, in which she always kept a single bullet. She refused to carry an unloaded revolver, but it was too dangerous to keep a round in the firing chamber. This was a satisfactory compromise. Adira's gun was perfect for her—it was lightweight and accurate, with a two-inch barrel and a Neoprene grip that made recoil manageable. The gun store clerk had shown her the same gun in pink, but Bubbie had waved it away. The black was far more appropriate.

Favoring her bad knee, Bubbie spread her legs apart, the right slightly ahead of the left in an exhaustively perfected power stance. She held the gun in both hands, bouncing as lightly as she was she was able, her weight on the balls of her perpetually aching feet. Bubbie locked her eyes on the front sight of her gun, took a deep breath, and let it out slowly. She squeezed off three rapid shots, nodded, and slowly reeled her target in.

A single, bullet-size hole pierced the man-shaped paper.

"Suh-wish, Mrs. Cohen! Nice one!" Three bays over, the kid who wanted to be a cop brayed Bubbie's triumph.

Bubbie smiled grimly. "Yes!" she yelled, thrusting her left fist awkwardly into the air.

The kid laughed and ran to tell the manager about Adira's perfect grouping. Debbie jumped up and down and cheered while the recorded fanfare the gun club played to celebrate such a feat blared from the loudspeaker. Bubbie sat on the bench at the back of the shooting lane, the accomplishment having made her unsteady.

"Sons of bitches," she murmured to herself. She smiled.

"Doda... Doda... Adira! Over here. Over here. Over here. Damn it!" Yigal yelled. He was a head taller than the melee of aimless passengers who had, half an hour ago, disembarked the plane from Ben Gurion Airport. Several turned to look at him, caught by his angry tone, then returned their gazes to the opening of the baggage belt, where their luggage had consistently not appeared for the entire half hour.

"I said 'Moo, moo, moo-moo-moo'!" he told a slatternly type with the temerity to continue looking at him. "Don't tell me you don't speak cow, I won't believe it." He detested people like her. The words "I Visited the Christian Holy Land" were all but tattooed on her forehead.

"I'm sorry? I don't understand," she said. Her eyes darted around, avoiding his.

"Oh, never mind. Go back to sleep." These people were no better than herd animals; they drove him crazy. They reminded him of the Palestinians. They all thought the same, looked the same, smelled the same: dirty. They bred like rabbits and every single one of them insisted he had a claim to prime real estate in Jerusalem. That was one of the reasons Yigal had wanted to be on patrol. Teach the Arabs a lesson that the lefties were too weak to deliver: Israel was for Jews. It was a Jewish state for a reason, and the Arabs who insisted on staying chose their own lot.

Yigal's spine stiffened as he thought about the incident that had caused his commander to recommend him for non-combat service. They were on patrol along the Gaza border when they were called to a house that had been reported to harbor a Hezbollah operative. The house was crowded with small children all approximately the same age. The lady who'd answered the door—rather nervously, Yigal thought—explained she was running a daycare. Yigal knew this must be a lie. What better place for a terrorist to hide than amongst these little rats? But he, for one, would not be deterred by their presence. He'd said so, loudly, yelling at the dirty little Arabs and pointing his gun at the lying woman. That was when his commander's leftist tendencies became apparent.

In front of that entire houseful of *Araboushim*[17], she'd demanded that Yigal wait in the Jeep while the others searched. She told him off, in front of the rats, when he was clearly in the right. You needed to put these stone-throwing devils in their place when they were young—that was the best approach. Otherwise how would they know whom they were dealing with? They'd continue to throw their rocks, reveling in their impunity.

But the lesbian bitch whose squad he'd been unlucky to join disagreed. She'd filed a report against him, and recommended he be taken off patrol duty immediately. He'd waited most of his young life for the privilege, eager to serve his country, and one weak, foolish woman was able to take it away with a few strokes of her pen.

While it turned out the report of the Hezbollah member was false— the house crowded with Arab children had indeed been a daycare—Yigal still considered it a lost opportunity to rattle some teeth. Pacifist army officers were the front edge of the anarchy that, Yigal felt sure, would destroy the Jewish State of Israel. They were the ones who, based on the lies of the psychiatrist he'd been forced to see, assigned him a Profile 21, deeming him the lowest of the low, too weak or too crazy to serve his country. Discharge due to Profile 21 was a black mark in Israeli society; employers discriminated on the basis of it, weapons permits were denied because of it, drivers' licenses had been revoked in light of it. To think of it made him so angry he became dizzy. He shook his head to clear it.

When he looked up, he could see Adira searching for him through the glass partition on the other side of the customs desks.

"Doda. Doda." Yigal waved both arms at her. "Doda! I'm right here, damn it!"

---

[17] *Araboushim* / ah-rab'-bU-shEm / n. *Hebrew*. A racial epithet used against Palestinians. Roughly equivalent to "Dirty Arab."

Almost lost in the growing crowd of people waiting to greet the passengers, Adira finally noticed him and waved back. She'd probably had trouble recognizing him with his standard number-two blade, army-issued hair. At that moment, he could tell, she was lamenting the loss of his "sweet black curls." Well too fucking bad. They'd grow back, soon enough. But what would he do?

"What the fuck?" he yelled at a passing stewardess. "Have you all decided to steal my belongings? What's happening here?"

"I'm sorry sir, I work for United. Perhaps you could call your airline." She hurried away with a worried backward glance. He watched as she approached a guard by the wall and indicated Yigal with an oblique jerk of her head. Yigal stomped up to the two of them, surprising the stewardess as she turned toward him. "What's going on here?" Yigal asked the guard. "Is there something wrong with the baggage system? I've been waiting for an hour."

"I'm sorry. I can't help you with that. Sometimes it just takes a while. Return to the turnstile and try to be patient."

"Patient!" Yigal spat in disgust. "Ridiculous. "Glaring at all around him, he walked back to the empty turnstile. "Fine. I'll just wait here, with the rest of the sheeple." This time, his glares were returned.

Yigal glanced toward the guard, and saw him staring back, with no attempt to hide his gaze. Yigal increased the intensity of his glare, but the guard continued to stare, his face calm. After a while Yigal turned his eyes back toward Adira.

Where was Salla? His beautiful, beautiful cousin—he wanted to see her so badly. She was now an assistant professor at the university—how he'd love to take her classes. He'd share his expertise on Israel, a world where Hebrew wasn't a dead language. He'd heard she might spend a year there as part of her rabbinical studies. Who better to introduce her to the country than he? Although things had been tense when Salla had last seen him, Yigal was certain they'd be smoothed over by now. He now realized his callow advances on her were immature—and premature. He was a boy, then, and now he was a man. Although he'd always be younger than Salla, he was probably much taller than she, now. Now, she would have respect for him.

The problem was, people didn't understand him. His first—only—girlfriend had said it was because *he* wasn't able to care. This was a lie. He cared very much, had cared very much for that girl. It's just that she was always making demands of him—demands that he say things properly, buy the right present, look at her in special ways—it never made sense to him. It seemed to Yigal that she was the one who hadn't cared. He'd never asked *her* to change the way she looked at him. As she'd said a last goodbye, with tears in *her* eyes, she shook her head and walked away, never looking back. He'd been in agony for months—she'd changed her phone number, stopped responding to email, un-friended him on the social networks. She'd been so sweet, so kind to him, before. And yet, after only two visits to implore her to come back, her parents threatened to call the police if he—as they said—ever darkened their door again.

None of that mattered, though, now. He had survived the pain of first love and was stronger for it. He saw, now, that the girl had simply been practice, to teach him how he should be with Salla. It wasn't a mistake, it was a lesson. One that had finally been learned.

By the time the conveyor belt began to deliver their luggage—a broken gear was blamed for the delay—Yigal had calmed down, and was able to muster a smile for his Doda Adira. She was, after all, rescuing him from a bad situation, and she'd always been his favorite aunt, feisty and understanding in the correct measure. They'd had their differences, certainly, but she understood him in a way other people were too weak, too cold, to understand.

As he picked up his bags and headed toward her, he was intercepted by the guard.

"I'm sorry, sir, but you're going to have to come with me." The guard grabbed Yigal's arm and directed him toward frosted glass doors on the other side of the baggage claim.

"Yigal!" His aunt's voice grew faint as he was walked away from her. On the other side of the glass, three security guards, a customs agent and an RCMP officer waited to interrogate him.

Two hours later, after everything in his luggage and on his person had been thoroughly scoured, Yigal was allowed to leave. The experience had calmed him, and he was in reasonably good spirits when his Doda Adira stood to greet him as the guard ushered him through to the other side.

"Doda." He held out his long arms and she hugged him awkwardly, her head no higher than his chest.

"Yigala. Finally! I thought you'd never get done."

Yigal decided not to get her started. "Yes, well, they can't be too careful, with terrorists on the loose."

"Yes. Well." Her expression turned to sorrow as her eyes moved over his head. "What happened to your sweet curls?"

"Military issue, Doda. Don't worry, it will grow back." He wheeled his large suitcase along the airport sidewalk.

"Well, they didn't make us shave our heads for the Yom Kippur war, I'll tell you that much."

"Doda!" Yigal said, smiling, pulling his luggage behind him, "you were never in the Yom Kippur war. Come on. Admit it."

"Well, not officially, perhaps. Women didn't serve back then. But I could cook up a pretty nice Molotov cocktail, you know. Unofficially."

"Really? Please tell me all about it." He'd forgotten how much fun Doda Adira could be.

Ian shifted his weight in the uncomfortable folding chair, a Styrofoam cup of terrible coffee in his hand. The setting was familiar. Having attended years of AA meetings all over the world—with no notable change in his drinking behavior—the odor of moldy plaster and aging linoleum set a scene he'd been part of for decades. If this were an AA meeting, Ian's introduction would go something like this: "My name is Ian and I'm an alcoholic. Also, I'm a Muslim now, which really bollockses it up." Fortunately, no such speech was required. Ian had seen the flyer for this meeting at the mosque, and he recognized several congregants among the seated. This audience would be particularly unreceptive to Ian's tales of booze-fueled debauchery.

Ten minutes later, Ian's impatience was mounting when a small man with a tidy beard, tweed blazer, and expensive jeans stepped up to the wood podium. He cleared his throat, and began.

"Hi, and welcome to the first meeting of the Toronto Chapter of the IPBC. The Irish Palestinian Brotherhood Campaign—for short." At the polite laughter, the speaker's benevolent gaze swept the crowd.

"I'm Tom Bryant and I welcome you all to join us. The IPBC aims to raise public awareness about the human rights abuses in Palestine's occupied territories. The more people we can bring to the cause, the more likely those abuses can be stopped."

Ian's irritation rose again and he considered walking out. In his opinion, Tom's namby pamby tone served to illustrate exactly why the occupation had gone on as long as it had. Groups like this only made people believe they were doing something—the something being, in Ian's opinion, whining and wasting time—when they should have been working toward real change. As the IPBC bloke nattered on—something about raising funds by walking up a fucking hill, for God's sake—Ian decided to give it another minute before he left.

Ian had always wanted to go to Palestine, the place where his father was born, to fight the good fight. He wasn't sure what a good fight would entail—he'd certainly done his part for soccer hooliganism—but he was increasingly convinced he was meant to be involved in one. A cursory study of a few passages in the Qur'an supported his belief that involvement in some kind of struggle was encouraged. The Imam in his grandfather's mosque in London had seemed certain that blood-letting was proof of real commitment to Allah's will.

The small mosque Ian had joined in Toronto wasn't as uplifting as the one he'd attended sporadically in London, but he had hopes it could offer real meaning amongst the *"Allahu Akbar"* this and the *"Bismillah"* that. What the Imam lacked in fire, he made up for in learning. There wasn't much talk of the struggle, though, mostly just a great lot of praying, studying and salaaming. But the place reminded him of his grandfather, "Giddo," and that was enough for now.

Giddo had loved Ian in a sporadic, grudging way. He'd earned the boy's adoration with a silken prayer rug, a visit to his tailor shop—where Ian's father had been raised—and the occasional outing to Giddo's mosque in Luton. There, the Imam's blazing rhetoric made a lasting impression on a boy who was accustomed to being impressed upon with slaps and kicks.

When Ian was eight, his father died and his eternally apostate mum hit the road for the last time. With no place else to go, he was shipped to south England, to be raised by his mother's parents. To Ian's everlasting sorrow, he never saw Giddo again. A search for the elderly man, when Ian was in his twenties, led to a terse gravestone listing Giddo's name, and the dates spanning his life—nothing more.

Ian's maternal grandparents were proven parenting failures, as evidenced by his mother. His grandfather had been on the dole since before anyone could remember. His grandmother was addicted to Harlequin Romances and cheap sherry. When Ian turned fourteen, they'd made him get a job to subsidize the rent. They kicked him out at sixteen when they decided they could make more money—with less trouble—by simply renting out his room.

"As-Salāmu alayka[18]." An awkward young man took the metal folding chair next to Ian.

---

[18] *As salāmu alayka* / a-sah'-lam ah-lech'-hem / phrase. *Arabic*. A greeting, lit., "May peace be upon you."

"*Alayka salām*[19]," Ian replied, proud to know the response code. He recognized this young bloke from the mosque. Ian watched as the other ran his eyes from pierced eyebrow to sleeve tattoo, aware he wasn't your garden variety Muslim. The young man's eyes lingered on the large gauge holes in Ian's earlobes, which Ian had stretched until they were large enough to accommodate the thimbles he wore as earrings.

Waiting patiently for this examination to finish, Ian inventoried the young man's oversized yellow-and-brown-striped soccer shirt, tucked into high waisted, pale blue jeans. Ian's eyes lingered on the other's green socks, framed by an expansive gap between cheap gym shoes and frayed hem. He noted the young man's smooth hair, which looked as though it had been cut by someone's grandmother and was held in place by Vaseline.

Ian held out his hand. "Ian. Hi ya."

"Hi, I'm Akil." They shook hands, Ian somewhat limply, Akil approximating a management-textbook approach.

"Ian—I've seen you at the mosque, I think. What do you make of all this?" Akil waved his arm to indicate the speaker, the room, the apathetic audience. "Weak, eh? I was hoping for a chance to actually *do* something for a change."

"Ah, yes, I know," said Ian. "I was thinking that exact thing me self."

They sat and listened to the lecture, each expressing restlessness in his own way. Ian's right leg bounced to a rhythm he did not seem to hear, while Akil bit at his cuticles.

"So—you're English, eh?" Akil sounded like a typical Canadian kid, the type who might speak a bit of Arabic at home.

"Irish, although I've lived all over. My accent's probably a bit of everything by now. But, by birth, I'm mostly Palestinian." Ian had acquired this little affectation since formally converting to Islam several months earlier. 'Mostly Palestinian' helped him forget his English grandparents' indifference to anything other than football and booze, and his Palestinian grandfather's seeming indifference to him. 'Mostly Palestinian' seemed to prevent further questioning, while prompting instant camaraderie in some circumstances.

"Wow, Palestinian! Cool." Akil contemplated this for a moment. "So, you travel for work, eh? I'm looking for a job, right now. I even got a certificate in office applications, but, no luck so far."

---

[19] *Alayka salām* / ah-lech'-hem sah'-lam / phrase. *Arabic*. Response to a greeting, lit., "And upon you be peace."

"Well, yes, I work for Aubrey Bishop, actually." Ian waited to see how this would go over.

"Wait, you mean *the* Aubrey Bishop, that guy they put the fahtwa out on?"

"Well, yes, although I don't think it's an official fahtwa. More like a condemnation, really. Yeah?"

"Uh, yeah. That's weird, man, you working for a hater." Akil shook his head.

"Not really, mate. Most people misinterpret what he says. I should know—he's my best friend, and I'm a Muslim. Aubrey's a bit of a wanker, yeah, but he's certainly not a hateful one."

"I bet he's super rich, though, eh?" Akil wasn't going to argue.

"Well, he's doing better than you and me, let's put it that way." Ian leaned in, and lowered his voice. "But, you know, the economy hasn't been kind to him, either."

"Huh. Okay. Anyways, Ian, some friends of mine are getting together this political group, and we're looking for a few people to join. Want to check it out? The next meeting's tomorrow night."

"Uh, not sure, mate. I'll think about it, yeah?"

"Okay, yeah. But these are really serious guys—they don't mess around, you know? Like—have you ever heard of Roger D—" Akil raised his elbows in an awkward approximation of a rapper stance—"the rapper wit da rap sheet a hun'red miles long?"

At Ian's blank stare, Akil laughed. "I guess not—he's had some of his stuff on the radio, though. He's totally from the streets—you don't want to mess with him. We've been friends since grade one."

"All right then." Ian was smiling.

"No, I mean it. We're planning some big moves—you should join us."

"Okay. Good enough, mate. I'll let you know, all right?"

At the front of the room, the presenter was going on about some film he was about to play for the forty or so people in the room. Something in the speaker's tone caught Ian's attention.

"The documentary 'Through My Broken Camera's Eye' is a piece of non-violent resistance in film-making," the small man was saying. "It shows us the kind of impact we can have by simply bringing the truth to light." He gestured to the screen behind him. "This is what it's like, in the Israeli Apartheid of the West Bank. Our brave young Palestinian filmmaker did his part in documenting the abuses. We can do our part by sharing his work with the rest of the world."

As Ian watched the short film, his left leg jerked to the staccato beat of his thoughts. His anger, never fully tamped, was fanned by each new assault. Farmers held at a checkpoint for hours on their way to work their own land. A sobbing boy, restrained by Israeli soldiers as his father is taken off to jail. A young man rolling in the dirt, dying from a close range, "non-lethal," rubber bullet. The audience gasped and booed as the images jerked past.

At the end of the film, the speaker turned up the lights and stood looking at the people blinking in their seats.

"Do you see the impact of this film? An excellent use of our funding, don't you think? This is what the world needs to see. We can effect real change. Now we need to get it into theatres, onto television screens—we need it to go viral. Why don't we have an open discussion on how to get that done?"

"Oh for fuck's sake." Ian, muttering, leaned in to Akil. "I'm done with this rot. You want to get in a pint or two at that place across the street?"

"A pint? What do you mean—beer?"

"Well, yeah, mate. Surely you're legal?"

"Are you kidding me? I don't drink! I mean, we can't drink. It's, like, prohibited in the Qur'an! In three different passages! It's called—I don't know, like, the devil's handicraft, or something. It's a big deal, eh?"

"Well, yes—I know, but you do know that lots of Muslims drink, yeah? You should see Morocco—it's a country-sized piss tank."

"What? Are you fricken' serious, man?" Akil's harsh whisper had the people around them staring.

At the front of the room, the speaker stared at them, his hands on his hips.

"Excuse me? I can barely hear myself over you two. Could you please keep it down?"

"Fuck you, mate!" Ian stood. "Fucking wasting people's time— there's a war out there and it needs soldiers! Not—movies and—hill walkers!"

Ian grabbed his denim jacket, struggled it on and strode out of the room, missing the smile that crept across Akil's features as he jumped up to follow.

Within a week, Ian was the newest member of "Activists for Allah," a group that, like Ian himself, was fervor lacking expression.

Chapter 8

Of the people there are some who say: "We believe in Allah and
the Last Day;" but they do not believe.
Fain would they deceive Allah and those who believe,
but they only deceive themselves,
and realize it not!

~Surat Al Baqarah 2:8
The Holy Qur'an

Adira sighed and settled herself on the couch as her granddaughter nattered on at the other end of the line. They'd had this discussion so many times that she no longer had to listen to Salla's words to respond in a way that suggested she was listening. Salla's tone—confident, bossy, zealous—told Adira she didn't have to pay attention just yet.

"Ach," Adira said, "ach," by way of keeping the conversation going. Salla droned on.

From her quiet row house in a quiet section of Toronto, a quiet city, Adira inhabited every single story in every issue of the *The Jerusalem Post*. Her imaginary life as an Israeli was all the more vivid, superimposed on her actual routine of shopping, bridge, and target practice. When a mortar fell in Tel Aviv, it landed on *her* house, assaulted *her* ears, threatened *her* quiet way of life. Blood from a blast victim sprayed *her* cup of coffee as she sat on the patio of an overpriced Toronto cafe. Palestinian children threw rocks at *her* ancient Ford sedan when she backed it out of her garage. When Sean Hannity thanked Bibi

Netanyahu for coming on his show, it was *her* prime minister whose hand he grasped so warmly.

Adira was never far from her internal Israel. It lay under all her thoughts, motivated her most fervent actions. She considered it her duty, a Jew who did not believe in God, to follow the strictures of the Passover Seder, which emphasized that *she*, Adira, had escaped slavery in Egypt. Not some mythical ancestor but Adira *herself* had walked through the desert to the Promised Land. Not some far flung relative's but Adira's *own* was this blood and milk and honey refuge from threats one couldn't imagine, but could certainly anticipate.

Adira, *herself* could—if finances and health allowed—float overly buoyant in the Dead Sea, sample the pomegranates in the Tel Aviv Market, join the struggle for land in the settlements. *Next year in Jerusalem* was, for Adira, not just something one said twice a year as part of the Passover seder, but a mnemonic for the Jewish escape plan.

While Adira's imaginary Israel informed her present, a single moment in her childhood, in the late 40's of deceptively placid Toronto, eclipsed her past. This vivid memory became darker with each remembering, staining all her memories of childhood.

On a fine Sunday, in her seventh year, Adira had been taken to visit her Aunt Ruth, who lived within a small pocket of Jewish families in a predominantly Catholic neighborhood. In celebration of the perfect spring day, Adira's mother had pushed her out the door and told her not to come back until lunch. A well-equipped playground was just around the corner, and Adira skipped toward it happily. She had a much anticipated book—an extravagant gift from a favorite uncle—in one hand, and a couple of Aunt Ruth's still-warm cookies in the other. Adira's joy turned to disappointment, though, when she arrived at the playground to find the swings locked up, the slide and the monkey bars barricaded. The Lord's Day Act, enacted in 1906 and still enforced this sunny morning in June 1947, prohibited all activity besides prayer on the Christian Sabbath.

If Adira was lucky, some custodian might unlock the playground after people left church. More likely, the playground would remain off limits until Monday morning. Having observed her own Sabbath on Saturday, Adira was respectful but impatient. Perhaps that's why, when she noticed a gap in the fence around the swing set, she allowed herself to squirm through. Wrapping an arm around each of the swing's chains, she cracked the spine on her brand new copy of "The Little Hunchback Horse" and proceeded to read, munching the cookie in her other hand.

She sighed in contentment.

Adira had been floating in this idyll for twenty minutes when a shout broke it apart.

"Hey!"

Two boys, wearing faded and stained dungarees, stared at her, their faces pushed up to the fence. Adira jumped out of the swing, dropping her cookie. She held her book behind her, leaving the cookie in the dust.

"What are you doing on our playground?" The bigger, meaner looking of the two grabbed the chain link with both hands and climbed over in a few quick leaps. He walked up to Adira, stood too close, and spoke slowly, and deliberately, inches from her face: "You're not supposed to be here on a church day."

"But you're here," Adira pointed out, her voice shaking. She didn't back away.

From behind her, the other boy snatched the book from her hands. He grimaced at the book. "Hey, get a load of this," he said, reading the subtitle. "What'cha got there? 'A Russian Fairy Tale', eh?"

The other boy grabbed the book to see for himself. Adira winced perceptibly at the smear the boy's greasy hands left. She stiffened, hoping vainly to keep her dismay to herself.

"Well I'll be a monkey's uncle. What, are you Russkie?"

"N-no." Adira, resenting her own stammer, kept her eyes on his broken and dirty shoes.

"She's not even dressed for Church. I bet she's a Kike!" the other boy offered.

It was probably Adira's eyes that gave her away. The boys laughed, and the one holding the book threw it against the fence. They pushed her back and forth, laughing. Then one of them lifted her skirt and grabbed at her through her underwear.

"Dirty little Jew girl!"

Adira screamed, and the custodian whose job it was to enforce the Blue Laws in this particular playground appeared, shouting. The boys scattered. The man yelled again, and Adira bolted for her aunt's house, snatching up her sullied book and shoving it under her arm, scratching herself on the fence as she scrambled through. She would never finish reading "The Little Hunchback Horse," but she kept it all her life, a smeared reminder of this ugly lesson.

If only her granddaughter could understand the portent of moments like these, could have some respect for the lessons of the past, Salla would be safe. But, like everyone who was too young to know, she was so busy worrying about the future that she couldn't see behind her. Adira sighed.

"Bubbie? Is that what you're saying? That the Palestinians *want* to be marginalized? That they *want* be treated like second class citizens?"

"*Hok a chainik*[20]! Listen to you, Salla. You may know Torah backwards, but you don't know *dreck* about the history of Israel. If you did, you wouldn't be so quick to judge."

Salla groaned, quietly, and switched her phone to the other ear. Bubbie had been convinced, for years, that Salla would cleave to the Zionist position, if only she would take the time to understand the damage the world had wrought on the Jewish people. The Diaspora, the ghettos, the pogroms, the death camps. The pitying snickers of other children when they realized you don't have a Santa. Those damned Catholics and their movies portraying Jews as Christ's killers.

"I can hear you moaning, you know. Salla! I'm not *kvetching* about a stubbed toe, here. This is serious. If another Hitler were to rise today—did you know that Neo-Nazism is popular again in Germany? No you didn't, did you? If—when!—another Hitler arises, Jews will at least have a place to go. Where we can't be turned away, like the MS St. Louis."

The MS St. Louis was a German vessel that had, ten years before Bubbie's birth, attempted to secure safe haven for close to a thousand Jewish "souls," as they were described on the manifest. To the travelers, their corporeal selves were likely of a greater concern, although, as the Good Friday Prayer of the time suggested, it was a spiritual lack in the "perfidious Jews" that warranted persecution. The one-thousand passengers of the MS St. Louis were turned away from every country the ship approached, including the US and Cuba. Canada, after some debate, chose not to respond to the ship's pleas at all. Eventually, the journey of the MS St. Louis ended in Antwerp, Belgium, having traded its visions of the free world for the terra firma of the Third Reich.

"I'm just tired of the Palestinians pretending to be victims. Poor victims who strap bombs onto the backs of their children, so they can kill other people's children."

Salla had had enough. Usually, she could tune out of this conversation without losing her place, but once in a while Bubbie would escalate to a height she was forced to meet.

"Palestinians are *not* evil baby killers, Bubbie. In fact, I'd be willing

---

[20] *Hok a chainik* / hok'a-chainik / phrase. *Yiddish*: Literally, to "hit a tea kettle." Colloquially, to make a useless noise; to talk nonsense.

to bet there are approximately the same percentage of evil Palestinians as there are evil Jews. To paint all of them with the same brush is morally wrong, and, I think, beneath you." This conversation followed a pattern established over Salla's life, taken up where Salla's father had left off. Once his bravely-fought battle with cancer had been lost, his struggle with Bubbie was passed down to Salla.

"Oh, Salla. Why can we never talk about these things?"

"Because whenever we get into it, that old definition of insanity comes to mind: doing the same thing over and over and expecting different results."

"Well, maybe we just need to find a new way to discuss?" Bubbie's voice was hopeful.

"I'm not talking about this discussion. I'm talking about Israel's approach to the peace process. Insanity. In a nutshell, it's 'Keep Fighting'."

"My God in Heaven, Salla! What would you do if your neighbor thought it was perfectly acceptable to throw rocks at you?"

"Oh, I'd bomb him into the stone age, Bubbie. Grumpy old Greek guy that he is. Totally worth it. Believe me, I'm thoroughly repulsed by the smell of roasting lamb." Salla paused, smiled wickedly. "Then, as an afterthought, I'd dismember his cat."

"Salla, I can't believe you sometimes. This is not funny. It's serious. I'm going now." Bubbie hung up the phone, the better to cut off Salla's irritating chuckle.

Aubrey stopped by Salla's on a Saturday afternoon, knocking hesitantly on her door. He thought he heard cello music echoing through the apartment, but all the lights were off. He gave one last knock. The music stopped, and she stood at the door. Her luminescent skin glowed in the half-light, her form outlined by the darkened room behind her. He stood and stared, as always taken aback at the effect of her presence on him.

"Hello! *Shabbat Shalom*." Oblivious, Salla ushered him in. "Sorry about the light. It just takes your eyes a moment to adjust."

Aubrey looked around the dim living room, puzzled.

"Oh—'*Shabbat Shalom*' means 'Happy Sabbath', which probably is a good place to start." Salla offered a brief glimpse of her crooked smile. "I'm really glad to see you actually. I was getting a little desperate. If you don't mind, I'm in dire need of a *Shabbos Goy*."

"I'm sorry, a what did you say?"

"*Shabbos Goy*. There's a proscription against working on the Sabbath—you know: 'remember the Sabbath and keep it holy'?" At Aubrey's nod, Salla continued, hesitantly. "Well, many observant Jews hire gentiles to do the things they cannot do themselves on Shabbos."

"Like what—eat pork?"

"Funny! No, more like driving, turning off lights, lighting candles—that sort of thing. Paying overdue parking tickets online before the fine doubles."

Aubrey laughed, and leaned against the doorway. "The last's pretty specific, as general examples go."

Salla's chuckle was tinged with chagrin. "True. The problem is we're not supposed to ask a gentile to do these things directly. It's a lot of trouble, though, because I can't turn on my laptop to pay them online. But I can't afford $150 in fines—$75 is already crazy enough. It's my own fault, of course, I should have paid it right away. I'm so annoyed with myself." Absently, she did finger stretching exercises, looking at her hands. "Anyway, I take the proscription against using electricity seriously. I really love the idea of giving the earth a day of rest, you know? It seems a particularly meaningful way to observe the Sabbath."

"It does sound a bit of alright. Quite the green thing to do and all." Aubrey groped his way to Salla's couch and sat, giving her leave to launch into one of her lectures. He loved it when she did this—and not solely because of an atavistic sexy librarian fetish he might have been harboring, although that certainly didn't detract.

He looked at the photograph of the stained glass tree on the opposite wall. Light from Salla's living room window lent it an ethereal air.

"Conservation does seem to be a common thread in Judaism, one I really treasure." Salla was delighted to see Aubrey sit down, and she quickly joined him on the couch, accidentally sitting closer than she would in such circumstances. "Have I told you about the concept of *Tikkun olam* yet?"

"I don't believe so, no." Aubrey smiled at her in the weak light. When she hesitated, he nodded her on.

"Well, it literally means to 'perfect the world' and many Jews take it to mean it's our responsibility to do so, through good deeds, conservation of the planet, and heeding the laws of the Torah. It's something we say three times a day as part of the *Aleinu*—you know, my daily prayers?" Salla paused and swept her long hair behind her back, waiting for his smile. She smiled back, and continued. "In *Kabala* it's been suggested that the prayer itself brings the world closer to perfection. The *Aleinu* itself says, basically, that when all the world recognizes the one God, the world will have been perfected."

"And do you believe that to be true?" Aubrey didn't usually risk interrupting, but he felt compelled to ask.

"What—me?" Salla paused a moment, taken aback. "Well, yes, of course."

"You sound doubtful."

"No. I don't think everyone must convert to Judaism, if that's what you're wondering. I just think the world would be better if we all shared a reasonable set of values. Like the concept that healing the world is our main goal."

"Well, I would be remiss not to aid in such an honorable goal." Aubrey's eyes crinkled faintly, but he gave Salla's problem serious consideration.

"Okay, here's a thought. I was planning a stop by the library after I visited with you a bit. I'm sure the computers there are on all the time, anyway, yeah? So you wouldn't be turning anything on. And since I was already heading that way, ahem, you wouldn't be using extra gas if you hitched a ride. Right?"

Salla hesitated, considering this idea and all its implications. At her quick nod, Aubrey held out his hand. "Come along, then, your—what did you call it? *Shabbos Goy*?" She smiled, the corner of her mouth forming a point on her cheek. "Your *Shabbos Goy* is at the ready."

As Aubrey opened the door to help Salla into his steel blue Ferrari—which he'd ferried from London at great expense—he stole a look at her form. She drew the seatbelt on, defining her thin waist, her long legs outlined through the length of skirt that fell to her calf.

She looked exactly right in his beloved car, somehow, her smooth, tall form juxtaposed against the car's plunging lines. Salla's beauty was of the type that couldn't be defined with a simple itemization of assets. Wide, deep-set eyes, gleaming hair, clear skin, plump lips; these she possessed in correct measure, but Aubrey's attraction to her sprang more, he thought, from the cadence of her voice, the length of her bones; the shape of her ears and their position on her head. The tilting, quixotic smile which she released in sweet, intimate bursts.

She was the only person he'd ever met that made faith sound like a vaguely respectable intellectual pursuit—when she spoke of her faith his critical mind was unusually quiet.

As Aubrey pulled out onto the street, Salla relaxed. He handled the old car with a pride and confidence that charmed her. More importantly, he seemed to know exactly the quickest route to Toronto's Reference Library, a litmus test that many of Salla's potential suitors would have failed. He parked at the curb—taking up an entire lane and risking the wrath of angry Toronto drivers—and gallantly leapt out and ran to her side of the car to open her door.

"Your library computers await milady. I'll locate a parking space for the chariot and return anon." Running back to the driver's side, Aubrey jumped in and pulled away.

"Hey, Bishop! You fucking Nazi! Don't you know when you're not wanted? Go the fuck home!" A young, slim man, of a type that one would not imagine yelling at strangers, jabbed his middle finger at Aubrey's car as it retreated.

A pang of sympathy for Aubrey caught Salla unawares.

"What are you talking about—Nazi! Have you even heard his music?" She stared at the man, daring him to respond. He dropped his eyes, returned to unlocking his bicycle.

"I don't need to. He's a world-class asshole—where have you been?" he said, his voice less certain.

"Why don't you try listening to his lyrics instead of judging him in ignorance?" Salla winced at the edge in her voice. She'd assumed that something like this might happen, if she was going to be with Aubrey in public. She'd planned to come across as the reasonable one.

"I don't need to read Mein Kampf to know Hitler was a monster. What are you, his PR team?"

Stepping back from the man, Salla went to the library entrance to wait. She kept her head down, her hands shaking, until she was sure the man was gone. When she looked up, Aubrey was striding toward her, a smile warming his features.

"Aye-up. Shall we commence?"

Salla looked at him, taking in his weathered skin, his blue eyes, the thick tuft of hair, greyer than the rest, that grew up from his forehead.

"I've just had a rather uncomfortable experience, Aubrey."

Aubrey's smile dropped. "Oh. I see. I assume you've met one of my, er, *not*-fans?"

"Is that what you call them?" Salla's smile was stiff. "He was screaming and gesticulating at you as you drove away. Compared you to Hitler. I guess you're used to that sort of thing."

Aubrey frowned. Crossing his arms, he leaned back against the wall of the library.

"Honestly, it's not the sort of thing one gets used to, so much as something one rises above."

Salla's sad eyes caught his. "Something *one* rises above?"

He smiled into them.

"Okay, so I'm very good at distancing myself. Salla, it's been over a decade. Surely there's nothing I can say, or do, at this point that's going to change anything."

"But that's—"

"Salla. Please. Let it go."

Salla threw up her hands. "Okay! Okay." And yet she felt she was abandoning a friend.

Ignorant of or oblivious to Salla's quandary, Aubrey took her hand and swept her through the library's revolving doors. The parking ticket he was incurring at that moment would fall behind his hotel dresser where it would sit for years, accumulating overdue penalties. It would never be paid.

Chapter 9

Satan's plan is but to excite enmity and hatred between you with
intoxicants and gambling, and hinder you
from the remembrance of Allah,
and from prayer: will ye not then abstain?

~Al-Maeda 5:19
Holy Qur'an

"So, what's up mate? You want to grab some pints tonight? Or are you too busy again?" Ian, leaning in the doorway of Aubrey's hotel suite, sounded tired.

"Yo, Hadji-man," Aubrey said, smiling. "You want to make a few toasts to Allah while we're at it?" Aubrey picked up his guitar from its stand, and made for the sitting area of the suite. Reaching the Victorian-era settee, he sat and placed the guitar on his lap.

"Oh, sod off, Aubrey. What's a bit of the lash got to do with my religious beliefs? I read the other day that alcohol's an Arabic word. Didn't know that now, did you?"

" No, I did not. But it's not me who cares how much you put away. It's your eternal damnation, not mine—just one of the many advantages of atheism." Aubrey tuned his guitar, cocking his head as the harmonics rang out.

"Anyway, it's been a while, mate. We need to catch up. To attempt such a feat without large quantities of a decent ale—well, it's unheard of."

"Right, yeah." Ian didn't laugh.

Looking Ian in the eyes, yet somehow past him, Aubrey picked out a tune.

"What's that you're playing?" Ian's voice was tinged with a peevish suspicion which they both heard. Ian fought to lighten his tone. "Sounds foreign."

"Oh. Well, it's an Israeli folk tune." Aubrey felt silly, for no reason he could think of. "You've probably never heard it."

"Aye, probably not." This was drawn out in Ian's unique brogue. "Okay, well, I'll arrange a cab. Meet me in the lobby around seven—how's that?"

"It's a date, sweetheart—" Aubrey made kissing noises as Ian shut the door.

A few hours later, Ian and Aubrey stood at the bar of the Nag's Head, a scruffy English pub on Toronto's post-bohemian Queen St. West. Each had a Guinness in hand.

"So, how's my little Mohamedan?"

"Ach, Aub, would ya just lay off? I put up with so much crap from you about this."

Nevertheless, Ian told Aubrey of his studies; how he'd mastered the ritual of *wudhû*—the cleansing ceremony that was the prelude to Islamic prayer. He was so proud of this accomplishment that Aubrey was taken aback, guilt forming in an unfamiliar place.

"You know man, that's brilliant," he said. "I can see you're getting something out of it, and I'm happy for you."

"What are you going on about now?" Ian put down his beer, and looked at Aubrey, his eyebrows comically high in his forehead.

"I know I've been a pill. I'm going to try to stop. From now on, nothing but respect, yeah?" Aubrey, with little success, tried to sound as though he believed what he was saying. Ian was having none of it.

"What a load of cack. What the fuck's going on with you these days, Aubrey? I swear I can't tell."

"I know. I don't know! I always denounce religion as the root of all evil. Right? It breeds intolerance, divisiveness and, well, you've been treated to the diatribe. Now, though—well, I'm wondering if *I'm* the intolerant one."

Ian was looking at Aubrey, his expression bemused. At Aubrey's last words he laughed, perhaps angrily. "Really? You—intolerant, now? Surely you're having me on. You're a model of brotherly love and acceptance, you are. Next thing, you'll be filling out an application for sainthood."

"Never," Aubrey declared dramatically, his finger in the air, and waited for Ian to laugh, which he did, dutifully, after a pause. "It's not that I feel I was wrong—I'm still convinced religion's a load of bollocks—it's more that I'm realizing I've sort of been just as bad, in my own way. A self-righteous arsehole, some would say." They shared a genuine laugh, remembering a time—in the still painful past—when it seemed everyone in the entire world was saying exactly that.

"Wait. This sudden change wouldn't have to anything do with that Jew girl?"

"Forsooth. Another pint, fair maiden," Aubrey called to the purple-haired bartender, "No, make it two, in the event you're otherwise disposed when we're ready for the next round."

"Aubrey?" Ian was not so easily put off. "Well? Is that it? She's converted you, now?"

"'Course not. Now you're being completely daft. I said, I still think it's all a load of shite; I'm just trying to be more respectful of other's beliefs. Like Salla is of mine."

"Oh, ho ho. I knew it." Ian's triumph had a bitter edge. "Salla, eh? Looks like it's hotting up between you and the rabbi, yeah? It's not like you to keep in mind any old random scag's name. Who's the one that stayed the night last week? Remember? Super totty? What was her name?"

"It was Colleen. She has a small part in 'This Night', herself. And it was the week before last."

"Right—Colleen. She played the cat creature. In heat."

"That's her. She's coming to the wrap party, actually."

"Okay, so you remembered her name. She must have had manna flowing from her quim. I guess that's why she was still here in the morning. Well, you'll be having some good times at the after party, at least."

"Yes, um, that's something I wanted to talk to you about, old son. Salla's coming to the wrap party. I've invited her, and she accepted. All right? And I don't want to take a lot of shite about it from you."

"Fine, mate, don't get your knickers up your arse. I can get off your back, if you're planning to stay off mine."

"I am. But I'm sort of going to need your help."

"I hear you, mate. Too many birds, too little tonker. I'm happy to help you, my friend. Want me to give the rabbi a good rodgering? She'll have a night she'll not soon forget."

"Ian." Aubrey found himself much angrier than the situation called for. "Fuck off—got it? Salla is off limits. She's my friend and I won't have you slagging her off." Aubrey leaned toward Ian, pinning him down with his eyes. "Ever. All right? She's one of the most decent people I know, and she deserves your respect. Don't forget it."

"Hold on there, mate—who the fuck are you, today? I don't respect anyone I don't have to, and she's never done a thing to earn it—from me, anyway. You might be the gaffer, but no one tells me how to think." His tone was so uncharacteristic that Aubrey was taken aback. He paused.

"Okay. Sorry." Aubrey looked Ian in the eyes, again, and put down his beer. "You're right, about that, certainly. But if you knew her, you'd have more respect, I promise you that."

Aubrey paused a moment, gathering himself for a speech that would have been easy to give to any other person he'd ever known. "Ian, I want to make a point of telling you that I don't like it when you say these bigoted things and I'm supposed to just pretend they're benign. I really can't stand it. Jews are people, just like you, just like me, just like him." Aubrey jerked his thumb at a chubby drunken urbanite bent over at the bar, glowing neon in tight pink jeans and a lime green t-shirt two sizes too small. They looked at the guy, and then at each other.

"Okay, maybe not him. But you hear me, don't you?" Aubrey put his hand on Ian's shoulder. "It's getting old. I know Israel's not your version of Disneyland—nor is it mine—but I don't like your anti-Semitic tirades. I'm beginning to feel that silence on my part is tacit agreement, yeah?"

"Tacit?"

"Yeah, like I'm agreeing without saying anything. It makes me feel dirty. Watch the anti-Semitic shite."

"Right, I'm supposed to just smile and wave my little hand when they murder Palestinian children? As a response to rockets that fizzle on impact?" Ian swallowed his beer, grimacing.

"Look, by 'they' do you mean Jewish people, or are you talking about Israel? Because it's not the same thing."

"Oh, that's brilliant, The lot of them are responsible for crushing Palestine."

"That's just not true. Salla, for example, is against Israel's military policy."

"Well isn't Salla just the bee's knees?" Ian's knuckles were white around his glass. "You're with her every waking moment—you even sound like her! She's got you by the bell-end, Aubrey."

"What are you going on about? My views haven't changed one iota. We haven't even spoken of these things. Salla's seeing me, you stupid git. That should tell you something about her, right?"

"Wait. Do you love her?"

"What?" Aubrey was startled.

"She's 'seeing you'? When the fuck did you start talking like that? You sound like a little girl—'she's seeing me, she's seeing me—oh goody, goody gumdrops.' What the fuck, Aubrey? Are you, falling for her? Or not?"

"Well, no. Of course not. She's studying to be a fucking rabbi, for God's sake. Can you imagine anything more tedious? And she's never smoked a joint in her life, I'd wager." Aubrey's laugh was hollow. They sat in silence for a moment.

"She's only ever been drunk twice, she told me, but she said she 'wasn't sure about the second time—she may just have been tired,' for God's sake."

"She shags like a nun in a fiberglass habit, too, I bet."

Aubrey laughed, despite himself. "I don't know. And that's all I'm ever going to say on that topic."

"Oh, now, look at the cute little gentleman. Isn't he sweet?"

"Sod off and drink your beer," Aubrey said, gloomily. They drank. Ian didn't bother to hide his smirk.

Chapter 10

And Ruth said, "Do not entreat me to leave you,
to return from following you,
for wherever you go, I will go, and
wherever you lodge, I will lodge;
your people shall be my people
and your God my God."

~Ruth 1:16
K'tuvim

Salla entered the main hall of Ahavas Sholom, the Orthodox synagogue she'd joined that year, breathless at the two-stories of space looming above her. The temple she'd been raised in had begun in a former elementary school and lacked the grandeur of a building designed specifically for the purpose of worship. Almost in spite of herself, Salla was awed by the soaring ceilings and the detailed stained glass friezes. While she supposed the Almighty would have no preference, human beings seemed to expect a certain degree of opulence in a house of G-d. It helped put them in the proper frame of mind for prayer. Salla had expected the space to have this affect on her, but as the weeks went by she just felt out of place.

Adjusting her father's old *tallit* [21] around her shoulders—she'd worn

---

[21] ta'leeth / n. *Hebrew.* A shawl-like garment
with fringes,at the four corners, worn around the shoulders by Orthodox and
Conservative (and sometimes Reform) Jews during certain prayers.

68

the white prayer shawl every morning for the past several years, but it sat awkwardly on her here—Salla re-inserted the bobby pin that kept her pretty new *kippah*[22] in place atop her tidy chignon. She carried her father's antique *siddur*[23] in her right hand, hoping the weight of the old prayer book would make her feel less conspicuous. She ignored the sidelong glances and tried not to fidget as she climbed the stairs to the *Ezrat Nashim*—the segregated section in which the women of this synagogue sat. The women were allotted this separate area, as far from the *bihmah* as possible, Salla imagined, to emphasize the fact that they were not to touch the Torah in the presence of men. As she took her seat in a front row pew, Salla tried to smile at the curious faces turning toward her. She knew that the rabbi frowned on women donning the vestments of men—he'd said so in exactly these words—but she wasn't overly concerned. His appreciation for the depth of Salla's learning softened his resolve on this point, and she considered herself a good influence on him. The rabbi's learnedness had drawn Salla to Ahavas Sholom; the seating arrangements certainly had not.

The woman beside her, every hair on her head encased in the traditional snood—the *mitpachat*—as well as a closely fitted hat, peered at Salla curiously, then quickly looked away.

"Hello. *Vos iz es faran neyes*?" Salla said, catching her attention and smiling broadly.

"Oh," the woman laughed. "Nothing much. What's new with you?"

"You know, the usual," Salla chuckled, relieved. A bit of Yiddish went a long way. In Orthodox circles, it was a social lubricant rivaling wine in efficacy. Accepting Salla's gesture, the woman relaxed, and patted the seat beside her.

"So, welcome to Ahavas Sholom. I think I've seen you around before. I thought maybe you were *baal teshuva*?"

"Well, no, not really. I've been practicing all my life, in a Reform synagogue."

"Hmmm. Reform. I see."

"Well, yes. In fact my father was the rabbi at Or Hadash, before he died."

---

[22] kee'pah / n. *Hebrew*. A skull cap, yarmulke. Used by Jewish men and boys (and Reform women) to cover the head in the presence of God.

[23] sid'ur / n. *Hebrew*. A Jewish prayer book designed for use chiefly on days other than festivals and holy days; a daily prayer book.

"Oh. Your father was Yosef Avi Kahn?—may he rest in peace. I remember reading about him in the paper. He was a very good man. Such a loss. So many wonderful things he did for his community. And all the money he raised for Israel!" The woman paused, then went on in a conspiratorial tone. "I'm sorry for what I said. I'm not one of those who thinks the Reforms are heretics, I promise you. I, for one, am glad you're here—I don't care what they say. And to learn you're the daughter of Rebbe Kahn..."

"Yes, well, he was an inspiration to me. In fact, I'm going to start my *Aliyah* year in April. That's why I joined this *shul*[24]: I wanted to belong to a temple that was rigorous in its commitment to *Halakha*[25]."

"What do you mean, your Aliyah *year*?"

"I'm going to Israel to become fluent in Hebrew, and immerse myself in the culture." Salla was puzzled to be answering this question.

"Well, of course I know what Aliyah means dear." The other woman laughed and patted Salla's arm. "I just don't know why you'd go for just a year."

"Oh. It's a requirement for Rabbinical Studies. I've applied to Rabbinical School, and I'm planning to start in the spring. You never know, maybe someday I'll be Rabbi, here."

The woman laughed heartily, and patted Salla again.

"Well, that's not going to happen, dear, but good for you for trying. I'm sure the Reforms would love to have you—they're pretty lax about that sort of thing."

"What do you mean, *lax*?" Salla said, poised. "I don't think including women in the pursuit of education is a sign of moral laxity. Do you?"

"Women should pursue education that is appropriate for their duties. Of course. We have men and women for a reason. I understand why you would want to follow in your father's footsteps, but there are just some things that are better left to men."

"I'm not following in his footsteps! It's just—never mind. I simply couldn't disagree more. I hope you wouldn't stop your daughter from entering the Rabbinate, if that was something she truly wanted to do."

Salla had gone over this argument many times in her head. She was mortified that now she had an opportunity to air her views, she was coming across as confrontational. She'd been hoping to educate, to lead

---

[24] shUl / n. *Yiddish*. Synagogue.
[25] Huh-luhk'-khuh / phrase. *Hebrew*. Lit., "the path that one walks." Jewish law; i.e. the complete body of rules and practices that Jews are bound to follow.

by gentle example. This wasn't going as planned.

"I most certainly would stop my daughter from acting like a man. She'll be a dutiful wife, as is proper. And I've never been yelled at by a Rabbi. You're very emotional—that's one of the reasons women should not obtain *semicha*[26]. They just get too emotional."

"I am not emotional, and I wasn't yelling." Salla said, too loudly.

Just then, the doors opened and Rebbe Efron strode into the prayer hall below, his grey beard pointing the way. The woman put her finger to her lips, shook her head at Salla, and slid down the pew until she was sitting several feet away. With a final sidelong glare, she opened her prayer book. As the rabbi began the service, Salla closed her eyes, rubbed her temples, and, sighing, opened her own book. Gradually, she relaxed into the solitude of prayer.

As Salla walked from Bubbie's house—it was her custom to borrow Bubbie's old car to drive to the temple—a familiar green Mercedes pulled up beside her. The woman in the driver's seat—a very young fifty-something with a colorful scarf and a carefree tilt to her head—cocked a crooked smile at the girl.

"Mom!" Salla, startled, stuttered to a halt. "Hi!" It was time to vary her routine, if it was this easy to track her down.

"Salla!" Esther smiled gaily. "Hop in! Let me take you out for lunch?"

They made themselves comfortable at Esther's favorite booth in her favorite restaurant, an overpriced eatery in the financial district near her second husband's offices.

"So. Is it true? Your Bubbie tells me you might have a new man in your life?"

"Oh, great." Salla's voice was flat. Her mother surprised her by laughing, and, after a pause, Salla found herself joining in.

"So, come on now, tell me. Have you really been dating Aubrey Bishop?"

Salla's eyes wandered over her mother, noting signs of age, tiny changes indicating cosmetic corrections, a subtle weariness of posture that was new. She leaned forward, her elbows on the table. She missed her mother quite a bit, some days. More these days than at any time in the past.

---

[26] *semicha* / sem-E'-khah / n. *Hebrew.* Derived from "to be authorized", in reference to the ordination of a rabbi.

"Well, yes. I have. And I must say, right up front, that he's not, by any stretch of the imagination, an anti-Semite!"

"Oh dear!" Esther pronounced with a gasp of laughter. Her brows, perfectly shaped with the aid of an expertly wielded eyebrow pencil, stayed perfectly still. Salla watched, wistful, as she realized that her mother felt herself aging and was fighting it.

"Salla, please! I was never one of those who called Aubrey Bishop an anti-Semite."

Esther was silenced by the arrival of the waiter, a dignified man, probably gay, in his late sixties. The staff in this restaurant was aging along with its patrons, along with the velvet banquettes, along with the ornate trim. They gave their orders—the best Eggs Florentine in the city, Salla was assured—and paused until the waiter was out of earshot.

"As I was saying, Aubrey Bishop does not hate Jews. I get it. That God album was just his way of rebelling against the Man."

Salla tried to hide her smile. She'd never understood Esther's self-image as a child of the sixties, but maybe it wasn't as far off the mark as she'd thought.

"That album was a little punk rock, for my tastes, but I remember thinking it was a respectable achievement—although in a rather antagonistic way. I believe your father would have agreed."

Salla agreed.

"Anyway, I bet he's an exciting date, at the very least," her mother said, leaning forward, her smile conspiratorial.

"Well, yes, he definitely is that." Now that her guard was down, Salla's happiness was evident to anyone looking on.

"But I also really like him, as a person, Mom. He's funny, and kind and—wise." Salla said this as though it was only now occurring to her. "Not in a showy way, mind you, but he's a very intelligent man."

"He sounds very nice. Is Bubbie giving you a hard time?"

Salla laughed and sipped her excellent coffee.

"What do you think, Mother?"

"I thought as much. Listen, my darling, that's why I stopped by. I wanted you to know that your mother, at least, is happy for you. It sounds like so much fun! *Variety* says his new movie's going to be a big hit, did you know that?"

"I wouldn't be surprised. He's very talented. You should hear him play Daddy's guitar. You'd be impressed."

Salla, warming to her topic, went on in this vein for a half an hour, between bites of egg and smoked salmon dripping with hollandaise.

Aubrey never failed to bring a perfectly appropriate gift, for example—yesterday's had been a lovely bottle of kosher wine, imported from Israel. He'd taken her to the library, to the movies, to the opera. He always opened her doors; he'd given her a single guitar lesson which revolutionized her playing. He laughed—heartily!—at every single one of Salla's jokes. He was sweet and kind and a good companion in a way she couldn't define so much as itemize.

Esther laughed at this list of virtues. She'd never seen her daughter so animated, and it both charmed and alarmed her.

"You sound just like me, talking about your father—may he rest in peace—thirty years ago."

This gave Salla pause. She put down her fork.

"What do you mean? I never heard you talk about Daddy like that."

"Oh—he was always a wonderful man. You know that, darling. He could do no wrong. He said every single one of his prayers, every single day of his life."

"Mother." Salla's tone contained a warning.

"Sweetheart, you know I would never say a bad thing about your beloved father. It's just that—as you know—we weren't a very happy couple."

It had taken years for Salla to forgive her mother for this.

"And why *was* that, pray tell?"

"Oh, my darling. I had nothing but admiration for him. I do hope you know that."

"Yes. I know." Salla studied her neatly-bitten fingernails.

"Yes. Well, but I think it's important you understand these things. You know that my leaving was a mutual decision?"

Salla had heard this but had never really believed it. Her father would have lived through the most untenable of situations, if only to continue to be an example for his congregation. The fact that her mother had remarried three years later, well, that was damning evidence, though of what exactly, Salla tried not to ponder.

"Marriage to your father was like a chicken marrying a duck. I had nothing but respect for him, of course. That, in essence, was the problem. I'd always wanted to be a rabbi's wife. What decent Jewish girl didn't, back then? We were trained for it from birth. By the time I realized what marriage to a rabbi really meant, I was pregnant with you. So I stayed, and I loved you and admired him. But in the end, admiration really wasn't enough."

"But you guys had so much more. You played together so

beautifully. It was completely transporting, for everyone who heard you."

Salla had sweet memories of her lovely mother standing in front of the ark, wearing a simple dress, strumming a simple guitar, accompanying the cantor in a simple harmony, the congregation singing the responses. Temple Or Hadash was renowned for the quality of its music program.

"Yes, we made music for the *shul*. Every single Sabbath for the entire eighteen years of our marriage we sang at *shul*. We almost never made music at home—don't you remember? Because I didn't feel like it, anymore. Music had become my day job. In a setting where applause is frowned upon."

"But Marty doesn't even play. Don't you miss it?"

"No, not at all—because I still play every day. And I sing anything I want—not just songs from some list approved by a Ritual Committee. And you know what? Marty applauds."

"So what are you saying? That you left Daddy because no one applauded when you performed?" Salla hadn't meant this as coldly as she'd said it.

"No. My God, Salla—you're just trying to pick a fight. Our marriage failed because I came second. You came second. Everything came second to the Temple. It's really how it had to be, with your father. And good for him! He was born to it. But I was not. It was never how I'd wanted to live. I wanted to be Mary."

"Mary!"

"Of '*Peter, Paul and*' fame. I wanted to write important songs and perform them at protest rallies and sleep in on Saturdays. I wanted to go to *shul* only on Yom Kippur, like the rest of my family. I mean, of course we had a *seder*[27] every year, like everyone else, but when have you ever known Bubbie to attend services?"

"Well, never, but, you know—"

"Know what, my darling?"

"Well, I'm pretty sure Bubbie's an atheist."

"Exactly. She sent me to Hebrew school, made sure I was ready for my *Haftarah* reading, threw an extravagant *Bat Mitzvah*. All of it. And your grandfather went along, although I think he spent most of his life angry at God." Esther sighed. "But your Bubbie is just not a believer.

---

[27] *seder* / sA'-duhr / n. *Hebrew*. A ritual dinner held twice during Passover, during which prayers are said and symbolic foods are eaten.

74

Myself, I always believed in the substance, but the ritual? Not so much."

"Hmm," Salla agreed.

Her mother reached across the table to grab her hand.

"But you, you always seemed to love it all—just like your father."

"Mom. You do know I've applied to rabbinical school." Salla steeled herself. Again, her mother surprised her.

"You have, dear? I wasn't sure if you'd changed your mind. Well, I think that's marvelous! The Rabbinate could certainly use more people like you. I'll even come to your Temple for High Holy Days. What do you say?"

Salla smiled. "When the time comes, I'll say thanks for coming, Mom. And *L'Shana Tova*[28]."

They finished their meal in companionable silence.

Aubrey and Salla sat in her favorite restaurant, waiting for their wine. "C'est What" was an underground establishment, Toronto having the kind of weather that encouraged tunneling. It had limestone walls, a unique and ever-changing menu, and an excellent wine list. Usually Salla would order a glass of their decent house red and make it last. Aubrey, however, had just ordered a bottle of the restaurant's finest. It was turning out to be Salla's idea of the perfect evening. The weather was fine, Aubrey was funny and attentive, the movie they'd just seen—a small French film about the inevitability of war—had sparked a lively debate.

"Surely you jest, my sweet. I couldn't disagree more." Aubrey was leaning forward, his expression earnest.

"No, I'm completely sincere. I think man, at his heart, is basically good. Truly." Salla enjoyed arguing with Aubrey. He was even more attractive when animated by his own rhetoric.

"Have you learned about Pol Pot, in any detail? How about the Massacre of Nanking? Did you consider the Third Reich? I mean, come on." Aubrey threw up his hands "You're one of the smartest people I know—you cannot be this naive."

"I don't simply pull my opinions out of thin air. Of course, I've thought about it a great deal."

"Well? Have you? What was the Holocaust, if not a countrywide effort of pure evil? I mean, we say 'Hitler' as though it was the work of one man. But he had the support of a majority—a majority!—of the

---

[28] Shi-nah' tO-vah' / phrase. *Hebrew.* Lit. "May you be inscribed (in the Book of Life) for a good year." Colloquially, "Happy New Year".

German people."

"You don't think I've considered the implications of the German people's support of Hitler? Aubrey. Darling." Salla threw out her arms. She enjoyed mimicking his dramatic style. "I'm a Jew, for heaven's sake. I'm not saying that evil doesn't exist, or that a small percentage of people are not truly evil. I just think humans—as a species—tend to do right by each other." She propped her elbows on the table and rested her chin on her hands. Inasmuch as it doesn't adversely affect our own fortunes. Man is a social creature. Our biological imperative impels us toward altruistic acts."

The waiter brought the Malbec, held out the bottle for Aubrey to inspect. At his nod, the waiter poured two glasses and left.

Salla put her hand over Aubrey's. "Just a moment—you wanted to hear the blessing?"

At his nod, she recited:

> *Barukh attah Adonai*
> *eloheinu melechk ha-olam,*
> *borei peri hagafen.*

"It means, literally: Blessed art thou, lord our God, king of the universe, creator of the fruit of the vine," she said.

"And does that make it safe to drink?"

Salla raised an eyebrow. "Cynic. What's wrong with expressing gratitude for the things we receive? We're about to enjoy this really lovely bottle of wine—thanks, by the way—is there some rule that we have to take the gifts we're offered for granted?"

"You're welcome, my dear, and thank you for enjoying it with me," Aubrey said with a grin. "As I was saying: To what do you attribute the almost overwhelming and willing, co-operation of an *entire people* in what was one of, if not *the*, single greatest work of evil in our entire history?"

"Well that was a mouthful. Do you need time to recover?" Salla smirked her sidelong smile. As he shook his head she lifted her wine glass, inhaled deeply, sipped, and continued.

"Yes, the Holocaust was a work of great evil; ergo, humans have the capacity to do great evil. But people are just as capable of great acts of kindness and sacrifice. I think Germans under Hitler were able to distance themselves from his atrocities, through a sort of turning their faces from the facts. From their humanity. You know?"

Aubrey shrugged.

"It's a sort of mental showing of their backs to the things they could not control. I think most people, when they feel threatened, become very frugal about the things they will take responsibility for. In a safe, perfect world, we look out for the entire community. In a dangerous world, we look out for our friends. In a deadly world, we look out for ourselves."

"Okay, sure, but what would you call that, if not a tendency toward evil?"

"I think it's more like the imperative of self preservation. Don't forget, we're capable of great sacrifice, as well. Everyone talks about Hitler, but very few non-Germans have heard of the White Rose society."

"Sounds familiar, but…"

"Exactly, see? They were a group of students from the University of Munich—none of them older than twenty-five—who decided that, morally, they had no choice but to fight the Nazis. They did so with the only weapons at their disposal, the printing press being mightier than the war machine. They distributed pamphlets, sprayed graffiti propaganda, recruited like-minded students. They did everything in their means to empower the German people—or at least the students at the University— to resist the Third Reich."

"So, what happened to them?"

"Well, after a show trial in which the judge acted as the prosecutor, haranguing them for presenting a threat to the dream of German supremacy, the three ringleaders were executed." Salla slumped back in her seat, unsure where she was taking this. "The Gestapo hunted down and executed several others. Many other students from the University of Munich were sent to concentration camps."

"Of course," Aubrey said, trying not to look triumphant.

"But that doesn't mean they didn't represent a much larger group. They called themselves members of the 'other' Germany, comprised of poets and thinkers, who found Hitler's policies reprehensible. They weren't afraid to fight." Salla paused and gazed at stone walls.

"Anyway, why are we always talking about how the world affects Jews? I'm starting to feel more like a tour guide than an instructor."

"I think of it more as how the world affects Salla, actually." His smile made its way into her and brought out one of her own. He really was a very lovely man.

"And what about you? What effect does the world have on my favorite fallen rock star?"

At his sad face, Salla winced and shook her head. She was such an ox, sometimes.

"I'm so sorry Aubrey—I didn't mean to be callous. You seem so sanguine about your life, I—"

"—no, please don't apologize. I've had a decade to get used to falling. I really don't care about it anymore. But I do care about what you think of me."

He reached across the table for her hand, traced her palm and smiled at her. Salla shivered, his touch taking her out of her mind and into her body.

"Besides," he said, "I love to hear you rant. Sometimes I have at you just to hear your response."

She smiled into his eyes, her mouth tilted, and snatched her hand back to swat him with it. "Just for that, let's talk about love," she said.

"Love?"

"Yes. Love. And marriage. And housefuls of children, each one with a diaper demanding immediate attention."

Aubrey's laughter was both genuine and muted.

"So you think that's the way to shut me up, is it? What if I like talking about love?"

"Well, let's see. You've never been married—I think your longest relationship was with that singer who likes to tie things up and ignite them on stage—a *match* made in heaven, apparently. Pun *int*ended!"

Aubrey groaned but Salla was undeterred.

"Where was I… Oh! You *live* in a *hotel* room. And you drink, daily, to riotous excess."

Salla held out her glass of wine to Aubrey, who refilled it to the top, ignoring the hand she held up to stop him. When he was done, she poured half of it back into his glass.

"The upshot is, Aubrey, that you're perfectly content with this state of affairs. Blissfully unfettered, I believe you've been quoted as saying."

"Someone *has* done her homework." Aubrey was daunted by this array of facts. Salla was not.

"There are approximately as many fan sites as there are flame sites devoted solely to you, and they have all come to the same conclusion in this area at least: Aubrey Bishop is not marriageable."

"Wow… You know, Salla, you're not supposed to discuss this with me, right? I mean isn't it rather forward to mention children on a third date?"

"Oooh, is this a date? And here I am, without a copy of the rule book." Salla looked steadily at Aubrey. "The thing is, I *do* want marriage. And children—lots of them. Four, or so. And I *am* crazy about you—to a degree you can't imagine, because I make some effort to hide it." Aubrey met her eyes, then cast his at the table.

"The thing is, dear friend." Reaching across the table, Salla grasped his hand in both of hers. "I know you're not the one with whom I'm going to have the life I want. There's no point in being oblique. You're a forthright person, and you deserve nothing less."

"Oh, Salla, Salla, Salla. I thought I lacked artifice. You, my sweet, are thoroughly devoid of it. One of the many things I love about you."

She released his hand, and they sipped their wine in silence, Salla contemplating, then dismissing, his use of the word 'love'.

Aubrey cleared his throat.

"Of course, this conversation does seem kind of awkwardly premature. I mean, we haven't even—"

"Fucked?" Salla's quirky smile crept up her cheek again.

"Salla!" Aubrey quickly glanced around the room, checking to see if anyone else had heard.

Salla laughed. Only those who didn't know her well would find it ironic that *she* had the capacity to shock *him*.

"I was going to say… made love." Aubrey said. "We've never made love." At Salla's quick laugh he stared at the table, and put forth an uncomfortable chuckle.

"Yuck. Made love," Salla said, her expression mock-sour. "You know, I've never been comfortable with that phrase. Ever since my mother used it in reference to her and her husband." She allowed herself a delicate shudder. "I prefer to call it something else; 'boinking' or, 'making the beast with two backs' or, I don't know, 'bumping uglies'—I'm particularly fond of that one." She smiled, waiting for Aubrey's laughter to subside.

"I don't think anyone's mature enough to talk about sex with a parent."

At Aubrey's emphatic nod, she had a new thought.

"But isn't making love something for people who *are* in love? It's considered a great *mitzvah*[29] to give your wife an orgasm. But Judaism's not as approving on the subject of friends with benefits."

"I don't know, Salla, I just know I'm glad you're my friend, with or without benefits."

A little sadly, they got back to arguing about the inherent

---

[29] *mitz·vah* / noun. *Hebrew.* A good deed done from religious duty.

benevolence—or lack of same—of human nature, and, not long after, Aubrey took her home. She opened her door, kissed him on the cheek, thanked him sweetly, and ducked into her apartment. From where he stood on the pavement, Aubrey smiled at the sound of the deadbolt as she locked the door behind her. He shook his head as he drove away.

Chapter 11

*O ye who believe! stand out firmly for Allah, as witnesses to fair
dealing, and let not others' hatred of you make you swerve to
wrong and depart from justice. Be just: that is next to piety, and
fear Allah. For Allah is well-acquainted with all that ye do.*

~Surat al-Ma'idah
The Holy Qur'an

The Activists for Allah sat on white plastic chairs, elbows propped
on a plastic picnic table they'd brought in from the back yard. They'd
forgotten to knock the snow off the chairs and a couple of them were
sitting on wet spots, shifting, uncomfortable in the cool dank air.

The small brick house owned by Akil's parents sat in a neighborhood
of identical buildings, each unique only in the items the occupants
displayed in front. Akil's parents had placed in their tiny half of the yard
a glittering plastic snowman outlined with of tiny colorful lights. The
neighbors who occupied the other half of the building had chosen to fill
their porch with a teetering collection of broken appliances, discarded
clothing, odiferous garbage bags, and other household ephemera.

The Activists met only when Akil's parents were out of the house,
but since both Mr. and Mrs. Khoury worked evening shifts at a local dry
cleaner, the group met often.

Ishmael, tall and thin, sporting a thick beard and a dirty red toque,
put his arm over Akil's shoulders and gave him a shake. "So how's the

81

job hunting coming along, Akil? Get that fifty-thousand dollar desk job yet?" In unison, each Activist issued a hollow laugh; irony on a chalk board. Akil looked at the ground, and shook his head.

"Yeah, right," he said, his mouth a grimace. "I was sitting in the waiting room with this other guy and he's, like, forty, and wearing a suit. He's even carrying a briefcase, eh? And I'm like, no way are they going to hire me over him. The guy was in there for like half an hour. And they spent ten minutes on my interview, tops. I'm like, no way? and they're like, yeah, well sorry, see ya!" He waggled his fingers in the air. "After I spent ten weeks learning those office applications. I got straight A's in the class on Excel!"

Sympathetic noises issued all around. They'd all been there; those who were still trying were still there. The latest dip in the US economy had pulled the Toronto job market down with it. You needed both education and experience to get hired. None of the Activists had either. But they did have a saying: "Petty theft for petty cash." Lifting things that rich people didn't appreciate seemed to even the score.

Roger D, tall and thick, his baseball cap tilted sideways to keep a blue and white *keffiyeh*[30] in place, elbowed Akil in the ribs. "Yo, you'll have plenty of time to go legit, little brother. What I want to know is, what about that tight little hoe nex' do', Akil? She spreading any of that *koos* around?"

"Yeah, right. She'll give it up for anything that walks, besides me. Her old man called my dad a rag-head. To his face!" Akil's face was tighter than any of them had ever seen it. "If I'd been there—pow!" He plowed his fist into an imaginary face, but his eyes were sad. His parents worked so hard, and the mortgage was up for renewal. The current interest rates would push the monthly expenses far beyond the family's ability to pay. And the evil scum next door just bred like rabbits, collected their welfare, and threatened his family. They'd pay with eternal damnation, but it wouldn't come soon. Akil clenched his hands as he thought of the pig who'd insulted his father. No better than filth, the man would keep his house, while the Koury's lost theirs. Unless Akil could help it.

Roger D clapped Akil on the back, shaking his head.

"I'm sorry man. That sucks. Even if the bitch don't." He stood, looking around. "All right, men. Let's call this meeting to order. Akil—

---

[30] *keffiyeh* / keff-E'-yeh / n. *Arabic*. A headdress worn by Arab men, made from a square of cotton fabric, held on with a band tied around the crown of the head.

read the minutes of the last meeting for us."

"Uh, sure." Akil shook his head, then looked around for his notepad, purchased for just this purpose. He opened it to the first page, and squinted at the scribbles there.

"Well, we watched those videos from that Habib guy and we thought we'd try to raise some money to send for weapons. I was supposed to do some background research, but I haven't had a chance." He made a note.

"And Fareed's going to be released from jail on Friday—his parents are working, so we've got to pick him up. Theft over five—good thing he's a young offender—he'd be getting out in ten instead of two. And I told you guys about my new recruit, Ian Al Habib."

At this Roger D leaned forward. "He's the cat who works for the BishoPrics?"

Ishmael was smiling, his thin face split by a crooked grin. "English guy, right? I saw him at the mosque—he's one messed-up looking mother fucker."

"When they let you back in the *masjid*, Ishmael? I thought Imam Safar tossed you out."

"Yeah, well—he's not always around, eh? Besides—with that big new mosque in town, he can't afford to be rude. My dad's kind of a big donor."

Of them all, Ishmael was the only one who had access to funds, in the form of an inheritance he was spending as fast as he could while his parents were alive. While a few of the Activists wielded their pick-pocketing skills on the streets of Toronto, Ishmael had no farther to go than the wallet of his rich father. Akil stole because he had no other way of getting money. Ishmael did it for fun, rather than profit.

"Anyway, Ian's okay," Akil said. "He kind of looks like a punk, but he's cool."

"Yeah, well, no props for the company he keeps. How come he's working for that hater?" Roger's arms were folded across his chest, and his eyes held Akil fast. The question wasn't rhetorical.

"I don't know. He's been with him for years. Like, twenty. He says he's trying to convert Bishop to Islam."

Roger D snorted. "No way in hell's that gonna happen. Aubrey Bishop is one evil son of a bitch. He hates all believers—don't you forget it." He nodded at Akil's earnest face in approval. "That's fine, though. He can join us next week. I think your recruit is going to make a big contribution to the cause."

Roger's proposal that they adopt the Hamas charter slogan was passed unanimously, with a great deal of congenial backslapping. They smiled at each other with pride as Akil read: "Allah is its goal, The Prophet its model, the Qur'an its Charter, jihad its path, and death for the cause of Allah its most sublime belief."

At these last words, Roger D thumped his chest with his fist. "Inshalla, y'all!" The others echoed, more quietly, perhaps, than he.

Chapter 12

Let us walk in the woods, says the cat.
I'll teach you to read the tabloid of scents,
to fade into shadow, wait like a trap, to hunt.
Now I lay this plump warm mouse on your mat.

~From The Cat's Song
By Marge Piercy

The cat leapt to the Blanket Lady's window, as was his custom of late, to continue his investigation of the goings on in Her den. If he continued to find them to his liking, he would intensify his courtship of Her.

Without her blanket, she was an odd combination of predator and prey. While her body held a lanky grace, her movements were bird-like, simple. He'd seen her remove the blanket only once before—tucking it away like a molly cat careful with her new kitten, resisting the urge to bat at the dangling fringe—and here she was, bare of it again. He suspected she shed the blanket when her heat approached.

A Man, the one who'd left his scent at the Lady's door many mornings ago, was with the Lady, his eagerness evident in his leaning in her every direction. The Man took up the Lady's long-necked box, striking its strings to make it sing, and the two caterwauled over it.

The cat tucked his forepaws under his chest, relaxed enough to allow a faint rumble to issue forth. His Blanket Lady was very enamored of this male, and it was working out well for the cat. An hour before, he had watched through the kitchen window as She prepared for him a small dish of the cooked flesh of a bird—a welcome departure from the dried, crunchy fare She usually served.

Ordinarily, the cat was wary of male humans. They were far more likely to offer him their foot than were females of the species, and far less likely to offer him food. The Blanket Lady's new companion, however, kept his territorial instincts in check, and, in a strange twist, was the one who had placed the bowl of delicious bird remains on the step. The Man was probably hoping this display would induce the Lady to mate with him.

As he watched from the windowsill, the cat cleaned himself, gleaning from his whiskers another fragrant hint of bird. While he groomed, he watched the Lady and Man cavort, their mouths moving relentlessly, their sharp bursts of humor always a little startling.

As the sky darkened, the cat was pleased to note the Blanket Lady took the male's arm and sidled him out the door, closing it firmly behind him.

Yes, the cat decided, this seemed quite an appropriate situation. Over the next weeks he would make a detailed feasibility study of joining the Blanket Lady in Her den, before he decided whether to move. Meanwhile, he would make her an offering—the head of a mouse perhaps, or the entrails of a squirrel. Squirrels were plentiful this year and he knew she was fond of them. On more than one occasion she'd tried to trap a juicy black female that lived in a tree near her door. While she'd been able to coax the prey to her, holding out hard little fruits that the creature consumed with relish, the Lady's smooth paws were ineffectual weapons and she'd merely brushed its fur with one clawless digit before it leapt free.

There was still a chance the Man's treatment of the cat would change if the Lady accepted him as her mate, so the cat would proceed cautiously, but he was optimistic. The den seemed a happy, calm place, and he'd made note of a pillow near a south-facing window.

As the sky darkened into night, an Angry presence joined him, creeping up to peer through another window. At this unwelcome company, the cat's ears lay back while his fur stood up, freezing the rumble in his chest and leaving prickles down his spine. He stole off.

Chapter 13

I will incline my ear to a proverb;
I will solve my riddle to the music of the lyre.

~Psalm 49:4
The Holy Bible

His cell phone tucked between ear and shoulder, Aubrey pulled apart the raw silk curtains, opening his room to the city view he was paying a premium for. The lights on the skyscrapers twinkled as the dusk dimmed into night. His hotel room reeked of good whiskey and imaginative sex. The girl had left, reluctantly, several hours ago, but traces of her lingered. Salla's voice message, the only way her phone was ever answered, played, then beeped.

"Salla? Hi, it's Aubrey. Listen… can I come pick you up, tonight, around nine or ten? Give me a call when you get this. Cheers."

He lay back on the brocade cover on his king-size hotel bed, nursing a mild hangover that had lingered through the day. He'd had far less than his normal daily intake the night before. He made a mental note—of the kind that would flutter away the moment he stopped thinking about it— to stick to Guinness. If he was going to get healthy, it was definitely the way to go.

A familiar two-handed rat-a-tat-tat on the door reminded him that Ian had gotten it together to set up some publicity time for "This Night, Mine." Aubrey had promised Jerry he'd flog it to death, and flog he would. This project deserved more than his usual half-arsed bodging.

"Aubrey, would you fucking open the door for once—before my knuckles fall apart?" Ian's voice was peevish, even muffled by the door.

Aubrey rolled off the bed and went to the door. "Come in, ducks."

Ian pushed into the room, looking around him suspiciously. "Good evening to you. What've you been up to, today?"

"Sleeping, mostly. I think I'm going to lay off the Scotch for a while. I'm still not a hundred percent."

"Ah. Turning into a bit of a lightweight, are we?"

"Yeah, right-o."

"Aubrey, really: Are you not well? I don't mean that as a joke. I'm truly concerned."

"Ian, old boy, I appreciate it. I really do—the fact that my reduced alcohol consumption worries you—but I'm perfectly fine. I promise."

"Right. Okay. You're perfectly fine, you're just turning a bit of a Nancy boy, yeah? That's lovely, then."

Ian handed Aubrey his schedule for the month—mostly local TV, but he'd managed to book him for a spot on Conan. This was good news on multiple levels, as it ensured his first class fare to New York would be taken care of.

"Brilliant! I'm impressed, I have to say. Great score—thank you."

"Oh, it weren't much, really. I think there may be a bit of a buzz in the air. A lot of publicists had already heard tell of you taking the role— all I had to do was make the calls, and they got back to me right quick. Bit of a change from before."

"So, no lynch mobs, then?"

"Well, no more'n you'd expect." Ian was lying, but that was fine with Aubrey. That's how it worked, between them. Aubrey didn't need to know about the latest spate of hate mail filling up his website servers and overflowing the offices of everyone who had anything to do with him. This was a regular occurrence anytime he appeared in the news. A tacit agreement existed among about six people to shred correspondence that had even a hint of negativity.

"Right. Well, thanks, Ian. This is really great."

"So, want to get some dinner? Or I could grab some takeaway, if you'd rather stay here in front of the telly."

"Can't tonight, mate. I've got plans."

"Plans?"

"Yep. Can you make sure the door's closed all the way behind you when you leave?"

Ian's face slowly registered that the message had arrived. "Oh. Right.

Will do. See you later."

Ian left, closing the door behind him with more force than was necessary. Back in his room he climbed into the unmade bed with his motorcycle boots on. He folded his hands over his chest, frowning, then grabbed his laptop from the side table and checked his email. A new message had come from his Activists for Allah group with the subject line *Look at These*! He hesitated over the delete button for a moment. Sometimes the Activists sent something worth looking at, but too often it was just a poorly written diatribe based on nonsensical misinformation. That, or pictures of women—of the quality one's cousin might marry— with their baps on display. These were sometimes funny, but not intentionally so, and Ian had seen enough great breasts in person to have lost interest in viewing mediocre ones on screen. Or maybe not. He opened the email. It contained a single link to a YouTube channel, and a note from Akil which said "Hey, this guy looks just like you and he's got the same last name—any relation?"

Ian clicked on the link. The page that opened, titled "Habib in Hell", appeared to be a collection of videos taken by a young man named Aaban Al Habib. As Ian's eyes settled on Aaban's image, he was taken aback. With his well-formed features and stylishly rough hair, Aaban could have been a young movie star. Ian loosened his belt, slid his hand into his pants.

A knock at the door sounded and Ian jumped up from the bed. An accented voice sang through the door: "Room service."

"Piss off!" Ian yelled, self-conscious and angry. "Do not disturb!"

He stomped to the door, grabbed the "Do Not Disturb" tag, and thrust it at the maid who peered through the opening. He slammed the door, locked it, and rattled it a few times to ensure it stayed that way.

Falling back on the bed, he grabbed his laptop and clicked on the most recent video.

Aaban stood in front of the camera, his eyes casting furtively around him. He adjusted the lapel microphone he wore, hiding it in his collar, and looked directly into the camera.

"Hello Habib fans," he said, smiling. His raspy voice delivered this in a strong Birmingham accent.

"I thought we'd have another peek in at our favorite Israeli Defense Force Nazis, as they go about their business, which, as you know, consists of harassing my people." Aaban indicated three boys wandering over the rock strewn ground behind him. Occasionally, one of the boys would bend over a plant, swipe it with a small, hand-held scythe, and place it in the plastic bag he had tied to his belt loop.

"Now, you see these boys here, right? They're collecting *Salvia fruticosa*—an herb for cooking. Took me a while to find the Latin name—it's called Greek Sage back in London. Here, it's some unpronounceable thing with lots of rolling 'r's. Goes well with lamb. Anyway, if you're new here, I should tell you my Arabic is coming along, but I still only understand about half of what I hear. No matter. I'm just here to document. You decide what it means."

Aaban glanced over his shoulder and, reaching toward the lens, changed the view to frame a rutted road running up a dusty hill. A utilitarian green Sufa jeep bounced along it toward the camera.

"So here come the occupiers, as expected. Remember, these children are picking herbs for their mother. Not exactly a threat to the Zion Nazi cause, right?" Aaban nodded into the lens, smiling tightly.

"I'll leave the big camera here as a distraction. It's seen enough action that I don't care if they smash it." Stepping back from the frame so his upper body was included in the shot, he made a square of his hands around a small hole that had been cut into his vest. "This camera," he said, pointing to a lens just barely visible in the hole, "is more discreet."

Smiling, he walked backward a few steps, then turned toward the boys, who watched the jeep bounce up and down the road toward them. The scene switched to a clouded, jerky image, as the camera in Aaban's vest filmed him walking toward the boys who stood their ground, watching the soldiers approach. The next thirty seconds of film were chaotic; a lot of shouting in what Ian assumed was a combination of Arabic and Hebrew, jumpy images of the soldiers emptying the boys' plastic bags on the ground, stamping on the contents, and confiscating scythes.

Finished, the soldiers stood amongst the debris and pushed the boys on their way. The tallest boy turned and said something—judging by his body language—in protest. By way of response, one soldier grabbed him by the hair and jerked him backwards to the ground, delivering an angry, guttural diatribe. The boy picked himself up, glaring at the soldier.

The boys ran off, the smallest crying loudly, and the soldiers turned to the camera in Aaban's vest, yelling. One jabbed a finger at the camera on the hill. Aaban continued to film as they headed for the camera, sitting on its tripod a hundred feet away. The soldier who'd grabbed the boy pushed it over. The scene switched to the viewfinder of that camera, lying on its side, as it filmed the boots of the soldiers walking away. The scene faded to black, then faded up to Aaban, his wide shoulders draped over a shabby brown couch. A charming, wry smile wrinkled the corner of his eyes, but his voice was sad.

"So there you have it. Three boys picking herbs are the most pressing concern of the Israeli Defense Forces, aka, 'most moral army on Earth'. It's obviously not the most shocking clip in my collection, but it really underscores how seriously the IDF take the job they're doing. Nice work, men. Tomorrow you can find a sweet old granny to harass." Aaban's raised eyebrows spoke to the camera. "This is Aaban Al Habib, signing off." The image froze.

Ian shook his head angrily and scrolled down the comments section. As he read, he grew angrier. Comments from Aaban's fans were interspersed with angry blurbs calling for the soldiers to gun him down, saying that the IDF were charged with protecting Israel, that the weed-gathering boys were encroaching on Israeli territory, and that Aaban should be treated as an enemy of the state. Many comments were in Hebrew. Ian sneered. He couldn't read those, but he was certain he knew what they said.

Returning to the list of videos, Ian opened one that showed IDF soldiers breaking up what appeared to be a peaceful protest by threatening young Palestinians with their clubs, and grabbing women by the hair to yank them to the ground. He grew angrier as he watched, knowing that many people watching this video—perhaps even at this moment, as he himself watched it—were cheering the soldiers on. "Evil motherfuckers," he said under his breath. He watched every video on the site, feeling a kinship with Aaban. He wished he could help him in some small way.

Before he closed his laptop, Ian signed up to Aaban's feed, to be sure not to miss a moment of his work.

Aubrey whistled as he rode the elevator down to the hotel's underground parking garage, his trusty Enriquez slung on his back. Belting it carefully into the back seat of his old, steel blue Ferrari, he set off.

Less than ten minutes later, he was parked illegally in front of Salla's building. She appeared at the door, glowing and lovely in her unassuming way, and as he hugged her he breathed in her scent—soap and little else—and enjoyed the feel of her smooth hair against his cheek. As always, she pulled away first.

"So, what's up? You have plans?" As she looked at him, her hand resting lightly on his forearm, he was hyper-conscious of her casual touch. It often took him by surprise, the effect this inconspicuous woman had on him.

"Grab your guitar and let's go, my dear. We have a gig."

Soon thereafter, they were walking past the shops and restaurants of Toronto's West Queen Street, a Canadian Mecca of all that was urban hip. Aubrey wore his red plaid fedora down over his eyes, and his scarf pulled up past his chin. He led Salla to the back of a former warehouse, notable for the army of dog-size, metal ants climbing up the side. Beneath the ants, a woman's face, a full story tall, loomed over the pair as they found their way into the back room of Toronto's famous Cameron House.

Inside, a hammered metal bar showcased a ceramic gallery of gaily painted, slightly parted buttocks—all from an identical mold, each one decorated in a different theme. Salla's eyes fixed on one in a gay biker pirate style, complete with backless chaps and a pink jolly roger. A sequin-festooned butt plug emerged from the ceramic cheeks.

Aubrey, oblivious to the surprising décor, headed directly into the arms of an aging Rastafarian with several gaps in his huge smile.

"Maks! So great to see you." Aubrey grunted quietly as the bigger man squeezed the air out of him.

"Aubrey Bishop! You make it! I figure you were pass out in some pricy hotel room somewhere. Good to see you, old man." Makonnen Johnson leaned his head to the side, examining Aubrey from different angles.

"You're looking pretty good. Respectable, now, with your ears showin' and all."The big man laughed, his sausage-thick, foot-long dreadlocks swinging, and let Aubrey go with a slap on the back.

Aubrey examined him. "You're just as lovely as ever, my friend. Bit more grey around the edges. Very dignified." Aubrey reached behind him to grab Salla and pushed her at Maks.

"I'd like you to meet my friend Salla Kahn," he said with a flourish.

Salla's small pale hand disappeared into Maks' dark brown ones.

"Salla. Very nice to meet you. Any friend of Aubrey's is all right by me."

"Thank you. Likewise." Salla's smile tilted up at him.

Aubrey reached up to squeeze Mak's shoulder. "I still can't believe you're here, Maks. You do realize this is the northern hemisphere?"

"I know, man—it's too damn cold, eh? But this my city, now. I love Toronto more than I hate the winter. I tell you, some time, I don't go adoor for a week, just waiting for the sun to shine. Last year I take a trip back to Kingston in March, so as not to be here when hell literally freeze over."

"I hear you. Not ready for the Jamaican Bobsled team then?"

Maks laughed in a basso profundo burst. "No, man. Never."

"I know. It's a lot colder here than in Provence, that's for sure."

"Yes—I hear you hide out in France a lot of years. What make you leave that beautiful place?"

"Finances, my friend. Pure finances. Or, lack of same, actually." Aubrey laughed ruefully. "Seems you don't get royalty checks when no one's playing your music."

"Right man, I hear you. Well, you not be pay for this gig either, let me tell you that up front. No one pay you to play in Toronto, nowaday."

"Things certainly have changed, haven't they? What did we pay you for doing sessions on 'Enter the Fray'?"

Maks sighed. "Man, I live off my conga back then. I probably make enough to cover rent for years ahead. But those day, I spend every cent on my buddy."

"Ha. Right, mate. I think all our buddies got a working out in those days."

"Hey, speak for yourself, man. I don't know about yours: mine still in commission." They laughed again."But they had beautiful girls in that Belgium. They sure like a Rasta with bankroll."

Aubrey became aware of Salla, fidgeting beside him.

"So, you're still with Joanne? How many children do you two have now?"

"Oh, we're together now almost twenty years now. The fourth and final is gwine to high school next year. If you can believe it. What about you, man? I read about you and that Alisha Freaksa goin' bad. I'm sorry."

"Yes, well, it got ugly for a while, but things are good now. I've got this new singer I'm working with." Aubrey smiled and winked at Salla. "She's going to sit in with us tonight, if you don't mind?"

"Not at all, man. How you feel about working for tips, young lady?"

Salla's smile had a fixed quality. "Sit in? I haven't even rehearsed. Do you have a song list, or...?" Her voice leapt to a higher register.

Aubrey was laughing, unconcerned. "I was thinking of an Israeli folk song, or two—maybe some Nirvana. A little Aubrey Bishop, perhaps. Sound good?"

"We never do spend a lot of time rehearsing," Maks, equally unconcerned, reaasured her. "We play for a lot of years together— nothing can surprise me now."

Salla's laugh sounded as though it had escaped without her permission, but she allowed Aubrey to lead her to a mike on the left side of the stage. He pulled her guitar from its case and, placing the strap over her shoulder, he motioned for the sound guy. They had Salla's guitar set up with a pickup of its own in what seemed like seconds, while her hands fluttered in impotent protest. Aubrey cupped the back of her head, kissed her on one tense cheek, and whispered. "No worries—you'll be great, because you *are* great."

A thin, red-haired man with a handle bar mustache and a trumpet in one hand took position at the microphone beside her, while another player positioned a double-standup bass next to Maks at the drum kit. Aubrey strode to the center of the stage, threw on his own guitar, and the show began.

They played for hours, an eclectic outpouring of tightly percussive ska fused with the odd, punked-out Israeli folk tune, the chord changes coming naturally to Salla. Sprinkled in the mix were Aubrey Bishop tunes, ones that were popular before the meltdown, Aubrey calling out the key changes where necessary. Toward the end of the evening, Salla delivered a few songs in her own husky soprano, as comfortable, somehow, as she was in her own living room.

A surprised crowd quickly filled the backroom, and then, after a hundred cell phones had been employed, made its way into the street, and, eventually, around the corner after the fire marshal's capacity limits had been exceeded. By the time Aubrey and Salla crept out the fire exit, both sated and replenished, Maks' band had emptied the tip jar five times. Salla and Aubrey refused to share in the bounty.

In the car on the way home, Salla was mostly silent. She smiled at Aubrey when he spoke, but it was obvious her mind was elsewhere.

Aubrey walked Salla to her door, waiting while she unlocked it.

As he turned to go, Salla grabbed his hand and pulled him back to her. Holding his hands, she stood on her toes and kissed his mouth, her eyes open, probing his. He groaned, and wrapped both arms around her. After a moment, she wriggled out of his arms and pulled him inside.

Chapter 14

Come I will teach you to dance as naturally
as falling asleep and waking and stretching long, long.
I speak greed with my paws and fear with my whiskers.
Envy lashes my tail. Love speaks me entire, a word

of fur. I will teach you to be still as an egg
and to slip like the ghost of wind through the grass.
~From The Cat's Song
By Marge Piercy

The orange tabby sat outside the smudged window, willing its mile-long stare to yield another offering. The Man was in the Lady's den again tonight, but He was not scratching the stringed box and wailing. This was unfortunate, as the noise was usually a sign the Blanket Lady's beneficence would be at a maximum. Missing, too, were the startling bursts of hilarity that the two tended to emit together. While the cat found the noisy expression of the humans' unseemly joy unnerving, he'd come to welcome their cacophony as another indicator that table scraps would soon arrive. The cat settled down on the sill and made himself comfortable while he waited to see what bounty this new, quieter behavior might yield.

As the Blanket Lady pulled the Man through the small apartment, the cat followed along a ledge on the outside wall. Its whiskers pressed against its cheek as it leaned for purchase on the narrow windowsill of the bedroom. The cat peeked through a crack in the curtain as the Man followed the Lady into her sleeping room. Nuzzling the lady's bare neck, he began removing the pelts She cloaked herself in. First, he removed her top layer, pausing to gaze down the length of her before gently starting on the layers beneath. He peeled off one covering then another, all the while grooming her length with his lips. Finally, He was still, gazing at her furless body glowing in the moonlight.

She responded in kind; removing the man's layers, stroking him with her gentle paws, nuzzling him with her quiet mouth. Standing to face him, tenderly stroking his face, his back, his flanks, She grazed the front of his body with hers. Looking at his eyes from inches away, nuzzling his mouth with hers, She grasped his distended member with her wandering hands and observed the effect on his face.

As the two stood at the foot of the bed, their naked skin exposed to the air, the Man petted the Lady slowly, methodically, with great care. Murmuring against her neck, he began to groom Her, gently, teasing down her luminous length; licking, lingering, his mouth remaining at the spot that made Her murmur back with growing intensity.

The cat cocked its head and kneaded the rough wood of the windowsill as the Lady softly moaned her delight in that stifled way humans had of expressing their pallid pleasures. Finally, the man laid Her on the bed and mounted Her from the front, cupping the back of Her head as they nuzzled each other's mouths. He stroked Her haunches like he was petting a cat, held Her face to hiss quietly in Her ear. Gradually their whispering discourse rose to discordant song.

As they finished, then began again, the curtains were closed against his gaze. The cat jumped down from the window, leaving them to their pleasures while he sought food elsewhere.

Chapter 15

O you who have believed, when you rise to prayer,
wash your faces and your forearms
to the elbows and wipe over your heads
and wash your feet to the ankles.
And if you are in a state of janabah,
then purify yourselves...
Allah does not intend to make difficulty for you,
but He intends to purify you
and complete His favor upon you that you may be grateful.
~Surat Al-'Aĥzāb 33:33
The Holy Qur'an

Ian joined the other men at the row of taps as they performed the meticulous ablutions of *wudhû*[31]. He was particularly taken with this *wudhû* room in his Toronto *masjid*, with its gleaming, multi-hued tile and built-in stone seats along the trough. The taps were spaced enough apart to allow the degree of privacy that full absorption in the ritual cleansing required. The low evening sun lent the room a warm glow.

To the background of the others, each praying at his own pace, Ian recited the words he'd learned from a "Coloring Book of Wudhû and Salah", a gift from his Giddo when he was seven.

---

[31] *wudhû* /wu'-dU / n. *Arabic*. The Islamic practice of cleansing parts of the body in preparation for prayer or for handling and reading the Qur'an.

"Bismillah ir-Rahman ir-Rahim[32]."

Ian washed both hands three times, scrubbing carefully between his fingers. He rinsed his mouth three times, then snorted water into his nose from his right hand, and allowed it to drain into his left. He was thankful he'd remembered to remove his nose ring—this part was difficult as it was. Twice, it went smoothly, but the third time a droplet of water tickled his windpipe. Coughing quietly, so as not to invalidate his *wudhû*, he washed his face three times, then his arms, starting with his right. He smoothed back his hair with his wet hands, and then smoothed it forward, fighting the urge to push his hair into some semblance of a style. He ran his wet fingers on the inside and outside of his ears, self-consciously avoiding the dime-sized gauge holes in his earlobes. He needn't have worried; each man was engaged in his own cleansing, careful not to nullify the ritual by thinking about anything else. Laughter during the process would invalidate not only the rite of *wudhû*, but also the prayer that followed. It was a busy world. No one had time to do everything twice.

As the setting sun darkened the windows and the *adhān*—melodic, faintly mournful—sounded over the mosque loudspeakers, Ian tucked his new silk prayer rug under his arm and made his way to the prayer hall. He was moved, as always, by the faintly melancholic, wailing melody of the call to prayer as it echoed throughout the mosque. Taking his shoes off outside the hall, he placed them with the others lined up along the wall.

Several meters away, the women entered the hall through their own door. They would partake of the prayers in their own section, separated by simple white dividers. Islam did not condone the sexes praying together—it was seen as an unambiguous way to take the focus from Allah.

But women were not the only potential distraction. Ian held back as he watched Akil's awkward form enter the hall in front of him. He watched from the doorway as Akil found a spot in the hall, then headed for the opposite side. It was difficult as it was to immerse himself in prayer without the odd energy of his new acquaintance complicating matters.

Several visits with IslamMadeEasy.com had allowed Ian to

---

[32] *Bismillah ir-Rahman ir-Rahim* / bEss'-ma-la E-rahk-man' E-ruh-hEm' / phrase. *Arabic*. The first words of the Holy Qur'an, lit. "In the name of God, most gracious, most merciful."

memorize a few short *Surahs*[33], and to mimic the postures of the men around him as they performed *salat*, some barefoot, some on the plush carpet, others in socks, most kneeling on their own, worn prayer rugs.

At a gesture from the Imam, the men stood. Cupping their open palms behind their ears as if to hear the voice of God, they intoned *"Allahu Akbar*[34]*"*. This rumbling chorus never failed to stir Ian.

In silent unison, the men crossed their arms at the waist, right hand clutching the left. They began to recite the sunset prayer, Ian reveling in his own, slightly garbled, quite serviceable version. For the next position, the men bent forward at the waist, placing their spread fingers over their knees, their eyes fixed on the floor. In keeping with the detailed instructions he'd found on-line for this position Ian held his back parallel to the ground, as though holding a glass of water between his shoulder blades. As Ian lost himself in the Arabic it became less awkward in his mouth and he thought of nothing—the position and the sound of the voices and his own part in the chorus filling him with the feeling he'd been seeking.

Then it was time to change position, and the awkwardness of the *Sajjda* brought him back to himself. The low bow, in which hands, forehead, nose, knees, and toes must all touch the ground together—it took concentration. The scent of his still-new silk and cotton prayer rug further distracted Ian as he intoned with the other men. He tried not to think about anything but the sound of the Arabic and relaxed when he succeeded.

In closing, *Allahu Akbar* was intoned a final time, again with hands outspread from the ears.

The Imam, hitherto engaged in his own *Salat*—always a few beats before the other men—now rose and moved gracefully to the front of the room, where a simple podium stood. He spoke in measured tones, his warm voice resounding in the voluminous hall.

"Today, my friends, as we continue our series on Islamic Life in the Great White North, I thought it would be meaningful to revisit the precise words of prophet Mohammed—*blessed be His name*—in the very last sermon he left for us. It started like this:

"'Oh People. Lend me an attentive ear, for I know not whether after this year, I shall ever be amongst you again. Therefore listen to what I am saying to you very carefully and take these words to those who could

---

[33]*Surah* / sU-rah' / n. *Arabic.* Any chapter or verse of the Qur'an.
[34] *Allahu Akbar* / a'-la a-wahk'-ba / phrase, *Arabic.* Lit. "God is great."

not be present here today.'

"Now remember: The Messenger—*May Allah honor Him and grant Him peace*—knew this would be his very last talk with his people. He understood the import. Make no mistake: he wanted to ensure that these words were engraved in their hearts. He said:

"'Just as you regard this month, this day, this city as sacred, so regard the life and property of every Muslim as a sacred trust. Return the goods entrusted to you to their rightful owners. Hurt no one so that no one may hurt you. Remember that you will indeed meet your Lord, and that He will indeed reckon your deeds. Allah has forbidden you to take usury (interest); therefore all interest obligation shall henceforth be waived'." The Imam's deep voice resonated with the conviction in his words.

Ian fought to keep his attention on the sermon, certain that this man would eventually offer answers to the questions Ian had not yet formed.

"The prophet Mohammed—*peace be upon Him*—went on to caution his followers to 'beware of Satan for the safety of your religion. He has lost all hope that he will ever be able to lead you astray in big things, so beware of following him in small things'."

The Imam paused, sweeping his deep gaze the breadth of the room. "Satan has lost all hope. Remember that. 'Beware of following him in the small things.' Small things. These are the things that creep into your heart, unannounced. Unbidden. These are the pathways by which Satan enters."

Once again, the Imam paused, searching the faces before him. The congregants stared back, or allowed their eyes to wander, each according to his nature. Ian met the Imam's direct gaze, then slid his eyes away.

" 'Oh People,' the Prophet said, 'It is true that you have certain rights in regard to your women, but they also have rights over you. Remember that you have taken them as your wives, only under Allah's trust and with His permission. If they abide by your right then to them belongs the right to be fed and clothed in kindness'.

"Now consider this: Only under Allah—*most gracious, most merciful*—do you have rights over your wife. He made this point even more clearly later, saying, 'Treat your women well and be kind to them, for they are your partners and committed helpers...'"

It was at this point that Ian lost control of his wandering attention and allowed his eyes to meander around the room. Akil, sitting on his haunches, was looking intently his way. Once Akil saw he had Ian's attention, he tapped his watch three times. Ian gazed back, puzzled. Akil repeated the gesture; three taps, three times, with increasing impatience. Remembering, Ian gave a sharp nod, waved Akil off, and tried once again to focus his attention on the Imam's words.

"And the Prophet—may peace be upon him—assured us that *all* mankind is from Adam and Eve! No Arab has superiority over a non-Arab nor does a non-Arab have superiority over an Arab. A white has no superiority over a black, nor has a black any superiority over a white; except by piety and good action. Every Muslim is a brother to every Muslim and the Muslims constitute one brotherhood. Nothing shall be legitimate to a Muslim, which belongs to a fellow Muslim, unless it was given freely and willingly... "

Ian returned to his own thoughts, letting the Iman's words move over him, their meaning less important than the fact that he listened to their sound. More immediate were the events in the latest Aaban Al Habib video. It had shown a group of Israeli settlers, fighting to prevent Palestinians from returning to their homes. Israeli soldiers were in attendance, but it seemed their only capacity was to protect the settlers from reprisal.

In the melee, one settler—a small woman in her twenties, her pretty face marred by the savagery of the act—shoved a Palestinian woman of equal build and approximately the same age, to the ground. The Palestinian, her pretty face peering from the black *hijab*[35] over her hair, looked up at her attacker in puzzlement. The Israeli standing over her, pink *tichel*[36] askew, shook a clenched fist in triumphant fury, and launched a guttural tirade that had an effect the shoving had not. The Palestinian's puzzlement turned to anger. She rose, slowly, pointing a finger directly between the other's eyes. Chanting a single word, over and over, she advanced on the settler. A thin man with red hair and beard stepped between them and shoved the Palestinian back. This time, she turned to the Israeli soldier observing it all, and yelled at him in obvious contempt. He returned her gaze, impassive, and gripped his M16 as though assessing its weight. She moved toward the Israeli woman again, her voice rising to a shriek as she repeated the word. The soldier barked out a single syllable. Glaring at him, she shook her head and left, following the other Palestinians, ignoring the smiling Israeli in the crooked pink *tichel* who continued at her heels.

---

[35] *hijab* / 'hE-jab / n. *Arabic*. Head covering worn by a Muslim woman beyond the age of puberty, in the presence of men to whom she is unrelated.

[36] *tichel* / tihk-'el / n. *Hebrew*. Head covering worn by a conservative Jewish woman after marriage, in the presence of anyone other than her husband.

The monologues that bookmarked Aaban's videos were becoming more weary, more shrill. After this one, he'd made a plea for money, his first. Aaban's perfectly arched brow was knotted—his handsome features were aging as the camera watched. He begged his supporters to get the word out, saying he was running out of funds.

The more Ian thought about this clip, the angrier he got. It was hard to concentrate on the Imam's words, when they seemed unrelated to anything that mattered.

Twenty minutes later, the sermon was finally over and everyone lined up to leave the prayer hall. Ian flinched when the Imam's hand fell on his shoulder.

"So, Ian, it is? Hello! You have been here several times now, I've noticed. Are you starting to enjoy our little community?"

Overwhelmed by contact with this tall, humble man, Ian ducked his eyes and tugged at the cuffs of his shirt. He had removed most of his body jewelry, but the Imam surely wouldn't miss the huge holes in his ears, or the cherry blossom tattoo peering out the top of his turtleneck. But a look into the Imam's dark eyes offered Ian a new calm. This man had the gaze of a teacher, not a judge.

"Yes, sir. Thank you. Everyone's been very kind."

"I'm glad to hear it. We want to make sure everyone feels welcome here. Each comes to Islam in his own way." The Imam's dark face was lit by a gentle smile. "Perhaps you'd like to join our *Madrasah*? It offers many courses you might be interested in. We've even had a few people become *Hafiz* after a decade or so."

"Havies?"

"People who have memorized the Holy Qur'an, in its entirety." The Imam's deep voice held a smile.

"Oh yes, my grandfather, my Giddo—he was *Hafiz*. I think he must have pronounced it differently, but he knew every word of the Holy Qur'an."

"Very good. Well, get started, and perhaps we'll be calling you Hafiz some years from now, *Inshallah*."

"Thanks, yes, *Inshallah*. I'll give it a think. I need to know more about the praying part, yeah?"

"Yes, perhaps. It's certainly a good way to make friends in the community. Check out our website, and call if you have any questions."

"Thanks again, I will. I've already managed to make a friend or two. There are some really interesting people here."

At that moment, Akil called Ian's name and waved him over. Ian held up a hand. He respected Akil's energy, but he wasn't about to be ordered around by a twenty-year old.

The Imam looked between Akil and Ian, his brow furrowed. He held onto Ian's shoulder and looked directly into his eyes.

"There are many *good* people here. I hope you will continue to feel comfortable among us." The Imam gave Ian's shoulder a final, gentle squeeze and left him to ponder his lingering over the word "good."

Chapter 16

And behold joy and gladness, slaying oxen
and killing sheep, eating flesh and drinking wine.
Let us eat and drink, for tomorrow we shall die!'

The Torah
Isaiah 22:13

"Oh, my, God!" Emily shrieked, jumping up from her chair. "That's totally amazing, Salla! I'm so excited for you!" She looked around the Queen Street café where they'd met for lunch as if seeing it for the first time and sat down, realizing she was at the precipice of what would constitute a major scene in emotionally understated Toronto. "What on earth are you going to wear?" she went on in a stage whisper.

Salla responded in kind. "I know! I don't know! Which, my friend, is where you come in." Clasping her hands under her chin, Salla batted her eyes at Emily.

"Help?"

Emily grinned broadly and clapped her hands.

"Absolutely! I'd be thrilled. It's practically what I've lived my whole life for, giving you a makeover." She looked at her underdone friend, her eyes crinkling roguishly. "But you have to make me one promise, okay?"

"Anything. I'm desperate. Not only have I never been to a wrap party, I don't think I've ever met anyone who's ever been to a wrap party. So state your demands. You may never get another chance."

"Okay!" Emily considered Salla. She reached out and lifted a hank of

Salla's long straight hair as though weighing it for market.

"You have to promise to let me have your hair cut. I want carte blanche—no negotiation. You sit in a chair and submit to my will. Got it?"

"Oh Ems, I love you dearly but sometimes." Salla looked at her friend's serious face. "Well, what do I care either way, right?"

"Right. You won't regret it, I promise."

"I know. I'm certain I probably won't."

"Convincing." Emily gave a little wiggle of happiness. "I have the absolutely perfect little black dress! Gucci of course, tasteful, yet funky enough for the most cutting edge of indie film parties. Oh! Or maybe the Cavalli. Equally hip, but might work better with those legs. This is exciting! I can't wait."

"Uh-oh. What have I signed myself up for?" Salla feigned irritation, even happier now that her friend was happy for her.

Emily looked at her for a moment. She opened her mouth, as if to say something, and swiveled her chair to face Salla.

"Salla. This is really big, right? Why aren't you absolutely freaking out? He's asking you to what's probably a really important night for him. Are you guys actually getting serious about each other?"

Salla's happiness dimmed.

"Ems," she said, as if the name were a sigh, "think about what you're saying, my dear. You know my studies commence in the spring. In *Israel.*"

"Well, yes,"

"Did you expect me to just change my mind about something so important to me?"

"Well—of course not, Salla, no."

"And do you think Aubrey Bishop's dream is to be married to some rabbi? Can you picture him converting to Judaism, attending shul every Shabbos? Yom Kippur? Sukkot? Getting a late-life circumcision?"

"Oh. Well, no, probably not. Wait—he's not circumcised? Is that *kosher*?"

"Never mind! But that's not even the big thing." At Emily's arched brow, they burst into laughter. "Pun *not* intended!"

"Whatever you say, Salla." Emily's smirk was triumphant.

"Anyway, that aside, you *have* noticed that he's a vehement atheist, I trust? He's practically an evangelist for the, um, not-cause."

"Well, of course."

"So, how happy would he be in the *Holy Land*? And what would I do—pretend not to know him in public? You don't bring your"—-Salla made air quotes with her fingers—"anti-Semitic boyfriend of world-renown to *Israel* with you. It's absolutely out of the question."

"Right. Not happening. No question."

"Exactly. And do you think I should drop everything to follow an alcoholic rock star through his haphazard existence, spending my days in hotel rooms, watching him drink himself to death?" Salla looked stricken, as though this thought had occurred to her just as she'd said it. She paused. "Living for wrap parties, spectacular sex, and his occasional dry spell?"

"Well, no." Emily was subdued, but had not yet conceded defeat. "Perhaps you should give him a chance to see what you see in Judaism. After all, that's what brought him to you in the first place. He might surprise you."

"You really have to give it up, Ems. This Salla Bishop routine—it's sweet, and I know it's because you love me, but it just doesn't work, in any potential universe, no matter how you look at it. I know: I've looked. Kind of obsessively." They were both aware Salla was aiming for a light tone. Neither was fooled.

"I'm so sorry, Sal. I wasn't thinking. Are you... do you...well, do you love him?"

Salla paused, and the silence went on for what, in another context, would have been an unnaturally long time.

"It just doesn't matter. I mean, I really don't have a choice. I can't afford to. Ems...I don't know how many different ways there are to say this to you: I have to get my feelings for him under control. Or I have to stop seeing him altogether. Which do you think is more plausible?"

"Oh, dear."

"Yes. I think you've got it."

"Sweetie, I'm so sorry." Emily sat back in her chair. "It's sad; such a terrific guy, such a terrible catch."

"Yep. Therein lies the rub, alright."

"Spectacular sex, you said?"

"Oh yes."

"Too bad."

"Uh-huh."

The following Saturday, Aubrey left the stretch limousine waiting in front of Salla's apartment and knocked on the door.

Emily answered, fighting for control of the smile that threatened to burst from her face. She took in his formal attire, set off by a pair of cutting edge cowboy boots and a hat she'd seen in Vogue, and laughed happily. She grabbed his hand and pulled him in the door.

"Please, come in! Make yourself comfortable on the couch for a moment." She shoved a beer into his hand, then ran to the bedroom, from which issued a flurry of frantic whispers, the occasional "ouch, hey!" and the rise and fall of excited laughter.

Almost twenty minutes, three beers, and about sixty dollars in limo fees later, Emily ran back into the living room. She threw her arms wide. "Tada," she sang, clinging to the last syllable, while Salla walked quietly into the room and stood, watching Aubrey for his reaction.

For ten full seconds, he had none at all. She looked much like any one of the super models he'd enjoyed and moved past, over the years. His concern that she'd feel awkward amongst the illuminati of Toronto's independent film industry was allayed, at least: her dress was just unusual enough to ensure that she would not simply fit in, but might, in fact, influence some trends. Then she smiled her sideways smile and Aubrey saw Salla herself. The black dress fit her long curves, her upswept hair scattered light across the angles of her face, her makeup emphasized—without caricature—her wide eyes, full lips, and flawless skin. She looked more precisely herself, like a pencil sketch outlined carefully in ink.

"Oh, my." Aubrey paused, sensitive to the import of this moment for her "You're a masterpiece." He turned to Emily. "I'd say you've gilded the lily, but I've always thought golden lilies must be very special flowers, indeed." He winced as this left his mouth, happy Ian was absent, rewarded by Salla's gratified smile.

"Phew," she said. "That's such a relief. If you hadn't pronounced me apposite, Emily was going to force me into these." She held up Emily's favorite pair of Manolo Blahniks, ankle boots with a poisonous heel that might have been designed by a snake. They were probably the sexiest shoes Aubrey had ever seen. They also would have made Salla tower over him. He grabbed Salla's hand and leaned in, to whisper through her silky hair, "Perhaps you can try those on when we get back." She smiled widely, leapt at Emily to give her a loud kiss on each cheek—pausing between to beam a look of gratitude into Emily's eyes—and grabbed a tiny, sparkling purse off the table. She stepped confidently out the door, Aubrey following in her wake, muttering, "Apposite? Appostite? Appasite?" He reminded himself to look it up as soon as he had a moment when it would not be conspicuous. At the very least, Salla had made a distinct impact on the breadth of his vocabulary.

Minutes later, the limo pulled up in front of the unimposing façade of Toronto's famous Opera House, a former Vaudevillian theatre known more for its acoustics than its glamour. Three lone protesters waited outside, bearing signs reading, respectively, "Nazi go home", "Boycott Anti-Semites", and "How do you like my God, now, Bishop?" Salla took Aubrey's hand and led him past, nodding and smiling politely at each one. The news the next day would show these same three picketers, their backdrop the crowd entering the venue. From this evidence, two local anchors would float the rumor that hundreds of people had shown up to protest Aubrey's presence. And all four of Toronto's news stations would be careful to zoom in from various angles on the unmistakable form of Aubrey Bishop entering the club with none other than the suddenly lovely—and, since the Dini interview, very recognizable—Dr. Salla Kahn on his arm. That particular impending unpleasantness did not, however, mar the evening for either of them.

As Salla followed Aubrey through the double doors of the lobby, her bravado proved short lived. She held her breath as she took in the small crowd, each one of them clad flawlessly in the regalia of the well-to-do Torontonian hipster. She'd always been uncomfortable around people like these; to them, her disinterest in fashion implied social ineptitude and they'd always tended to treat her as either invisible or as an interloper. Tonight, the fact that she was sporting the perfect camouflage didn't obviate her discomfort but the converse, in fact. Since she felt like an outsider but looked like an insider, everyone she met that night assumed her disdainful rather than simply shy.

"Oh .Salla, come over here." Aubrey pulled her along to the next person he was to greet. All the new faces were blurring together. .

"I'd like you to meet my friend Ian." Out of a discomfort stemming from a vague fear of Ian's behavior, Aubrey had not said a great deal about Ian to Salla. He'd mentioned that Ian looked after his schedule, and that he was staying in the same hotel, but little more. It was for that reason Salla's response to this important introduction was to smile, say a quick hello, and excuse herself to search out the ladies' room.

When she was well beyond hearing, Ian burst out with, "What the fuck was that? You'd think she'd be happy to meet me, finally. The famous Ian, your general factotum, and very best BFF."

Aubrey drew in a breath to laugh then noted that Ian was not smiling.

"I'm really sorry, man. I'd forgotten to tell her she was going to meet you, tonight. In fact, I forgot to tell her who you are, altogether, to be honest." Aubrey was a little chastened but no more. It wasn't his responsibility to smooth Ian's path; Ian would just have to turn the charm on Salla himself.

"Excuse me a mo, would you mate?" Aubrey said, seizing his chance to let Colleen down gently. She'd called him several times and returned to the set more than once; she'd been been expecting more from him than a single night and he owed her closure, at the very least.

When Salla returned from the bathroom—which she'd approached gingerly, as one must any such facility in a club in Toronto's indie entertainment circuit—Aubrey was talking to this tall blonde with intense eyes, who grasped Aubrey's arm and glared at Salla's approach.

"So, is this her, Aubrey? I haven't seen her hanging around the set," the woman said, trying for a smile that came out as a grimace.

Not one to be discussed in the third person directly to her face, Salla introduced herself, her expression several degrees cooler than Aubrey had ever seen, and slowly retracted her proffered hand in response to the woman's long stare.

"Aw, come on, Colleen, be polite. Salla's a really great person. You'd like her, under regular circumstances." Aubrey spoke quickly, his voice hinting at shrillness.

"What are these, unregular circumstances?" Colleen's laughter had a studio audience quality. "I think her being here is very unregular, actually. She's not in the movie, is she?"

"She's my guest, Colleen. Look, I should have told you about Salla before, but it's not appropriate for you to be rude to my friend simply because you and I slept together once."

"I'm sorry, I'd better go," Salla said, ducking away from this moment with no particular destination in mind. Although she'd been expecting a Colleen to crop up at some point, she wasn't prepared for it happening tonight. Aubrey was a dog—he'd never pretended to be anything else, really. She had never made him any promises—couldn't make promises, really—and she would either have to live with the way things were or not, as she saw fit. Since she wasn't ready to decide exactly what she saw fit to do, she simply lost herself in the crowd wandering up the wide staircase to the balcony.

Making her way to a seat along the railing, Salla sat on a decrepit, once red, velvet theatre chair, and gazed at the crowd below. She'd been here ten minutes, and met at least forty people, very few of whom she'd see again, and none of whom she remembered. She hadn't eaten a morsel of the interesting food or had a sip to drink, and already she longed to go home. There was no one to talk to, nothing to look at, and her feet already ached from the lack of arch support in Emily's "perfect" little flats. She helped herself to a martini from a tray proffered by a passing waiter and sat again. She'd had time for two gulps when she heard Aubrey's voice, ringing out from below.

"Salla. Salla! Salla Kahn! Wherefore art thou, my rose? Salla! Where are you?" Aubrey stood on a table beneath her on the balcony, his feet on either side of a large flower arrangement. He was cupping his hands, megaphone style, to amplify his naturally strong baritone. Everyone in the room laughed, clapped, and whooped, and it struck Salla that they all admired Aubrey. And that, despite two or three excellent reasons not to, she did as well. Forgiving him, she waved, her movement wan but her smile bright.

Aubrey drew a deep breath, the better to make the following proclamation: "O, that I were a glove upon that hand, that I might touch that cheek!" His voice projected to every wall of the venue.

Some wag in the lighting booth trained a spotlight on Aubrey, following his progress as he jumped off the table and raced up the stairs, taking them two and three at a time, to the balcony above. Everyone watched as he captured Salla's recalcitrant hand, kissed it, stole her martini and finished it and offered her the olive with a gallant flourish. The crowd whooped, whistled, and clapped, each according to his inclination, as Aubrey pulled her to her feet and headed back down to the stage.

"Please join me milady, anon, under the proscenium arch," he said in a voice as grand as the words. As the Opera House boasted an actual arch that stretched thirty-five feet over the stage, this wasn't hyperbole.

Aubrey had wanted Salla's opinion of "This Night, Mine" since he'd discovered she shared his fondness for black comedy. Post-production had ended that week, and Aubrey wanted to watch the film for the first time with Salla beside him. He led her to two seats in the middle of the theatre—one of which was decorated like a king's throne. "Most humorous!" he shouted to Jerry, writer/producer and director of "This Night, Mine", and the man most likely to have arranged a throne for Aubrey.

"No problem, Mr. Bishop!" Jerry's voice was faint, but still carried to the crowd in the large room. They all laughed again, accustomed to acting as audience to Aubrey's antics. Taking the microphone handed him by a smiling grip, Jerry walked up the steps to the middle of the stage and gestured to Aubrey to join him there. Aubrey settled Salla into the seat beside the throne, then ran up to the front of the room, jumping on the stage like one accustomed to falling from it.

"Come here, Aubrey. Don't be coy," Jerry said, reaching his hand out to Aubrey and then turning him to face the crowd. Jerry looked out at his people, shaking his head and laughing to himself. The Opera House became quiet. He cleared his throat.

"Once I heard Aubrey Bishop respond to a journalist's question about some altercation or other he'd been in. He was yelling, 'what did you expect from a blasphemous bastard like me—fucking unicorns?'"

Jerry paused for effect, smiling around the room.

"At the poor bastard's bewildered expression, Aubrey yells, 'I'll be glad to fuck a unicorn if you can provide one'." The crowd laughed—they'd all seen the YouTube clip.

"Well, that was it. I knew I had to have him in my film." There were murmurs from those assembled; they'd heard rumors to that effect.

"As you're all about to see, it was the best choice I've made in my life. As everyone who knows me can attest, I had high expectations for this film. No budget, a skeleton crew of brilliant, multifaceted people, of course," Jerry paused for the crew to cheer, "but far too few of them." The nodding of heads was almost audible.

"So there I was: no budget, almost no crew, and no marquee names to speak of, and I still had these expectations. Crazy, I know, but I don't think any movies would be made, ever, without the crazies in the world." Jerry paused, looking around the room full of approving faces.

"Anyway, there I was, script, skeleton crew, crazy expectations…and then, an incredible thing happened. Aubrey Bishop returned my call. My call!" A few scattered cheers erupted, as everyone leaned forward in their seats.

"He didn't just call—he actually accepted the part. That was big, but it wasn't all. He didn't just take the part. When he finally dragged himself here"—Jerry paused to smirk at the crowd's laughter—"he took over the part. He owned it. Wrested ownership right out of my hands. He became the Reverend Knight, as he was meant to be. Aubrey Bishop exceeded even my—crazy—unrealistic, expectations. So thank you, Aubrey. Thank you." Without further ado, Jerry hugged Aubrey, kissed him on the cheek, and forced the microphone into his hand. Aubrey took a moment to sweep his eyes across the faces, smiling. His gaze finally settled on Salla, and he began, as though practicing the speech on her.

"Wow. Well. It's just my luck to have to follow this man—the best writer I know—to talk about the film *he* wrote. I don't have a lot to say, really—or a terribly fancy way to say it—but I want you all to know that I'm very glad to be here. I'm very lucky to have been here." Aubrey paused, worried his voice would catch. He kept his gaze fixed on Salla.

"So, thank you." His eyes swept the crowd. "Thank you all! And I'll see you next year in Cannes." He punched his fist in the air.

They all cheered, and a few yelled "Cannes" as Aubrey handed the microphone back to Jerry. Jerry looked at it for a moment, looked at the audience and smiled. "What he said—next year in Cannes."

Aubrey joined Salla at their seats, and the curtains opened to an improvised movie screen set on the stage. The music swelled. From that moment, the audience was transfixed for the entire hour and thirty-six minutes. When the very last word of the credits had rolled off the screen—to this crowd, the credits were an important part of the show— they leapt out of their seats in a spontaneous standing ovation for Jerry, for Aubrey, for themselves.

Salla was so excited for Aubrey that right there, standing in front of their seats, she held his face while she whispered the *She-hehiyanu* in his ear. This prayer was recited in celebration of a special, rare event, and she couldn't resist.

> *Barukh atah Adonai*
> *Eloheinu melekh ha-olam,*
> *she-hehiyanu v'kiy'manu*
> *v'higi'anu la-z'man ha-ze.*[37]

When she told him what she'd said, Aubrey sighed and shook his head, looking into her eyes. "You're incorrigible. Thank you."

Laughing together, arm in arm, Salla and Aubrey crept out the back door, Jerry complicit in their escape.

Ian saw none of this. He'd spent the 90 minutes of the film's debut brooding, smoking, and pacing back and forth in front of the Opera House. His token, but well-rehearsed advances toward Colleen had been vehemently, rudely, and very publicly rejected. Aubrey, his supposed best friend, was too busy with his latest quim to even notice that Ian wasn't sitting with him in the audience. Ian's resentments mounted as he remembered that he was the one who'd found Aubrey the part in the first

---

[37] *Barukh atah Adonai* / ba-rUk' a-tah' a-doh-nl'... / phrase. *Hebrew.* Lit. Blessed are You, Lord, our G-d, King of the universe, Who has kept us alive, sustained us, and enabled us to reach this season.

place.

Pitching his cigarette to the street in disgust, Ian waved down a cab, took it straight to the hotel, stomped directly to his room and fell onto the bed. Grabbing his laptop off the night table he opened it to Aaban Al Habib's video blog and refreshed the browser. Seeing that Aaban had uploaded a new video, he made himself comfortable and clicked the play button.

On the screen, a new face: A young man Ian had never seen before, who lacked the startling good looks and the smirking good humor that made Aaban's accounts so compelling.

"This is a message for Aaban's supporters." The young man spoke in English, heavily accented. His expression was grim.

"Something has happened to Aaban. I don't know what exactly. The Zionists have taken him into custody, I think. I'm going to play you the last tape I found in his bags. I worry very much for his safety."

The screen changed to a view of what looked to be a rather dirty ceiling. Aaban's voice was faint; distorted, but he was clearly yelling.

"What do you want from me? I don't have to go with you—I'm an English citizen! No, I have not broken any laws—even so, what does the IDF have to do with it? No, I will not leave my home. What are you doing! Take your hands off me, Nazi! Let me go! I will come along, but do not touch me again!"

The sound of a door slamming, then footsteps fading, then the clip froze.

Ian slammed his laptop shut and jumped off the bed. He clenched and unclenched his fists, pacing back and forth in his hotel room; stopping occasionally to open his window and gaze at the indifferent city. He swore and resumed pacing.

"Salla! For shame!" Bubbie launched into full-throated hysteria the moment Salla answered her phone. Salla's croaky, "Hi, Bubbie" seemed to have ignited her grandmother's freshly banked fury.

"For shame! I cannot believe this, you, running around like some cheap *nafka*[38]! My own granddaughter! *Shanda fur die goyim*[39]!"

"Bubbie!" Salla sat up in bed, and glanced toward her bathroom, where Aubrey was using the acoustics of the shower to belt out a

---

[38] *nafka* / naf'-kah / n. *Yiddish*. Whore.
[39] *shanda fur die goyim* / shan'-da fir die goy'-yim / phrase. *Yiddish*. Lit. "a shame before the nations"; colloquially, embarrassing behavior engaged in by a Jew, within view of non-Jews.

raunchy Brittany Spears tune.

As angry as Bubbie could get, she had never, in Salla's entire life, directed her attacks at Salla herself. Salla stalled, her voice still. "What are you talking about?"

"What do you mean, *what?* I saw you on the *television*! Shaming me in front of the entire city! What am I supposed to tell people, *now*?"

Aubrey's voice grew louder, his fine tenor reaching through the apartment. As he bellowed, "Hit me baby, one more time," Salla covered the phone with her hand and shut the bedroom door with her foot. She longed to turn off her phone and enjoy the concert in the bathroom, but she didn't want to further inflame her grandmother. She sighed.

"What exactly have I done that's shaming you before the goyim this time, Bubbie?"

"Oh! Don't pretend not to know. Hanging off the arm of that *momzer*[40] like one of his little *koorvah*[41]! Do you think no one knows? Everyone knows, now. You're shaming our entire family with your *mishugina*[42] behavior! Yigal is appalled, too—we're beginning to think you've lost your mind, already!"

"Bubbie, it was just a cast party—a party for the film maker. Aubrey wanted me to see his movie, that's all." Salla kept her voice low, lulling, reasonable, as though soothing an injured animal.

"A party for the *devil*, only! Salla, Salla, Salla," Bubbie moaned. "What have you gotten yourself into? How can you ever be a rabbi, keeping this kind of company? The school will never let you in, now."

"I suspect the criteria of the Toronto Yeshiva differs slightly from yours, Bubbie." Her voice was still, but Bubbie had forced to the surface a worry that Salla had hitherto kept submerged. "Anyway, I never thought you were that happy with my plans."

Bubbie moaned softly through the phone, as though the pain from an amputation had subsided, briefly.

"I was afraid I would miss you, that's all. I thought you might take up with those crazy Orthodox and leave your Bubbie all alone. But never mind, I don't need to worry about that anymore. They won't take you when you disgrace yourself!" Her moan crested, her agony returning. "Oh, Salla, Salla. What have you done?"

Slowly, Salla disconnected the call, and turned off her phone, placing

---

[40] *momzer* / mom'-zer / 1. adj. *Yiddish*. Despicable, 2. n. *Hebrew*. Child born of an inappropriate sexual relationship, e.g. born fatherless.

[41] *koorvah* / kUr'-vah / n. *Hebrew*. Promiscuous woman; whore.

[42] *mishugina* / mish-uh-gin'-ah / adj. *Yiddish*. Crazy.

it on the night table with a gentle pat. She shook her head, then removed her robe, to join Aubrey in the shower.

Chapter 17

and when the LORD thy God shall deliver them up before thee,
and thou shalt smite them; then thou shalt utterly destroy them;
thou shalt make no covenant with them,
nor show mercy unto them;

~Deuteronomy 7:2
The Holy Bible

The Activists for Allah met once again in the damp basement of Akil's parent's home, lounging on the faded plaid couch, sitting cross-legged on the shag rug, or leaning against the cheap paneling on the walls.

"Ian? This is Ishmael, and that's Bill—aka Bilal. He's new, too." Akil handled the introductions, looking to Roger D first for approval. "That's Ahmed, over there. This guy right here's Roger D—that's his rap name. And you all know me: I'm Akil Khoury. So, hey."

"Hey," they chanted in turn. Ian said "Hiya."

"So, Ian, my brother Akil told you about us, right? How we going to call attention to the cause?" Roger D had a deep voice that was somewhat startling, emerging from his undersized head.

"Right, sure."

"And I think we all know the only way to accomplish that is to throw down with a major act. Like, show them we not just fucking around."

"Right." said Ishmael and Akil, simultaneously.

"But, I'm proposing we hit the Jews with some small shit, first. Just to shake 'em up. Let them know we're here." Roger D was comfortable in a leadership role, and Ian could tell he had the approval of all assembled.

"We gotta get them in the temple, you hear what I'm sayin'? That's what will get their attention."

"Okay," Ian said slowly. "It's to be a synagogue then. Define 'small shit' for me, yeah? Haven't decided how much I want to be involved."

"Nothing too over the top, man. Just, like, some graffiti that tells the Hebrews what we're about. Make some noise, maybe. Mess things up a bit. No one can afford jail time, nothing too serious."

"So what, graffiti's the main point? Get a message out?"

"No, I think fuckin with them is the main point. That's the message. Fuck with us and we fuck with you. That's the point, mother fucker. You get it?"

"Well, yeah." Ian held up his hands. "Take it easy mate. I get it. I just want to make sure what we're doing is meaningful, that's all. I didn't want to get involved in pointless drivel like that fucking IPBC shite. You know what I mean, Akil. Bunch of Nancies going on about how to 'discuss a solution'?"

"Yeah, that was pretty lame, eh? They were all like 'Let's try some activities aimed at raising public awareness'." Akil pitched his voice high to get the proper effect. "How about we have a hill walking drive at Blue Mountain." He snorted. "Like, public awareness is going to make them give us back our land—stop them from bulldozing our homes. Total waste of time bullshit."

"Well, I told you that's how that shit would go down, man." Roger D stood. "It's like 'Yeah, you can have your right of return—I got it right here'." He grabbed his crotch to illustrate.

"Problem is, you don't listen to your friends, Akil. Listening to them Jews tell you how to do things—distracting you with public awareness bullshit while they take more of our land. And we end up in that ghetto in the Gaza. Just where they want us. As I was saying, we gotta throw down a major act. Really make a statement. Like, I've got your public awareness right here." Roger D grabbed his crotch with renewed vigor.

They erupted into muted cheers, a couple of them grabbing their own crotches for effect.

Roger D, enjoying the momentum, went on. "Now, speaking of bulldozers: You cats ever hear the tale of Rachel Corrie?"

Ian had not. Roger D sat back on the musty couch and crossed his arms over his chest, warming up to the story. He smiled.

"Rachel Corrie was this sweet little American girl, joined a group of

Middle East activists. Wanted to turn the peace process around. She was playing for the right team, too. Known as the ISM: International Solidarity Movement. International." Roger D turned his head slowly, meeting the eyes of each man in the room.

"Solidarity. Anyone like the sound of that? Yeah. Well. So did little Rachel." Once Roger D was warmed up, he had the cadence and charisma of an old-time preacher in a modern-day mega church. "The ISM were engaged in real, actual, public awareness campaigns. Their people would put their own lives on the line for the cause. They would literally put themselves in front of a bulldozer—put their lives on that line—to save someone's house. Someone's home. Someone's land. Now, our tight little hero—Rachel—she'd staked out a house belonging to a doctor, no less. She put her little hot American body right there, right in front of it—wearing a bright little fluorescent orange safety jacket, of course—and she just refused to move." Roger D paused and looked at the ground, shaking his head slowly, nudging the suspense along. He lifted his head, stared into Ian's eyes, and continued.

"Now, in that part of the world, a bulldozer's not just a bulldozer. And a bulldozer driver—well, this particular bulldozer driver—was an IDF soldier. Familiar with the alphabet soup Ian? Driver was an Israeli Defense Force officer. So, you got your sweet little American civilian in her cute little orange jacket. You got her standing in front, protesting, protecting this respectable doctor's house—mighta been a pharmacist; accounts do differ—and what do you suppose that particular bulldozer driver took it in his head to do?" Another pause, as Roger D again met each man's eyes in turn. "He drove over her little hot body, wearing her little orange jacket, and he crushed her at the scene. Killed her, for trying to save someone's house."

"Wait, what? He killed her?" Ian's voice was quiet, disbelieving.

"Kill, her? Oh no. Admitting that might've meant taking personal responsibility. He didn't *mean* to kill her, he said. Dude lied, claimed he didn't know she was there. He was a *blind* IDF bulldozer driver, I guess. Motherfucker didn't kill her, no way. He just crushed her. Drove over her like she was day-old road kill."

The Activists were, for once, silent. Ian, picturing the scene, felt nauseous.

"Now, you wonder what kind of people we dealing with? That kind. Because that bulldozer wasn't just driven by a single soldier. It was driven by an entire people. An entire fucking people, called the Jews." Roger D was silent for a moment, looking at the ground. Then he lifted his face. "You got that?" The expression in their eyes said they had.

"So, who's in?"

They all were. It was agreed that their first act as a group would occur on a Wednesday night, three weeks from that day.

Chapter 18

Blessed are You, G-d, our G-d, King of the universe,
who has chosen us from among all people, and raised us above
all tongues, and made us holy through His commandments.
And You, G-d, our G-d, have given us in festivals for happiness,
feasts and festive seasons for rejoicing the day of this Feast of
Matzot and this Festival of holy convocation, the Season of our
Freedom in love, a holy convocation,
commemorating the departure from Egypt.
                                        ~the Passover Haggadah

"Hi, Aubrey?" This was the first time Salla had ever phoned Aubrey, and he was taken aback at how happy he was to hear her voice. She hadn't been answering his calls or texts for over a week—having been quite frank about how, as much as she wanted him, she didn't want a life with him, and she was trying to cool things off.

The right choice, certainly, but... he didn't seem to be taking it well. He'd been on a bit of a binge for the last three days, trying to shift the ennui that came from the cessation of filming and the absence of Salla. He was lying in bed, still a little drunk from the forty ounces of bourbon he'd finished, as the sun was brightening the sky.

"Salla," he said, trying to keep his voice from sounding as weak as he felt. "Hello, love. It's good to hear from you."

"Hi, um. Is everything okay? You sound... bad."

"Oh, just coming down with something, I suppose. I'll be fine. What's up?"

"Oh, well, not much. It's just that you expressed interest in Pesach, and I thought—

"Paysock?"

"Oh, you know, Passover?"

"Oh. Yes."

"Anyway, I'm going to have, what we're calling, a Pretend Passover, and I thought you might want to join us. If you're not...busy. It's usually in the spring but I thought it would be a fun dinner party, and you could meet my friends and learn a few things and..." Salla stopped abruptly. Silence sat between them for a moment.

"Oh. Well, I have been kind of busy with everything, but it sounds interesting," Aubrey said, interested in little but seeing Salla. He did his best to feign enthusiasm. "It's a ritual dinner, right? Something like the Last Supper?"

"Well, yes, the Last Supper was reputed to be a Passover Seder— although that's still up for academic debate. Really, if it was, a Seder, it was a pretty blasphemous one. But Jesus was a kind of rebellious Jew—"

"Well, that's if he existed at all." Aubrey sat up, regretted it, then lay down on his side and went on, more quietly. "I mean, you do know there's no historical proof of his life? No documents from the period in which he was supposedly performing all these miracles cite him in any way at all." This particular rant was one Aubrey had polished years ago, but he really wasn't up to delivering it now. "And off I go." He closed his eyes. "Sorry. Anyway."

"I don't know—Jesus isn't something Jews think about much, to be honest."

Aubrey laughed, then groaned and rolled to his other side, pulling the blankets over his head.

"Aubrey? Are you sure you're all right? You sound truly awful."

"Well, yes, thanks. To be perfectly honest, it's self-inflicted, really. So—"

"Oh." There was a long pause. "Well, I will have to pick up a few things if you're going to come, so if you could let me know—" Salla's voice faded.

"Salla. Are you saying that you're doing this for me?"

"Oh, you mean the Seder? No! Well, I suppose so. Yes. You've been so great with me—guitar lessons and helping me with parking fines and all the lovely wine and that wrap party—and I wanted to do something nice for you for a change. I really think you'll enjoy this. You like horseradish, right?"

"Well, certainly. Who doesn't? And I like you."

"Oh!" Salla's next words almost galloped out of her mouth. "Okay! So we'll see you then. Bye." The dial tone sounded. Aubrey gave a feeble chuckle and closed his eyes. He rolled on his side, groaning. His phone rang again.

"Hi Salla."

"Um, I'm sorry. I forgot. It's at 6:00, and it's at my friend Emily's house. This Saturday. She and her husband, Henry will be there. And me. They live in the Annex. Can you take down the address?"

"Sure. Salla, do you miss me?"

"Or I'll text it. Yes. That's what I'll do. Much easier. Bye!" She was gone.

Relaxing on one of the tastefully opulent sofas in Emily and Henry's sitting room, Aubrey plucked the olive from his perfectly crafted martini and waved it at Emily for emphasis.

"Surely you're joking," he said. "That unmitigated piece of tripe?"

"Tripe?" said Emily, sitting up in her seat beside him. "What are you talking about? I loved every word of that album. Some days, I felt like I was the one who'd written it. Tripe? It changed my world view!" Aubrey laughed, and she stood, folding her arms as she looked down at him.

This was not an unusual experience for Aubrey. He'd often encountered fans who saw design in his work that he hadn't intended. It happened often enough that it felt deceitful not to set them straight. But he just couldn't bring himself to disillusion Salla's best friend. So he fell silent. But Emily pressed on.

"I'm shocked that you'd say such a thing about it because, frankly, I've always considered it to be your best work."

Aubrey smiled up at her for a moment. When she did not return his smile, he stood as well. "Oh! You're not joking. Terribly sorry. I had absolutely no intention of insulting you—"

Salla and Henry, sitting on another couch, were trying unsuccessfully to stifle their laughter. Aubrey regarded them, puzzled, then turned back to Emily. She still looked peeved, if self-consciously so.

"Emily, please let me explain. I just meant that, if I'd know it would be my final act as a songwriter; or at least the work that I would be most known for, I would have spent a lot more time crafting, and less time carousing. I would have at least have tried to make it something worth bollocksing up my life for. I mean, imagine if *you* did a crap job at what turned out to be both your magnum opus *and* your greatest mistake? Especially if it was because you were solely focused on getting drunk and then laid? Although perhaps not in that order."

Everyone was silent as this thickened in the air. Salla stood and crossed the room to sit on the arm of the settee beside Aubrey.

"Trust me, there are worse ways to spend your time." She plunged in, patting his back. "Try denying yourself any hint of revelry for, oh, five years. Spend every last cent on housing and transportation. Subsist on ramen noodles, and handouts from your friends." She looked at Emily, who smiled at Aubrey and nodded as Salla went on.

"Eat macaroni and cheese out of a pot, while pushing such literary masterpieces as the 'Forms and Functions of Punctuation in the *Mishnah* out of your poor beleaguered brain." When the laughter subsided, Salla waggled her finger in the air, as though admonishing her younger self.

"*That* particular tome went on for a hundred pages, or more, by the way. I promise you, there is absolutely nothing more emotionally debilitating than grasping for new ways to dissect a text. Especially one that has been thoroughly eviscerated by much smarter people for thousands of years. Not to mention that you're perpetually weak with hunger because you've been saving your money for the subway."

Aubrey laughed happily and grabbed Salla's hand, kissing it, silently grateful.

"You see why I look up to her? A toast for Salla!"

They leaned toward each other to clink glasses while Salla ducked her head. Later, Emily would be able to pinpoint this as the exact moment she herself fell irreversibly in love with Aubrey Bishop. Grabbing his hand, Emily tugged Aubrey up from the couch.

"Speaking of hunger," she said, "Aubrey, come help me with the food, won't you? I'm sure Salla and Henry will be fine without us." Emily saw Salla wince, but she carried on, pulling Aubrey toward the heavy French doors that led to the hall.

"Come on, you two will survive apart for more than five seconds."

Aubrey followed Emily into her meticulously appointed gourmet kitchen, its gleaming marble countertops selected from pieces imported specifically to suit the 200-year-old Victorian Revival. Five years ago, she and Henry had bought the house from a reclusive writer who'd allowed it to disintegrate. Restoring the place to its original grandeur, and beyond, had been Emily's primary focus for an entire three years and she still basked in its reflected glory. Aubrey was dutifully impressed—

even correctly guessing the origin of the marble—and she was gratified.

Emily, having heard much about his disabilities in the kitchen, carefully steered Aubrey toward the large utilitarian stainless steel work surface, and handed him a peeler and a single potato. Then the real point of his impromptu sous chef apprenticeship began.

"So, what do you think of our girl Salla? Are your intentions honorable?"

"What? Oh shit!" Aubrey exclaimed as he peeled four layers of skin off the knuckle of his unsuspecting thumb.

"Oh! I'm sorry. I hadn't meant to scare you—are you okay?" The cut had done little more than exfoliate Aubrey's knuckle, but Emily confiscated the potato peeler, anyway, and set him up on a stool at the counter with a band-aid and a refreshed drink. She began taking covered dishes out of her restaurant-scale fridge.

"Anyway, I wasn't asking if you intended to marry Salla. I just wanted to brag about her a little, because not everyone sees how spectacular she is."

"You don't need to sell me on your friend, Emily. Her spectacular-ness speaks for itself."

Emily beamed at him. "I know, eh? Ever heard her play that old guitar of her dad's? She's a very serious musician."

"Yes." Aubrey chuckled. "And she was singing 'Spoonman' in the car the other day, which in itself was a revelation of sorts. I never would have taken her as a Soundgarden fan. She told me once she thinks Muse are the bastard child of Led Zeppelin, Stravinsky, and a Mellotron."

Emily laughed and nodded.

"Exactly. She is a living contradiction. She's also really accomplished in about sixteen different ways. Did she tell you she studied cello in university?"

"No! Her doctorate is in Jewish studies, I thought."

"Yes, but she did an honors degree in Music at U of T, first. Minored in French Literature."

"Est-ce vrai? Tu parles le Français aussi?"

"Oh no—I'm an *English* Canadian. Means I can conjugate verbs like nobody's business, but I can't speak a word."

They laughed.

"It's odd—I've never seen a cello at her place," Aubrey said. "She only plays guitar, it seems."

"Well, I have a theory about that." Emily peeked out toward the dining room where they'd left Henry and Salla, closed the door quietly, and lowered her voice. "I mean, when she switched majors from Music to Jewish Studies, she claimed she'd just lost interest in the cello. But her loss of interest coincided with her father's illness—you know he died of cancer?" At Aubrey's nod, Emily took a deep breath and continued.

"She won't acknowledge that there's any connection, but I know better. Poor thing. They were very close."

"I know she loved him very much. It's almost as though she's still grieving." Aubrey looked down, picking at the bandage on his thumb. "The topic is completely out of bounds, isn't it?"

"Yes. She *is* still grieving. I think we all are, to one degree or another. He was a lovely, lovely man. One in a million."

"So I gathered. Did a lot for the disadvantaged, did he?"

"Oh, it wasn't just that. I mean, he was a certainly a huge philanthropist; beyond his means. All he left behind was that ridiculously important guitar and enough money to get Salla through graduate school. But it was more than that. He was one of those people you'd go to when you were, like, going through difficult times, you know?" Emily searched his eyes. Satisfied with his nod, she went on.

"And he always said exactly the right thing. Or, more accurately, he always knew exactly the right thing to do, exactly the right way to be. It's hard to explain— Absolutely everyone adored him."

"So, did you meet Salla at the Synagogue then?"

"Me? Oh, no—I'm Catholic. We met at camp when we were nine. But I spent a lot of time at her place over the years. Her dad was like a second father to me. To hundreds of people, really. A spiritual advisor, in the truest sense. He would have been the same if he'd been an atheist or a Christian, or, like, a Scientologist. He was just that sort of a man."

"Hmmm. No wonder she misses him so much. So she took up Jewish studies after he died, yeah?"

"Yes, but don't make the mistake of asking her about it. She gets miffed if you suggest that she's doing it as some sort of homage to him. I really haven't figured out why. Perhaps simply because talking about him still makes her very sad. I do think there's something to the whole homage thing, though. Like, the world is short of people like him, so she genuinely believes it's her responsibility to fill his shoes."

"Wow. Big shoes. Enough said. Thanks for telling me this, Emily. You're right, she is more spectacular than I realized."

"Mm hmm," Emily nodded, opening one of three oven doors and pulling a meat thermometer from the brisket. "Glad I could help."

Pleased that all her talking points had been covered, Emily gestured toward the dining room. "Let's go see if they're ready for us, shall we?"

Salla threw a mock glare their way as they entered the dining room together. "What's she been telling you about me, Aubrey? I can only imagine the tales she's spinning."

"Well, I understand you're fluent in Hebrew—I was hoping you'd give me a demonstration, later?"

"Oh, is that the latest pickup line?" Henry joined in. "Never heard it before—'Hey there hot stuff—how about a Hebrew demonstration?' Not useful in many situations, but when the right one comes along—"

The others laughed politely. Henry was Associate Chair of Mathematics at the University of Toronto, and—consequently, perhaps—his sense of humor tended to favor puns. Emily's love for him was palpable, but it seemed she only laughed at his jokes ironically.

They sat at a table as painstakingly laid as a photograph in a high-end magazine. An odd clay platter with an assortment of disparate items sat awkwardly amidst the glinting crystal and gold leaf-encrusted place settings.

Salla followed Aubrey's glance, and smiled. "Oh—that's the Seder plate I made for my mother as a child. I can't stop using it for some reason, although it doesn't exactly go with Emily's Versace Barocco. It just feels homey, I guess." She chuckled. "Or, more accurately, 'homely'."

Aubrey smiled. "It's charming, although perhaps a touch uncomfortable amongst the rich relations, yeah?" Emily and Henry laughed, looking at Salla.

She tilted her chin, smiling her one-sided smile at them all. "Yes, very much like me, I know. Hey—it's Pretend *Passover*: I refuse to be baited into one of my old 'eat the rich' speeches." Salla threw a mock glare in Emily and Henry's direction, then turned back to Aubrey.

"As I was saying, my little Seder plate, or *ke'ara*, there, is a ceremonial platter we use to display the symbolic foods eaten for *Pesach*." Salla looked around the table, comfortable presiding over this type of gathering. "Shall we begin?"

They all took their places around the oversized table, Salla settling herself at its head. Beside her, Aubrey picked up the slim paperback prayer book sitting atop the small stack of china that marked his place.

"So, the primary purpose of this holiday is to commemorate the Exodus from Egypt, where the Jews had been enslaved. A celebration of freedom. Notice the pillows on our chairs? The idea is that free people can relax and eat comfortably, while slaves eat on the run, or sitting on the floor. More conservative Jews lean to the left, for certain parts of the meal."

Salla held up a small book. "You each have a copy of the *Haggadah*, which kind of walks us through the Passover feast."

"Kind of like a holiday instruction manual, is it?" Aubrey turned his copy over. Something about it was odd.

"Yes, exactly... er, this is the front." Salla turned hers toward him so that the spine was on Aubrey's right and pointed to the Hebrew there.

"In Hebrew, "Haggadah" means 'the Telling'. Because it's mostly in Hebrew, you read it from right to left, and you start at what most people think of as the back."

"Huh," Aubrey said.

As they started the Seder, Salla introduced Aubrey to the items on her little platter, starting with a mixture of chopped apples, sweet wine, and walnuts.

"Each of these will be eaten as part of the Passover Seder. *Charoset*, here, represents the bricks the Jews made under their enslavement in Egypt." As Salla gestured to the chunky brown dollop on the plate, Aubrey nodded, suppressing with some effort the urge to comment on modern archeological findings regarding slavery and the pyramids. He'd read that there was compelling evidence that paid workers, and not Jewish slaves, had built the pyramids. Salla, oblivious to his silent concession, gestured to the next item on the funny little plate.

"What we call *Maror*, here, is horseradish—the stronger the better. It symbolizes the bitterness of slavery. The parsley, or *Karpas*, is there to celebrate the rebirth of spring, and it's dipped into the salt water which symbolizes tears." Salla glanced over at Aubrey. "You look lost. Stop me if I'm going too fast."

"No, not at all. I was just thinking that this whole affair seems rather more complicated than the Last Supper, which was supposed to be the same thing."

"Well—I'm not well versed in the New Testament—Emily; help me out here?"

At Emily's derisive chuckle, Salla laughed. "Okay, sorry—I guess it has been a long time since your First Communion. I think you're right, Aubrey, biblical evidence seems to indicate that the Last Supper occurred around the time of Passover. The Eucharist is a ritual involving the eating of symbolic foods which commemorates the Last Supper. So it does have some passing resemblance to the Seder. Probably Jesus, being a Jew, got the idea of the ritual from the Passover meal."

"Hmm," Emily said.

"Too far? Sorry. Anyway, the *Z'roa*—in this case a roasted shank bone of a lamb, although a chicken wing would do—symbolizes the sacrifice at the Temple, and the *Beitzah*—the egg—symbolizes, well, both spring and mourning. Mostly mourning, really, as we're still mourning the destruction of the Temple."

"Ah... " Aubrey said, then subsided.

"Yes?" Salla prompted.

"No, nothing. Sorry, please go on."

"So, then, of course, we have *Matzo*, or the 'bread of affliction,' which is the only kind of bread we consume during the Passover season." Salla held up a plate with a stack of what looked like six-inch square saltine crackers without the salt. "Matzo is eaten to commemorate the exodus from Egypt, because the Jews fled so quickly, they couldn't wait for the bread to rise. Matzo's so integral to the idea of the Passover feast that regular bread is banned from the house for the duration. By the way, the bread of affliction is much tastier with butter."

Aubrey's smile felt donated, Salla noticed.

"Aubrey, I don't know how much—or little—you've heard about the Seder, so I may over-explain." She smiled at him. "Just let me know, okay? It's my favorite festival of all, so I may belabor it."

"Don't listen to her, Aubrey. She's the most engaging teacher on the planet and she knows it. She's trying to be humble, and it's almost killing her." Emily could be counted on to drain any moment of its gravity, Aubrey noted. She'd raised it to an art which she performed, it seemed, primarily for Salla's benefit.

As Salla wove the tale of the Exodus with the rituals and the prayers of the dinner, Aubrey became engaged despite himself. Although he could barely contain a chuckle in the presence of people who used the phrase "the Almighty" without a trace of irony—or even self-consciousness—he could see why Salla so loved a feast that, at its heart, existed solely to celebrate freedom from slavery. Whether or not it was based on actual historical events, the sentiments were rather grand. Certainly the four cups of excellent wine, drained quickly as part of this yearly celebration of freedom, were right up his alley. No one raised an eyebrow as he opened additional bottles during the meal. But he found himself consuming the last one alone.

The time came for the Four Questions, which were, Salla said, traditionally sung in Hebrew by the youngest child in the house. Emily stood and delivered them in a halting, wistful voice that told Aubrey all he needed to know about why children were missing from the table.

When Emily was done, Salla broke the gravity of the moment by whooping and clapping. She stood, and reached across the table to catch Emily's hand in hers.

"You learned that for me! You sweet, sweet friend. Thank you."

Emily smiled, and dropped into a stage bow. "Thenk *you*! Thenk you very mush," she said, her arms wide, her lip curled. "I'd also like to thank the all-knowing YouTube."

They laughed heartily, then, at Salla's cue, picked up their prayer books and got back to the business at hand, Aubrey sneaking a surreptitious glance at his watch.

He found the next part of the service disquieting enough to hold his attention for a while. Salla told them that 'Jehovah' sent a series of ten tribulations to the Egyptians for refusing to set their Jewish slaves free. These included plagues of boils, infestations of locusts, and rivers of blood, culminating in the massacre—via "Angel of Death"—of every first-born Egyptian male. Aubrey fought to still his inner voice, but his imagination had always been the sort to make him a character at the center of every story he heard. This particular one cast Aubrey as a charismatic Bronze-age huckster who'd founded his own religion. Aubrey as Moses leveraged algal blooms, solar eclipses, grasshopper infestations, and fatal viruses to attract followers proffering flacons of fine wine, herds of plump sheep, and tents full of beautiful daughters.

Oblivious to the alternate reality playing out in Aubrey's head, Salla assumed, by his off gazing eyes, that he was moved by her favorite celebration.

After the meal, Emily served cupcakes she'd decorated to signify each pestilence. The black ones representing a plague of darkness seemed edible, and the ones with images of hail and grasshoppers were quite tasty, but he couldn't bring himself to try the ones decorated with very authentic-looking boils, even if they were made of icing.

By the time they'd repeated the last words of the ritual, "Next year in Jerusalem," Aubrey had decided that, if one were forced to participate in any religious ritual, this one would get his vote, what with all the drinking and food.

As Aubrey drove Salla home—after consuming several cups of coffee Emily appeared to pour directly down his throat—an atypical silence rested uneasily between them.

"Why are you so quiet tonight, Aubrey? It's not like you to keep your thoughts to yourself." Salla's delicate hand touched his arm.

"I'm afraid if I talk, I'll say…things," he said, without thinking. He reached to hold the hand that had touched his arm.

"Well, now you do have to say things. Of course. What's going on?" Salla removed her hand from his and folded her arms, leaning sideways in her seat to look at his face.

"Salla, I hope you don't take offense. I mean, it really is a beautiful ceremony, there's no doubt about it."

"But?"

"Yes, but. But. Do you really believe all of it, I mean, literally?"

"All of *what*, Aubrey?" A glance at her lovely face, illuminated in flashes by the passing streetlights, told him he'd already gone too far.

"I mean—you know—divine intervention. That sort of thing—" Another glance at Salla told him only that she'd raised her eyebrows and nothing more. "God killing Egyptian babies to release the Jews from slavery." He went on, hurriedly, like someone speeding the wrong direction on a highway without exits.

"You do realize, for example, that the pyramids were unlikely to have been built by Jewish slaves. The real historical records—in other words, outside of the so-called holy books—make it clear that they were built by—you know—skilled, well-paid artisans. Yeah?" Aubrey was stammering, now.

"Hmmm," Salla said.

"Well, I just feel a little uncomfortable, when intelligent, articulate people with advanced degrees and otherwise, er, discerning intellects, believe in magic…I mean—"

"Yes, Aubrey, you do mean something. Spit it out. Please." Salla's face was completely still.

"Salla, I simply cannot believe that *you* truly believe in all of this religious claptrap. You're too smart, too analytical. To me, it seems like a passing fad that's lasted longer than it should have. I mean, eventually the Greeks gave up their myths. Why not everyone else? Why not you?"

"Aubrey, stop the car. Please. Pull over." Her tone was flat.

Aubrey was startled. "What—you're not going to let me drive you home? Come on, Salla, let's not do this."

"I have no intention of stomping off and walking home. This is too important a conversation to have in a moving car, that's all."

"Can't we have it at your place, at least?"

"No. It has to be now, I'm afraid. I'm sorry. And it's going to be a lecture, not a conversation, so be forewarned. Okay?"

"Okay." Aubrey sighed. He pulled the car to the side of the narrow street, parking in front of one of Toronto's ubiquitous Victorian row houses. He turned off the car, twisted in his seat to face her, and folded his arms. "Lecture away."

"Okay. First, I want to say that my faith is real. I don't—I have never—expected you to believe as I do, or even pretend to, but I expect you to respect that *I* do. I can't explain how I feel about G-d, or Judaism, in a specific way, because I don't question it a great deal. I have my faith and that, itself, is real to me."

Aubrey nodded, silent.

"Now, the Dalai Lama said something like 'if science proves a tenant of Buddhism wrong, then Buddhism must change'. I think this adage should apply to all dogma, whether religious or scientific, including that of Judaism. So, while I do not believe that Jewish slavery and the building of the pyramids, for example, were contemporaneous, I know, as my ancestors, and their ancestors did, that the Jews were enslaved in Egypt, and that G-d helped to free them."

Aubrey opened his mouth, but Salla held up her hand.

"Do I take every word of the Torah as literally true? Well, yes, and also, no—it is the Jewish way to interpret what we are told; to make sense of how ancient texts fit into our modern life. But I believe in the essence. I believe in the ritual. I believe it's necessary for me as a person and for the Jews as a people."

Salla sighed, tilted her head back, and closed her eyes for a moment. When she opened them, she was smiling. She turned to look into Aubrey's face.

"I like you, so, so very much. You're truly one of my favorite people." She sighed and shook her head. "But we absolutely must stop seeing each other."

"What?" Aubrey was not surprised. "But that makes no sense, Salla. We're so happy together."

"Well, yes. Well, no. No. I don't think we are, really. I mean, I enjoy you so much, but I haven't really been myself with you. I think I've been…I don't know…out of body, or something. Going to crazy parties. Having uncommitted sex. Wearing makeup. I just don't like myself like this."

"My God, Salla, you sound like a bossy old lady, lecturing your younger self for having fun. At least, I thought you were having fun. You *seemed* so happy. I thought I was seeing your real self emerge."

"You're right, in part—but it's my least favorite part of myself. I mean, I don't *want* to be that person. I have better things to do with my life. I mean, not better, maybe, but more important. Definitely more important."

"Wait, what you said about uncommitted sex—you do realize I have been monogamous with you? I hadn't slept with anyone else from that first time you kissed me."

She looked at him, then looked away.

"Oh Aubrey. Of course I know that. I'm not talking about your commitment to me."

"I mean, if you want some sort of formal…you know. I don't have the best track record but if anyone has ever made me want to settle down, it's you. Did you want me to make you some promises, my love? I'm good at keeping my promises."

"I know you are," she said, sighing again. "But I don't want your promises, sweet man. I want you to take me home, now, drop me off, and leave me alone. I want to move to Israel and become a rabbi and marry another Jew and have four children. I want you to pursue your acting career, and make music that's important to you. I want us to go on to live happy lives and remember each other very fondly, and, maybe someday, I want you to come visit my big family and sit down with us for the Passover Seder."

As she said this, Aubrey's face broke. He had nothing to say, so he lay across the seat and put his head in her lap. Salla waited patiently, stroking his hair from time to time, unshed tears heavy in her eyes. Eventually, he sat up, turned the keys in the ignition, and took her home.

Two weeks later, Salla sat on a bar stool in Emily's perfect kitchen, her head on her arms, her cheek against the cold marble countertop. Emily sat on a stool beside her, patting her back.

"Oh G-d Emily, I know it's the right thing but it's hurting so much. He's so incredibly lovely. He's such a good man."

"He's a *mensch*[43], all right." The two laughed; Salla, through tears. Emily's use of Yiddish never failed to elicit a chuckle, regardless of their state of mind.

"He called me this morning, you know," Emily said. "Ostensibly, just to see how you were doing, but also, I think, to check whether you really meant it. He's hurting, too, I could tell. He made it clear that, if you changed your mind, he'd be at your door, as he put it, 'with bells on'.

---

[43] *mensch* /mensch / n. *Yiddish*. A person, male, who is known to possess both great learning and integrity.

'Bells on'. I *do* love that man."

"Bells on? Huh." Salla lifted her head. She'd expected him to move on with only, perhaps, a backward glance or two, saddened but relieved she hadn't asked more of him. She dropped her cheek back to the cold, hard surface.

"He didn't mention wanting to convert and move to Israel for a year and marry a rabbi and be a dutiful Jew for the rest of his life, did he?" Salla asked with a creaky laugh.

"Oh, Salla, no. Don't joke about this. If you really wanted those things from him, you would tell him so. Anyway, you know I've never been a huge fan of the Israel plan. I want you here, near us."

"Well, don't worry. I'll still be here when it's time to baptize your baby girl. I promise." Salla sat up and made a creaky smile for her friend. "How are things coming along, anyway?"

Emily and Henry had finally begun the process of adopting a little girl from China, which gave Salla the perfect tool for distracting Emily from any subject on which she became fixated. As usual, Emily's response bordered on Pavlovian.

"Yes! Did I tell you that our dossier has been sent? So exciting! The Adoption Center is probably reviewing it, right now, as we speak. All we have to do now is wait. Wait—what time is it in China?" Emily checked her phone. "Oh. They're probably not reviewing it right this minute. But still! It's sitting on someone's desk, for review. I hope I didn't forget anything important! I've still got to get a reference from Father Sykes, and we're going to need a few more inoculations—oh! and I found the most perfect nursery pattern..." Emily went on in this vein for another ten minutes, with Salla doing a fair imitation of someone pretending to listen.

"Still mopin', man?" Maks came up behind Aubrey, sitting at their accustomed place at the bar of Toronto's Bovine Sex Club. The Bovine was a Mecca for local musicians who wanted to drink, talk about gear, find other players, and gossip about gigs. It was the kind of place where Aubrey was able to feel inconspicuous. This was increasingly important as he found the limelight on him growing once again. He lacked the funds for a security team.

Maks sat beside Aubrey and slapped him on the back. Aubrey looked up and smiled half-heartedly.

"Hey Maks. Moping? Yeah, I guess. Same old, right?"

"Yah, it a terrible thing to be star in the 'highest grossing Canadian film, in history.' Same ol', same ol', I always say."

Aubrey laughed. "Yeah, but some distinction, yeah? I get a kick out of that proviso: 'highest grossing *Canadian* film ever'."

"Yeah, man. Like, it's 'the tastiest *beetle*, ever'. Never fail to make me laugh."

Aubrey laughed.

"We just a colony here, in the eyes of Hollywood," Maks said, nodding. "They film at the Annex and say it's Boston."

Maks ordered a beer for himself, and another for Aubrey.

"But it's good to hear your laugh now man. Been a while."

"It doesn't come easy, these days," Aubrey said. "I guess the self pity I've been marinating in has pickled my sense of humor."

"Hey, but not your way with the words, now." Maks patted him on the back, again. "That got to be a good thing, no?"

Aubrey glanced over at him, his chin in his hands. "Most people would probably say no, I'm sure. I don't know. I left my car for ten minutes today. Ten minutes—not a moment more!—and someone had painted a swastika on it."

Their eyes met, and Maks nodded, with nothing to say.

"The worst thing is," Aubrey said, "it might have been intended as a compliment." He shook his head, then drained his glass, and motioned for another.

"Yah, well. You attract the wrong kind of fan with that one release, sorry to say."

"Yeah. Right-O."

They sat and drank, quiet for a moment.

"So, you missing your pretty Salla, still." It wasn't a question, but they both pretended it was.

"More than I would have thought, Maks. She's one in a million. You're a lucky one—found your woman early, and held on tight, yeah?"

"I don't know, man. Me an Sylvia, we're a team. Good one. She be faithful all these year, an never expect it back. It's funny—she used to say "it don' matter where you get your appetite, jus come home for dinner. Now, when she say, 'jus come home for dinner,' she actually mean, jus dinner."

Aubrey sipped his drink, his eyes downcast.

"But no matter. She good mother, great cook, good woman. But, an I be honest, now, she and I don't have the same thing as you an Salla. We laugh together, sure. But not for hour on end. We talk, too, but about kids. Bills. The news. We don't talk about life, itself. Don't talk about our

feelings. Not like the two of you. We be friends, but we're not close."
Maks peered at Aubrey, his expression gentle. "So go ahead and grieve,
man. It's normal. Healthy."

"Hah. Well, if it's healthy, I could fight off cancer, at the moment.
Sometimes I think I should have just put in my lot with hers. Followed
her to Israel. Maybe even converted. What do you think?"

"I think you look damn silly in one them Jewish beanies. An she
gwine be a Rabbi. Pillar of the community. Aubrey, you can't go there
an' still be you. An she can't take you with her an' be who she want to
be." Maks shook his head, his dreadlocks swinging. "I'm thinking we
have this talk a few time before, though."

"I know. I'm a man obsessed, yeah?" Aubrey thought for a while.
"It's amazing, really, that we wander about, thinking that love fixes
everything, when, really, the vast majority of the time it just bollockses
everything up."

"Now, I'm happy to drink to that one, man." Maks clinked his mug to
Aubrey's shot glass.

Chapter 19

Now the Lord God had formed out of the ground
all the wild animals and all the birds in the sky.
He brought them to the man to see what he would
name them; and whatever the man called each living creature,
that was its name.

~Genesis 2:19
The Holy Bible

Salla turned on her television to see Conan O'Brien address the camera. "My next guest is a man with a past. For at least a decade, he's been at the center of controversy." Conan looked into the camera and cupped his hand beside his mouth as though relaying a confidence. "That's why we've never had him on the show," he said in a stage whisper. "So this is kind of embarrassing." Conan paused while the audience laughed and murmured. Salla shook her head sadly.

"The thing is, he wasn't very popular with our demographic. Our demographic is, of course, people of every race, creed, and religion, somewhere between birth and 102 years of age."

The audience's laughter was louder this time. Salla pursed her lips, picked up the remote, and turned down the volume. She sat on her couch, put her feet on the crate that served as her coffee table, and crossed her arms over her chest.

Conan leaned forward on the desk, his long arm gesturing stage right, as though coaxing someone toward him. Salla leaned forward and turned up the volume.

"Everyone, here's Aubrey Bishop, former lead singer of the BishoPrics and star of the surprise indie hit, 'This Night Mine'."

The audience clapped, murmuring. Aubrey appeared in the parted curtains, paused for a moment, then walked toward Conan, his hands in his pockets, his chin down. It occurred to Salla that she'd never seen him uncomfortable before. She wondered if anyone else could tell.

Conan stood, shook Aubrey's hand, and gestured toward the chair beside him. Andy Richter, in the middle chair, made a show of jumping to the farthest one, as though in fear of Aubrey.

Aubrey smiled at him as he adjusted himself on the chair beside Conan. "Hey, no worries, mate—I've never written a single song about comedians." Andy and Conan laughed. The audience did not.

"Aubrey, thanks for coming on. So, it seemed the controversy surrounding you had pretty much died down, but I did see a few protest signs in front of the studio today."

"Yeah, they're always out there, Conan. They're objecting to my animal magnetism."

A few chuckles sounded from the audience, but for the most part they were silent.

Conan leaned toward Aubrey.

"So, I saw 'This Night Mine' the other day, and I have to admit, I was really impressed. You were fantastic."

"Aw, go on," Aubrey said, ducking his head. He glanced sideways at Conan. "No, I mean do go on. Please," he said coyly.

Conan reached out and grabbed Aubrey's hand in both of his.

"Aubrey, I've always considered you a very handsome man, and now that we've been together for five minutes…"

The audience laughed. One man whooped.

"Thanks Conan. It did seem an odd bit of casting though, right?"

"Well, you as a Baptist minister, it *is* kind of a stretch, you have to admit."

The audience laughed. Aubrey smiled at them ruefully.

"Yes—I know. When I heard he was a Baptist priest, I pictured him speaking in tongues and handling snakes. All bombast and brimstone. But the character's really nuanced. A gentleman, in the true sense of the word; devout and kind and deeply thoughtful. Then, of course, there's the element of Job, in the 'Why hath thou forsaken me?' vein. I was able to relate to that, for some reason."

The audience offered genuine, although quiet, laughter at this. They seemed to be warming up to Aubrey. Salla sat back on her couch and smiled.

"But it's not exactly all sweetness and light, now Aubrey, is it? Not to give anything away, but the film's got its fair share of people being ripped limb from limb, if I recall."

"Well, yes," said Aubrey, "shocking things do happen. It's earned its place in the horror film genre." His was face serious, but Salla detected the glint in his eye. "My virgin sensibilities were highly offended, I can tell you that."

The audience laughed politely.

"So." Conan slapped his desk. "I guess you've brought us a clip tonight?"

"Yes, I've heard clips are de rigueur. All the movie actors are doing it." Salla saw that one fall flat, although Conan gave a kindly laugh.

"Why don't you set it up for us then."

"Right, will do. So, this is near the beginning of the movie. My character, Reverend Thomas Night, has just learned he has an inoperable brain tumor, and he's only got a year or so to live. The diagnosis isn't much of a surprise to him, as he's been having all kinds of auditory hallucinations. But he's very depressed, yeah? In this scene, he's gone to the zoo to get away from things and have a bit of a think. He's sitting in front of the grizzly's cage when he hears a voice, and realizes it's the bear."

"Huh. That's odd. Usually when I hear a voice in my head, it's my mother. Or God." Conan delivered this quip directly to the camera. The audience's laughter was dutiful.

"Oh no—don't let's bring up God again, please." Aubrey smiled. This time the laughter was genuine. Salla could feel Aubrey's relief as he continued to set the scene.

"Anyway, Reverend Night hears the bear talking. And the clip shows what happens next."

"Okay, so, let's watch this piece from 'This Night, Mine'." Conan nodded toward the camera.

Aubrey, wearing a dated brown suit and tie, sits on a bench in front of a bear cage. A tiny boy absorbed in the gift shop toy in his hands, rests his forehead on the scratched Plexiglass of the viewing partition. On the other side, a grizzly bear's cheek is pressed against the glass. The bear's jaws are open wide, as though to poised to engulf the child's head. Its teeth scrape the glass.

"First I'd lift you by the head," the bear says, in a professorial growl. His mouth does not move. "I'd sever your neck in one snap, allowing the rest of you to drop to the ground."

Aubrey/Night, sits up on the bench, swivels his head around at the other people in the exhibit.

"Excuse me?" he says, a Southern drawl softening the words.

"I'd break through the crispy shell of your cranium, and slurp out your brain." The bear's voice is a plaintive whisper. "Then, I'd draw out your entrails, and savor the tangy sweetness of your intestines, sharing your last meal."

"Beg pardon?" Night is whispering, now, too. He stares at the bear.

"Just climb yonder fence, sweet morsel, and breach the river." The bear tilts its giant head, gesturing with its chin to the edge of the enclosure. "I'll wait for you on the other side." More a plea than a command.

The little boy raises his head and notices the bear, its jagged mouth inches from his own on the other side of the Plexiglas. He stares into the bear's jaws, then starts, and falls on his bottom. He begins to cry. The boy's mother laughs and picks him up.

Night leaps from his bench and runs at the bear, who stares at him from the other side of the divider.

"What in Sam Hill is wrong with you?" and suddenly the Reverend Night is hollering in a voice that rings of the pulpit. "Foul beast! Have you no mercy?"

As the other visitors turn to stare at him, the bear yelps and gallops to the other side of the enclosure, rolling its eyes as though fleeing an apparition from bear hell.

"That's right! Get out of here! You should be ashamed of yourself!" Night yells through the glass. The boy's mother, glancing at Night, hustles her son off to see the lions. Another woman, giving Night a wide berth, leaves the area, pulling her husband behind her like a poorly trained dog.

After sitting on its haunches for a moment, the bear lumbers toward Night in an indirect path, sniffing the air, the ground, a rubber tire hanging from a tree. Its movements are wary. The whites of its eyes are showing. It stops for a moment and turns to the black bears in the next enclosure.

"It speaks!" the bear yells. "Excuse me? It's speaking to me! That human in the brown—it is talking!"

The others raise their heads to sniff the air in Night's direction, then turn away in bored disbelief.

*The bear stops at the Plexiglass and stares at Night. "I'm sorry.
Were you speaking to me?" it says loudly, although Night is just feet
away.*

*"Of course I'm talking to you. Do you see anyone else here?" Night
replies.*

They stare at each other through the glass.

*"What did you mean, shouting at me about mercy?" The bear tilts its
head.*

*"What do I mean? I mean, how can you look at an innocent and
want to kill it? Don't you realize life is sacred?"*

*The bear shakes its giant head slowly, as though clearing its
thoughts, then lies down on the other side of the glass. It rolls to scratch
its back on the ground then rolls to fix its eyes on Night.*

"That's what we often wonder about you," the bear says.

"What in the hell are you talking about?"

*"Well, what are you doing here, for example, watching me endure
this sickly, diminished existence, instead of properly inhabiting yours?"*

*"I don't understand." Night's face belies his words. He sits on the
ground beside the Plexiglass. "That 'sweet morsel' as you called him—
why, he was little more than a baby!"*

*"Exactly... a young one's innocence. Its fragility. Its bursting
potential—that's precisely what makes them so delectable."*

"Well, I'll be. Would you eat a baby of your own?"

*"Why certainly!" The bear sounds surprised. "If I were to encounter
an unprotected, succulent young bear? The youngster would not survive
long without its mother, anyway. And although, like any good predator it
would fight for its life, it would prefer to become a meal for another than
to starve to death itself."*

*Night rests his forehead against the Plexiglass. The bear licks it on
the other side.*

*"I, myself, would be honored to go that way," the bear says. "In fact,
I'd rather you devour me this instant, than leave me here to wallow in
this cage." The bear sighs. "I'll die here anyway, never having lived."*

*As the clip ends, the reverent Night is sobbing quietly, his body
pressed against the scratched glass, his arms outstretched.*

The audience was quiet.

"Wow. I have nothing funny to say about that," Conan said, quiet
himself. "Although that bear is one heck of an actor." A few chuckles
issued from the audience as the solemnity lifted.

"That particular scene is what made me want to do the movie, actually." Salla nodded to herself. This was true. "It sums up in a few moments what I wouldn't have managed to say in an entire career," Aubrey said, his body still, his voice quiet.

"That's because people thought you were trying to say something else, entirely, my friend." Conan, reaching a long arm across the desk, shook Aubrey's hand. "Thanks for coming on, man. It's really a great achievement. And I mean that. Aubrey Bishop, folks. In his second life as the star of 'This Night, Mine'."

Salla saw the happiness on Aubrey's face as the audience broke into applause. She smiled, hugging herself.

Chapter 20

Prohibited to you are your mothers,
your daughters, your sisters, your father's sisters,
your mother's sisters, your brother's daughters,
your sister's daughters, your milk mothers
who nursed you, your sisters through nursing,
your wives' mothers, and your step-daughters
under your guardianship
born of your wives unto whom you have gone in.
~Surat An-Nisā' 4:23
The Holy Qur'an

Five sharp raps on her door snapped Salla from guilty reverie. Wielding her mouse surreptitiously, she exited the BishoPrics fansite she'd been browsing through and ran to the window to see Yigal—her first cousin once removed—smoking a clove cigarette and glaring at the door. Her movement brought his eyes to her window. He'd already seen her—putting it off was no longer an option. Cursing inwardly, she opened the door.

"Salla," he said, hurling his cigarette at the ground, grabbing her awkwardly around the shoulders and thumping her back a little too heartily, "how are you? It's good to see you, cousin."

"Yigal," she said, unable to feign enthusiasm with conviction. "I've been meaning to stop by and see you. I've just been so busy."

It was sad, she thought, remembering the odd, precocious boy he had been. They'd had something of a friendship, once—at least, an awkward camaraderie had been achieved. He'd taught her to curse in Arabic; a skill that would save her life, one day.

"Ah yes, busy, I'm sure," he said, his face skeptical. "Busy avoiding your Bubbie, to hear *her* tell it. Well, can't I come in?"

"Of course. Please do. I'm sorry. I'm just studying."

Yigal stomped into her apartment, staring around, making her belongings seem transient and fragile with the force of his presence. At six-feet, four-inches, height wasn't the only factor in his imposing facade. Yigal's youth was obscured by his perpetual stubble and habitual gruffness. Most people would have guessed him in his mid-thirties. To Salla, he looked much as he had when she'd last seen him four years ago, when he was fourteen. His mother had sent him to stay with Adira for the summer, in an attempt to get her little desert *sabra*[44] under some kind of control. He'd been expelled from school a second time, and she was at her wit's end. For Salla, that summer had been a particularly long one; she'd spent several unpleasant interludes fighting off Yigal's clumsy, forceful, and persistent advances. She'd ended the struggle by joining forces with Bubbie—over a long-winded two hours—to convince him that his behavior was not only unwelcome, it was inappropriate. This succeeded only in confirming his suspicion that, in this matter, too, everyone was against him. Privately, Salla and Bubbie had concluded the only solution was for him to enter psychiatric counseling, discussion of which, unfortunately, his mother refused to participate in. He was sent back home to Tel Aviv two weeks early, still considering himself unfairly put upon. Today, he seemed the same as he'd always been. Either he'd forgotten the incident, or he was keeping his feelings under wraps. This, she decided, was progress of a sort.

To Yigal, Salla's beauty—which he'd thought was a secret only he knew—was now disturbingly overt. The news that she had taken up with a famous musician had been distressing in itself, but to see she'd taken control of the way she looked—she was wearing *lipstick*, for heaven's sake—Yigal was appalled. She seemed, to him, both besmirched and elevated.

"So—studying were you? What more could you possibly have to study, Salla?" His attempt at a light tone was darkened by an ever-present edge of anger. "Is a PhD not as much study as one can do in a

---

[44] *sabra* / tsa'-bar / n. *Hebrew*. Lit. A thorny desert plant, with a sweet interior. Colloquially, a native-born Israeli.

lifetime?"

"Apparently not, considering I'm not yet thirty," she retorted, clinging tenuously to her good-natured tone. "I just want to make sure I have every 'i' dotted for my application."

"Oh, you must be joking. You will have no trouble getting into Rabbinical school. You've got credentials out to here, and you're the daughter of a rabbi. You speak Hebrew already! You are just wasting your time, studying. What you should be doing is learning how to behave like someone who belongs in the Rabbinate."

"What exactly do you mean by that, Yigal?"

"Aren't you going to invite me to sit down? I haven't seen you for a long time. Come on now. We're old friends, don't forget." The tinny bonhomie in Yigal's voice was missing from his face.

"Well, why don't you come in for a tea, then." Salla led him into the kitchen, pulled out a chair, and motioned for him to sit. "But after, I'll really have to see you out. As I've been telling Bubbie, I'm very busy, so I don't have a lot of time to visit. I'll stop by Bubbie's house sometime soon, so we can catch up properly." Salla did not want to discuss the reasons for their unofficial estrangement; Yigal, she knew, would see it from a completely different perspective, and it would only serve to dredge the underlying hostility directly to the surface.

"Well, you certainly should see your grandmother. She's worried about you, and she does not need more worry in her life. Salla, I'm concerned. As your cousin, I think it's important for you to hear my opinion of your current situation."

"I'm not sure what you're talking about." Once again, Salla fought to keep her cool. She filled the kettle and placed it on the stove, her back to Yigal. She would not give him, or Bubbie, the satisfaction of knowing that Aubrey was no longer in her life. She refused to allow them to think it was Bubbie's doing.

This would turn out to be a mistake.

"I mean you've been spending your time with that inappropriate man. That 'Mel—with a—Gibson' who wrote those horrible songs. I don't think you could find anyone worse to torture your grandmother with."

"That sounds like a direct quote. Bubbie didn't send you to talk to me about this, I hope?" Salla's voice rose and fell as she forced her feelings below the surface.

"No. No, she did not. But she did tell me she was concerned and I agree. We can't have you damaging the family name. I can hardly believe you're allowing this to happen. What about when word gets around about your new boyfriend?"

"For one thing, he's not my boyfriend." Salla stood. "For another, he's a good person, and he's also a good friend. Either way, it's none of your business, Yigal."

"You can't be serious, he's your friend. That man's an anti-Semite. Are you so filled with self-loathing you have to spend time with someone who hates you?"

"You don't know the first thing about him, or me." Salla was having trouble controlling her voice.

"I know that, sometimes, your liberal soft-heartedness confuses you about people's real intentions. You'd meet Hitler on the street and pronounce him a fine sort."

"That's ridiculous, Yigal." Salla got up to pour the tea, avoiding the thought that Aubrey had said something similar. "You—and Bubbie, for that matter—see malevolence everywhere. You two would distrust the motives of the Dalai Lama, for heaven's sake. Now that I think about it, Bubbie once told me that Mother Theresa's motives were suspect. Mother Theresa—who dedicated her life to ministering to the impoverished, the ill! The woman's literally beatified."

"Beautified?"

"I mean sainted!" Salla said. "She's one miracle from achieving actual sainthood."

"Oh, well—Catholics—what do you expect? Such hypocrites. Torture everyone who refuses to convert, then turn some crazy old lady into a saint for feeding the heathens."

"See, this is exactly what I mean. Yigal, the Spanish Inquisition ended in the fifteen-hundreds. It's probably time to let it go."

"Yes, well everyone would like to forget that it happened all together, would they not? Just like they would rather forget the Holocaust. Or pretend it never happened, like you."

"So, now I'm a Holocaust denier, is that what you're saying?"

"Well, no. That's not what I meant. I just think you would rather not know about the bad in the world. So you tell yourself it is not there."

Mechanically, Salla put sugar and milk in Yigal's tea and placed the mug in front of him. She scraped a chair from the table and sat.

"I see a lot of bad *and* good in the world, Yigal."

"What's your definition of bad? Cruelty to puppies? Or do you extend it to all cute animals?" Yigal's smirk sat awkwardly on his angry face.

"Why don't we start with defiance of the Ten Commandments, see how that goes?" Salla crossed her arms.

"Well, that goes without saying, naturally." Yigal sat back in his chair.

"Oh does it? So now you, *you* believe in strict adherence, do you? *Lo teer tsakh*[45]?" Salla's accent was flawless, a fact that surprised Yigal, as she'd never set foot in Israel. But he thought he knew where this conversation was going.

"Yes, what of it? Murder is wrong, certainly."

"Is it?" Salla put her hands on her hips. "But you have no moral compunction against killing."

"The commandment does not proscribe against killing. 'Thou shall not kill' is a Christian mistranslation—as you, of all people, must know. Anyway, I hear what you are saying. And it's true, I have no problem with war for the sake of self-protection."

"What about the murder of innocents? Because I've heard you say that's just an unpleasant cost of war."

"Israelis must protect our country from being taken from us. It's not our fault the Palestinians use their innocents as shields."

"First of all, they do nothing of the sort. Perhaps a few isolated sociopaths have done so, but that's far from a culturally acceptable practice. But sometimes it seems— " Salla paused and sighed, "sometimes, it seems as though Israel uses Palestinian children as propaganda to dehumanize their parents." She rested her chin in her hands, her elbows propped on the table in front of her.

"See, that's what I mean, Salla. You're so quick to defend the Arabs, you end up hating the country that would protect you from them."

Salla shook her head at him, fighting the urge to pick his entire sentence apart, opting for simplicity. "Yigal. I don't hate Israel. I love Israel. That's exactly the reason the situation there upsets me so."

"I think you would be less upset if the damned Arabs took it over. Then your liberal guilt would be assuaged. So what, all those Israelis pushed into the sea? You could dance, while that boyfriend of yours played his evil songs."

"Okay, Yigal, I think you should be going, now" she stated, tremulously. "You're not welcome." She stood.

"No." Yigal stated calmly, looking up into her eyes. "I'm not going anywhere."

"What!" Salla had forgotten whom Yigal thought he was. "I said

---

[45] *Lo teer tsakh* / lO-tere-sach' / phrase. *Hebrew.* Lit., "Not, shalt thou murder."

leave. Now!" She heard herself yelling, as if from three blocks away. She was furious, a feeling she'd experienced perhaps thrice in her adult life.

"And I said no! I will not leave!" Yigal yelled back, his loud voice reverberating off the walls.

The floor creaked in the adjoining apartment. A few sharp knocks sounded as the 72-year-old gentleman who lived next door picked up the baseball bat he kept under his bed and tapped it meaningfully on the floor. Salla had lived next to him for several years, and—a woman alone in the city—had been comforted by that sound more than once.

Yigal decided to try another tack. The incorrect one, he decided later.

"Salla—think of your father, for God's sake. He must be turning in his grave, may he rest in peace. If he could see you now he would grieve himself to death, again."

She walked over to pick up her cell phone on the table.

"Listen, Yigal, I mean it. If you don't leave right now, I'm going to call Bubbie." She held the phone at him as if it were a magic talisman.

Yigal, feigning indifference, stood.

"Fine. I'm leaving. You'd rather be a whore than a decent person, you just go ahead. I'm telling Adira. See what she thinks of you now."

Yigal stormed out Salla's front door, slamming it, twice, behind him. She ran to throw all the locks, in case he changed his mind and returned. "It's okay, Mr. Fotopoulos," she yelled through the thin walls. "I'm okay."

She dialed Bubbie, as much for closure as anything else. She didn't expect Bubbie to be able to bring Yigal under control. No one had ever had any success with that.

"Hello?"

"Bubbie. It's Salla."

"I know it's you, Bubbieleh. I do have call display, dear. What's going on? You can't come in person? I have to talk to a telephone all the time?"

"Bubbie, Yigal was here. He just left."

"Yes, I knew he wanted to stop by. He's been hoping to spend some time with his cousin."

"Wait—you knew he was headed over here? Unannounced?"

"Well, yes. You don't seem to mind it when that *goy*[46] stops by without calling first."

"I don't see what that has to do with anything. Aubrey is welcome in

---

[46] *goy* / goi / n. *Yiddish*. Non Jew. Derogatory.

my house."

"So, your cousin is not? What is this now, Salla?"

"Bubbie, for heaven's sake. Don't you remember how Yigal used to behave with me?"

"Oh dear. But that was years ago! He's a lot better now that he's grown up."

"That depends on how you define *better*. Or grown up. He wouldn't leave at first. He refused."

"Salla, Salla. I'm sorry Yigal was upsetting you. I'll talk to him. He's just worried about you, running around with that *fershlugina*[47] musician. You can't expect anyone to be *happy* about it."

"Bubbie, please. I've told you, over and over: Aubrey is *not* crazy. He's *not* evil. He's *not* an Anti-Semite."

"Maybe, but his music is. Those songs made people hate Israel."

"Look Bubbie, it's a sad fact, but the people who hate Israel are going to hate Israel. And of those, some will hate Israel for the sheer fact that it is full of Jews."

"Exactly!"

"But Aubrey Bishop is not one of them."

"Don't fool yourself, Salla. The world is not as sweet a place as you'd like. It wasn't that long ago that Toronto's Jews were banned from all the summer resorts outside of the city, you know. There was even a riot when I was young!"

"Oh here we go again." Salla sighed. "You're talking about the Christie Pits Riots? When you were *young*? Wasn't that in the 1930's? How young were you, minus ten?"

"Okay, perhaps not in my lifetime, but certainly my father's. In fact, I think he was there, fighting the Swastika Clubs with his bare hands."

"Bubbie, Bubbie, Bubbie." Salla held her temples in her free hand, her phone a couple of inches from her head. "When was the last time there was a Swastika Club in Toronto, of all places? You're living in the past, and blaming the present."

"That's what your father used to say, too, Salla. But what the Holocaust taught us, if nothing else, is that 'It happened before, it can happen again'."

And that, said with a flourish, was how Bubbie usually ended this particular argument with Salla. But not today.

"Yes, Bubbie! If it's happened before, it can happen again. Do you

---

[47] *fershlugina* / fer-shlug'-in-er / adj. *Yiddish*: Beaten up, no good.

forget what happened with Yigal before? There's something very wrong with him. He has no self control." Salla was breathing hard; she forced herself to slow. "Bubbie," she said, her voice controlled, "you really must send him home. I'm worried about you. I think he's dangerous."

"Oh, Salla, Salla. Always so dramatic. Yigal's just a confused boy. He left when you told him to, right?"

"Well, only after I threatened him with calling you!" As she heard herself say this, Salla could anticipate the ridicule she was about to endure.

"Oh, of course! Your worries are understandable now. Help! Help! Yigal's out of control! Call Nana!" Bubbie was jubilant.

"Bubbie!"

"Yes officer!" Bubbie interrupted. "Help! He's out of control! Call my grandmother!"

"Bubbie, I'm hanging up the phone, now."

"Hello officer? He only listens to my fearsome Bubbie! Help!"

Salla pressed the disconnect button and turned her phone off. She shook her fist at it, sighed, and went to bed.

Chapter 21

The Lord said, "If as one people speaking the same language
they have begun to do this, then nothing they plan to do
will be impossible for them. Come, let us go down and confuse
their language so they will not understand each other."
So the Lord scattered them from there over all the earth,
and they stopped building the city.
That is why it was called Babel,
because there the Lord confused
the language of the whole world.

~Genesis 11:6
The Holy Bible

The next morning, Salla tucked a towel around her hair and ran to grab her phone, chiding herself for having turned it on first thing. It had been ringing steadily from the moment she stepped into the shower. As she glanced at her call history, noting six calls from Bubbie, and, alarmingly, two more from Emily, it began to ring again.

"Salla! Thank God in Heaven."

"Bubbie. What's happening? What's wrong?"

"Oh, my darling, I'm so sorry. Oh my God! This is terrible!" There was a new intensity in Bubbie's tone.

"What? Bubbie, you have to tell me what's going on. Please—has something happened with Yigal?"

"Yigal? What are you talking about?" This unexpected question had the effect of snapping Bubbie out of the hysteria loop she'd been racing around. She sounded puzzled.

"Haven't you seen the news? It's even on Fox! It's been on all day." Bubbie's day began at five a.m.

"Bubbie—what's happened? Please tell me."

"Oh, Salla, Salla, Salla, Salla." Bubbie resumed her wailing. "It's so terrible. I hate to be the one to tell you!"

On Bubbie's fourth "Salla," her granddaughter ran to switch on her TV.

"Oh my G-d," Salla gasped, falling to her careworn couch. "Daddy's tree."

On the screen, in dimly lit footage, were images of Salla's girlhood Synagogue. Reaching to the ceiling behind the ark, the stained glass window her father had commissioned from a local artist was broken and warped, its angles twisted, its glass shattered. It looked as though someone had taken a crowbar to it. Someone had.

The "Tree of Life," as the piece was called, had been completed three years before his death, and Rabbi Kahn had loved it to a degree he himself considered unseemly.

"There's a fine line between art appreciation and idolatry, my dear," he'd told Salla more than once. "And I hope you'll remind me if I ever seem to cross it. But, I have to admit: I couldn't love this thing more if I'd created it with my own hands."

The congregation had worked diligently to raise the money for the piece and were just as proud as he. It was often cited as a masterpiece of the form.

The glass had been smashed in several places and the *came*—the lead wire seams which gave structure to the piece—had been badly mangled. To Salla, it seemed irreparable.

As the camera panned the scene, zooming in to better catalogue the destruction, Salla moaned and fell to her couch, clutching herself, aching with grief.

The image on the television switched to a reporter in front of the temple, her breath visible in the air, her expression sober. "Vandals smashed stained glass windows, destroyed religious artifacts, and defaced the walls of a Toronto synagogue last night. Or Hadash Temple, on Bayview near Leslie Street, was the scene of senseless destruction involving possibly hundreds of thousands of dollars in damage. The attack happened sometime in the hours between two and four. We interviewed the security guard who'd been hired to prevent this sort of thing. Although he declined to speak on camera, he told us the vandals had knocked him out and injected him with a drug. The cleaning staff discovered him bound and gagged in the temple's cloak room."

The scene switched to a series of images inside the temple, panning quickly past slogans sprayed in black letters several feet high. The words 'Jews Out of Palestine', 'Push them into the Sea', and 'Jihad for Israel' were visible.

"Hate messages were spray-painted on the walls of the synagogue, and in a disgusting turn, human excrement was found at the scene. Several prayer books were defiled. "

The piece closed with the grim reporter standing in front of the synagogue.

"Rabbi Ari Schusterman, who leads the congregation here, could not be reached for comment. Police are investigating."

Hours later Salla still lay on the couch, prostrate with grief, a blanket over her head. Her phone, which had been ringing incessantly, was now under the mattress in her room, the battery pulled and tossed on the floor. She rolled to her side, pulled her legs to her chest, and began, again, to cry.

Emily, a captive in Bubbie Adira's kitchen, marveled at the old woman's hyperbolic powers as she convinced herself that Aubrey was responsible for the destruction of Or Hadash. Leaning against a wall, arms folded, Emily watched Adira pace back and forth along the counter as she prepared food with her usual economy of movement.

"That evil son of a bitch. I'm absolutely, positively, *certain* he did it. I should just get my gun and shoot the evil *dybbuk*[48] now!" Bubbie's rage was escalating, in opposing reaction to Emily's calming tone.

"Bubbie Adira. I *promise*, he would never do such a thing. He didn't even have a motive, much less the opportunity." Emily hesitated. "Wait—back up. What was that about a gun?"

"My gun. I have a little black .38 special. And I'm not afraid to use it!"

"You have a what? Adira, are you crazy? You can't have a gun—you need a license! You could go to jail."

---

[48] *dybbuk* / 'dEbuhk / n. *Yiddish*. A malevolent spirit from Jewish mythology, believed to be the soul of a dead person, that takes possession of another's body.

"Emily Johnson. Who do you think you are speaking to? There is absolutely no need to be disrespectful, young lady! Do you forget where you are?" Bubbie was shrill with self-righteousness. Emily held up her hands.

"I'm sorry! I'm sorry. Adira, it's understandable that tempers are running high, but I don't like to hear talk of you shooting people. Guns *kill* people, I hope you realize."

"Well, for your information I've been a responsible gun owner for many years already. I got my license when you and Salla were still in grade school! I keep my firearm in a safe, under my bed."

Emily found this extremely worrisome, in light of Bubbie's paranoid bent. She was not, in Emily's opinion, the most appropriate candidate for gun ownership, being the type to shoot first and identify the victim later.

After a long half hour, as she repeatedly interrupted Bubbie's tirade to convince her of Aubrey's overall benevolence, his love for Salla, his lack of motive, and complete lack of opportunity (his alibi for the evening had been collaborated by stories in the feature sections of both of Toronto's daily newspapers, about five hundred of his fans, and at least three of his enemies), Emily had succeeded in wearing Bubbie down to the point where she was tired of talking about it, at least.

"Well, maybe he didn't do it. But I bet he's happy!"

Emily sighed. This would have to do.

"Hi Salla, it's Dini Fanshaw. I've been meaning to call and thank you for being on my show a few months ago. Listen, I hear you've been seen around town with Aubrey Bishop, and I was hoping you wouldn't mind talking about it. I was thinking perhaps you're trying to help him clean up his public image? Anyway, I'd love to chat. He's such a charismatic guy—I wonder if he'd consider coming on the show? Anyway, just thinking aloud. Give me a call back on this number, okay? It's my private line. Thanks girl! Bye."

"Salla? Did you call me? Er, it's Aubrey. Sorry. Perhaps you could call me if you get a moment? Right, yeah—goodbye."

"Hi, this is Roger Delanty calling on behalf of Mr. Bill O'Reilly. I'd like to invite you for an exclusive interview, Dr. Kahn, to discuss your relationship with one Aubrey Lionel Bishop. I'll try your email address, but please feel free to contact me at this number."

"Salla? Salla? It's Bubbie. Why won't you pick up? I'm at the shul and it's such a terrible sight. Your father—may he rest in peace—would have died to see it. Such a horrible, terrible, disgusting thing to do.

Please call me, I need you, my Bubbielah."

"Salla? Dini Fanshaw calling, again. I saw that you were at the wrap party for Aubrey Bishop's movie. How exciting. I'd love to chat with you on the air about it. Are you seeing him? He's quite a guy, that's for sure. So good looking and talented, too. Anyway, enough of the girl talk. Hope you're available. Call me at this number."

"This is Steve Stapleton of the Toronto Sun calling for Dr. Salla Kahn. Dr. Kahn, we'd like to have your comments on the outcry from the local Jewish community, regarding your relationship with Aubrey Bishop. I'd like to give you the opportunity to share your side of the story with the public. I'll try again later. Thanks."

"Salla! Your grandmother is very worried. You must call her right away. Are you so uncaring that you would allow her to worry? Call her! This is Yigal"

"Salla, what the hell? We're starting to worry now! I know you must be really upset—I am, too—but you've got to at least let us know you're okay. I'm at the Temple. Bubbie and I are trying to clean up. It's pretty bad—I'm sorry. Never mind. Call me."

"Dr. Kahn, this is Randall Turner, with the Toronto Star. I'm doing a piece on hate crimes in the Greater Toronto Area, and I'd very much appreciate the opportunity to talk to you about the events at Or Hadash. I've sent an email to you at the University, as well. Thanks."

"Salla, this is your grandmother, again. I'm sorry I said that man may have been responsible. I'm sure he probably wouldn't have gotten mixed up with something like that. I'm sorry. Okay? Emily said you would be very upset with me. So, anyway, I said it. Please accept my apology. I love you. Okay? Goodbye."

"Dr. Salla, this is Dini Fanshaw calling. I just saw the news about those terrorists vandalizing the synagogue. Wasn't that your father's temple? I'm so sorry; it's a terrible thing. Listen—dear—if you want to address the situation on the air, we'd really like to have you come on the show. Sometimes it helps to air your feelings, 'on air', so to speak. Really, we'll book you anytime you're available. I think it's important you give the community a few words; It may offer a chance for some healing. Call me at this number, or at my office, or at my email...whatever works. Thanks."

"Salla. Please call me. Please! I don't deserve this torture. Who treats her own grandmother like this! Give me a call. I've been going through hell and back!"

"Hello, Salla? It's Aubrey, again. I just saw the news. Was that your father's temple? I hope not. If so, God. I'm so sorry. Actually, I'm sorry even if it isn't. Such a terrible thing for those animals to do. I hope everything's okay? I'm going to call Emily and check. Okay my lovely? Talk to you soon."

"Salla! Call me! I'm so upset with you I can hardly believe it! I'm in agony! Please, please, please! Look, I'm sorry I said those about *him* destroying the temple. He probably didn't. Emily says he wouldn't, and she seems to know everything. As always. Please call me! I'm sorry! Call me, please!"

"Salla, Aviva, Kahn! I'm coming over there, right now. If you don't let me in, I'll be back with Bubbie. I mean it, Salla. Don't make me bring her over."

Chapter 22

But Jehoash king of Israel replied to Amaziah king of Judah: "A thistle in Lebanon sent a message to a cedar in Lebanon, 'Give your daughter to my son in marriage.' Then a wild beast in Lebanon came along and trampled the thistle underfoot."
~Chronicles 25:18
The Holy Bible

Yigal was whistling an old Beatles' tune as he pushed his cart through the aisles of Wal-Mart, marveling at the multitude of garbage available to every person every moment of every single day. Store hours? The place literally never closed for one moment, and hadn't, the lady on the phone had proudly informed him, in the ten years since its opening. He wavered between awe and disgust as he noted that there was literally no human need that could not be met in this garish fluorescent football stadium, this altar to the insatiable Frankenstein's monster of Chinese ingenuity and Western acquisitiveness.

"*Come together, right now, over me,*" Yigal sang, *sotto voce.*

"What's that now, dear?" a Wal-Mart greeter asked, her dentures gleaming at him.

"Not you," he bit out, gliding his cart past her.

"*He comes, grooving up slowly...*" Yigal was in such a wonderful mood, happier than he'd been in a long time. Happy to be doing something productive. He pushed his oversized cart purposefully to the supermarket section and selected items at random, casting his eyes about to see if anyone was watching. They'd said he had poor impulse control, but here he was, methodically executing a carefully conceived plan.

He bought two packages of Styrofoam cups, a package of cheap bar soap, and a funnel he found in the automotive section.

"He got, ju-jube eyeball, he one, spinal cracker..."

Taking a moment for himself, Yigal stopped by the video game section to try the latest *Call of Duty* release. The clerk, who pronounced it, "totally sweet—a *righteous* arsenal," received a scornful glance for his review. There was nothing like *Modern Warfare Three*, and there never would be. Yigal had achieved Prestige Level 10 a long time ago. If this clerk knew Yigal's game handle, he'd probably be impressed. But Yigal considered it a point of honor to keep his achievements to himself. He placed the controller carefully in its slot, and left, head held high.

Next, he made several circuits of the store, searching for the wine section to no avail. Finally he pushed his cart to the closest cash register in the wide bank of checkout centers and asked.

"What? Wine. Here? You can't get that in Wal-Mart, eh? Try the liquor store." The clerk raised her eyes at him. She smelled like stale cigarettes.

"Liquor? No, I want wine. Where is that kept?" Yigal was so tired of dealing with stupid Canadians. They were so slow moving, so dull. They seemed drugged.

"Wine is kept, along with all the other liquor, at the LCBO. Liquor Control Board of Ontario. You want booze, you have to get it from the government, eh?"

"LCBO? What are you talking about?" Although he'd come of legal age the same day he became eligible to join the IDF, Yigal wasn't really a drinker. He'd never had occasion to learn that, in Ontario, alcohol was a strictly controlled substance, sold only in government-run stores. One of which, it dawned on him, was less than a block from his aunt's place.

"Never mind. I'm finished now." He paid with cash and walked away with his bags, leaving his cart in front of the cash register. The teller shook her head as she watched him go.

After a quick stop at the LCBO ("How much? Is this your cheapest kind?") Yigal headed back to Adira's house, having added two oversized bottles of undrinkable wine to his load. Adira was away at her sister's house in Oakville for the weekend. She'd been avoiding him since his confrontation with Salla, he could tell, although they hadn't spoken about the incident. Women were so childish, he thought. Made you do their dirty work then accused you of being dirty. Salla's attitude had astonished him, though, helped him see what kind of person his sainted cousin had raised. She was practically fucking a Nazi—that's how far her father's liberal tendencies had taken her. That's what their sort of thinking wrought. These were the people who would be giving Israel back to the Arabs—wrapped up in a big blue and white bow—if they got their chance. Well, they wouldn't get their chance, if people like him had anything to do with it. Shaking his head disgustedly, Yigal went to work.

Taking one of his aunt's large pots down from the rack, Yigal carefully filled it one third full with gasoline. Heating it gradually over Adira's—thankfully—electric stove, Yigal then took up a bar of soap and a potato peeler. Humming, he carefully grated the soap into the hot gasoline, stirring with a soup spoon whenever the flakes were slow to melt.

As he worked, he thought about Salla. She *was* a good person, at heart. Of course. She'd just fallen into the wrong crowd. Women were malleable like this. That's why they were unsuitable for so many things— war, for example. Anyway, once the bad influences were gone, Salla would be more amenable to Yigal. Part of the problem, he acknowledged, had been his approach. He'd been too rough—too angry. She required a delicate touch, he'd remembered, too late. That was one thing the hateful Aubrey Bishop had going for him, Yigal thought—he was most likely *very* good with women. At the thought of Salla bending at the hands of the rock star, Yigal felt a nauseating rise of desire. His renegade penis, never completely under his control, throbbed as he pictured—and tried not to picture—the many ways Salla might be degraded by Bishop.

Once he'd used up all his soap, Yigal tore open the package of Styrofoam cups, breaking each one into pieces and carefully stirring it into the mixture. When his recipe had reached the consistency of jelly, he took it off the burner and allowed it to cool.

Smiling in satisfaction, he opened the bottles of wine, pouring them out into his aunt's white ceramic sink, carefully preserving the corks. When he noticed stains forming, he vigorously scrubbed away the evidence.

This accomplished, Yigal rewarded himself with a few hours of "Modern Warfare 2". His aunt's graphics card was out of date, but it worked well enough for him to run through the *No Russian* mission, for old time's sake. A happy nostalgia buoyed him along, as he and his comrades made their way through the Moscow Airport, killing every civilian they encountered.

Massacre accomplished, he placed the empty bottles in the sink, filling them halfway with the gasoline mixture. This part of the process was trial and error—the viscosity of the mixture prevented it from pouring through the funnel quickly enough, and a good portion went directly down the sink. No matter; he'd made extra for just such an eventuality. He'd always prided himself on his planning skills, and today's success was further proof of his ability. Pleased, almost happy, Yigal put the bottles in a plastic bag under his bed in Adira's guest bedroom, and returned to his game.

Ian, holding his fist like a rock, rapped an angry staccato beat on the metal door of the row house where Akil lived with his parents. Ishmael answered on the last knock as though he'd been standing inside waiting for Ian to arrive. Pulling Ian in the door, he made a show of swiveling his birdlike head outside ensure no one was watching.

"Right then, I need to know what the fuck," Ian said, pushing himself past Ishmael more forcefully than he'd planned. He'd been rehearsing for the entire half-hour subway ride, and was perhaps over prepared.

"What?" Ishmael asked, surprised. "What's your problem!"

"Is Akil here?" Ian said. "Where is everybody?"

"They're downstairs. What do you want?"

"I'm a part of this group, right mate? I want to talk about what happened. What you lot got me involved in." Not waiting for an invitation, Ian pushed past Ishmael to head for the basement. The TV in the living room was blaring—some lady newsreader going on about what the media was calling "the Destruction of the Temple". The press never seemed to tire of the story. Ian groaned, and took the basement steps two at a time.

In the cheaply paneled room that had become the group's unofficial meeting space, the Activists for Allah wore matching self-congratulatory grins.

"Hey—Ian! How about it, eh? Have you seen the news? They're really paying attention to us, now." Akil's smile broadened further. "I mean, what part of 'Jews out of Palestine' don't they understand, eh?" The group laughed, in unison.

Ian was unamused.

"Right. Well, if that's what you wanted to say, why leave cack all over the place, for god's sake? That sends a different message entirely."

"Hey, I had to take a dump anyway—I kind of just went with it," Ishmael mugged from behind Ian. The group laughed, uncomfortably, this time—their convivial mood dampened. While Ian had been diligently spray-painting his messages, things had kind of gotten out of hand. No one knew about Ishmael's contribution until Akil had stepped in it. He'd wiped his feet on the Jewish prayer book with a defiance that wrestled with fear.

"Well, I've never heard of anything so vile. And what was that with the window? We agreed: No permanent damage. What the fuck? We were just supposed to be painting messages."

"Relax Ian. You got your message out there. We all just decided a crowbar would talk louder." They laughed again—Akil was on a roll—until Ian cut them off.

"Yeah, your crowbar caused damage in more places than you know. My boss's girlfriend is freaking out—her dad was the one what commissioned the stained glass. It was a work of fucking art. And you lot, with your crowbar and your shite, destroyed it!" Ian struggled to keep his anger to a level he could contain. Aubrey's fury had been contagious. "After all your fine talk of Rachel Corrie, Roger! We're the ones who act like the bleeding bulldozer!"

"That's enough of that, man." Roger D stood, and walked toward Ian until his face was less than a foot away. Looking down into Ian's eyes, he lowered his deep voice. "No one was harmed in our action," he said, with a pause between every word. "Not a single hair on a single person's head. Do not dare compare us with that motherfucker who drove over an innocent. We're not even fighting fire with fire."

"Yeah, we were fighting *air* with fire! These people aren't part of the Israeli fucking power structure."

"First of all, nice of you to mention that now; second of all, so the fuck what?" Akil spoke from his seat on the couch, his hands awkward on his hips

"Yeah man, what are you talking about—your boss's girlfriend?" Roger D's attention was focused on Ian at an unnatural intensity. Ian hesitated before answering.

"Come on. You must know. My boss is Aubrey fucking Bishop. He's spitting tacks over this. He's been banging on about Muslims for years, and you've all just confirmed his worst bullshit."

Roger D leaned in. "What're you saying, now? You work for Aubrey 'Kill the Jew' Bishop?"

Ian nodded.

"And you're afraid you're gonna lose your job?"

"No—Aubrey'd never sack me. He's my friend—he looks out for me.

Besides, he needs me to do everything for him besides wipe his arse. But it's made the situation really tight. Aubrey doesn't need more bullshit."

"So, Bishop's girlfriend goes to that Jew temple?" Roger D's disbelief was blatant.

"Her father built it, or something. I don't know. She's a rabbi too, I think."

Roger D turned to looked at the other Activists. He shook his head. Then he returned his attention to Ian.

" No shit. A rabbi. Aubrey Bishop, fucking a rabbi. Wonders never cease. What's her name?"

Ian shook his head. "What? I don't know—who cares? Salla something. Salla Kahn."

Akil, Roger, and Ishmael turned and stared at Ian.

"Salla Kahn. And the wonders pile up." Roger D studied Ian.

"What?"

"She's that bitch on the Dini show a few weeks back, right Akil? The one who said a Jew's blood is redder?"

"Yep. That's her, Rog." Ian saw Akil's surprise turned to speculation.

"Yeah—you saw that too, did you? The moment Aubrey was smitten, I guess."

"Smitten with that fucking cunt! I don't think that's fucking funny." Ishmael strode toward Ian, his fists clenched. Roger D stepped between them to intervene. He put his hand on Ishmael's chest and patted gently.

"Cut him some slack, okay?" Nodding at Ishmael, he turned to the rest of the group.

"Ian's got a point, yo. We gotta watch what kind of impression we make in future actions. Ishmael—you know that was really disgusting, man. No more of that... shit, eh?"

The Activists' laughter was subdued.

"Fucking right. It makes us into just the kind of wankers they say we are." Ian's back remained up.

"Fuck you," Ishmael retorted quietly.

"No, fuck you, you fucking animal!" Ian leaned toward Ishmael.

"Ian! You made your point. Now back off." Roger D's face was grim.

"Fine." Ian turned. "I'm leaving. I don't want anything more to do with this shite, anyway."

Akil stood.

"Yeah, whatever—go drink your beers, alcoholic," he said, jerking his thumb at the stairs.

"Right—because a pint's the devil's work, but cack smells like roses."

"Yeah, whatever—get the fuck out."

"Gladly." Ian spun around, marched back up the rickety basement stairs, and ran directly to the front door—slamming it pointedly behind him—only to spend an anticlimactic half hour on public transit. And thus his association with the Activists for Allah came to an end. For exactly three days.

Chapter 23

How long will I take counsel in my soul,
having sorrow in my heart by day;
how long will my enemy have the upper hand over me?
Look and answer me,
O Lord my God; enlighten my eyes
lest I sleep the sleep of death.

~K'Tuvim, Scriptures
Tahillim, Psalms 13:3

"Damn it Salla, let me in." Emily's worried face peered into the corner of the window at the shrouded figure on the couch. She'd tried knocking, she'd tried yelling, she'd left messages, she'd cried, she'd freaked out. Desperate, she pulled out the last stop: "Don't make me come back with Bubbie!"

At that, Salla rose, opened the door, and returned to the couch, pulling the blanket she was wrapped in over her head. Emily galloped into the room like a bull through a gate and then, anticlimactically, turned and sat quietly on the couch beside Salla's prone form.

Barely holding back her own tears, Emily couldn't stop herself from expressing her thoughts aloud.

"Oh my God, Salla. Who did it? Who could have done it? Such a terrible, disgusting thing. Whoever it was, they're absolutely, completely, pure evil. It's so horrible. It's so…vile."

Salla's voice was a monotone croak. "I don't want to talk about it. I can't."

"Oh honey. I know, I know. But Salla, you can't just lie on the coach. Everyone is so worried about you."

"Fuck 'em."

"Salla, please."

From under the sheet, Salla's voice was defiant. "Do you know what Bubbie said? She said that Aubrey was involved. That maybe he'd—in her new gangsta lexicon—'bankrolled it'."

"What?" Emily feigned surprise. "Now she thinks he paid to have it done? That's so ridiculous. What did you say?"

"I hung up, and put the phone where I couldn't hear it."

Emily couldn't help thinking that Salla's approach was probably more effective than her own had been.

"Well she's safely ensconced at the temple, helping with the cleanup effort, so you needn't worry about her stopping by anytime soon. There's a lot to do." Emily's voice caught on her breath. She'd gone to see *Or Hadash* herself and been overwhelmed by grief, over and over again, at each new insult. She couldn't bring herself to look at the ruins of the Tree of Life. It broke her heart to even think of it. As Salla's closest friend, she'd been running around the synagogue since she was a child herself. Rabbi Avi had taken the girls with him many times as he met with the glass artist. They'd been enchanted as they watched the piece progress.

"Anyway, it looks much worse on TV, I promise you. Rabbi Schusterman already called the original artist—Sarah Berman, remember? She says she's pretty sure she can fix it."

"Really?" Salla peeked out above the sheet, the reddened rims of her eyes intensifying the green. Only Salla could look even more beautiful while crying her eyes out.

"Yes sweetie, she did, I promise. She said it looks worse than it is, and that it was due for some maintenance, anyway, because some of the colors were fading." The latter was pure fiction, but Emily felt sure she ought to press her advantage when it became available.

"Come on, Emily, I'm not an idiot. That window was designed to out-live the building. Why would you make that up?"

"No, no. *I'm* a total idiot. I'm sorry—I shouldn't have. I promise you, though, they did ask Sarah, and she did say it looked reparable. She quoted an outrageous price, of course." Emily paused, gazing at Salla's swollen face, considering.

"Okay, so," she rushed on, "I'm not supposed to tell you this, but

Aubrey has put up the money for repairs. He called her himself and arranged for her to get started on the work right away."

"He did?"

"He did."

"Oh, G-d." Salla rose to a sitting position, pulling her sheet around her shoulders and wiping her eyes and nose with the ends. "You know, what, Ems?"

"What, my dear?"

"I love him. I do."

"I know you do. I mean, he had me at 'Salla's spectacularness speaks for itself'." Emily's Aubrey impersonation was weak, but Salla's chilled body was warmed by the words, nonetheless.

"So, were you planning to tell him how you feel?" Emily asked the question gently, knowing the answer, but wanting Salla to articulate it.

Salla offered Emily a wan smile. "No. I mean, I've never really kept my feelings to myself, but—you know. I loved him before you told me about the Tree, and now, well—he's far from a perfect partner, but he's kind of a perfect guy."

"Yeah."

"Tragic flaws and all."

"Yeah. Tragic flaws and all."

They sat on the couch together, silently contemplating love's many enigmas.

Sighing, Aubrey walked into a flower shop almost one hundred kilometers from his hotel. Emily had assured him that daffodils were Salla's favorite flower, and he'd called everywhere before finding a place that had them on hand. This shop was an hour outside the city, but if it had the desired effect, the drive would have been more than worth it.

An hour and a half later, Aubrey was standing at Salla's door, a cartoon-sized bouquet of daffodils behind his back.

Salla opened the door. Her hair was unwashed, and she wore a scruffy graying bathrobe with a distinct coffee stain over the right breast. Her dulled eyes were swollen, crusted, and rimmed in red. And yet her face still glowed in the dark of the room.

"Come in, Aubrey," she said in a lackluster voice, returning to the couch, which was covered with evidence that she'd been residing there a week.

"Wait—look. I brought you something." He produced the massive bouquet of daffodils from behind his back.

"Thank you," she responded automatically. Taking them from him, she walked at an elderly pace into the kitchen. Having no container large enough to accommodate them, she selected a large stockpot, filled it with water and shoved the daffodils in, their crisp heads leaning. Leaving the whole affair in the sink, she headed back for the couch. Aubrey followed, alarmed.

"Salla? Are you in there?"

"Yes, I'm here, Aubrey. It's been a difficult week. I'm just a little depressed."

"Really? Is that what we're calling it then? A little depressed? Everyone is terribly worried about you." He looked around him, taking in the mess. Her father's guitar had been turned to face the wall.

Salla rolled over to face the back of the couch. Aubrey sat beside her at the edge of the cushions, her feet in the small of his back.

"You know that 'Bubbie' of yours actually rang me up," he said. It had been a trying discussion. Adira Stein had made it very clear that she did not like him—wanted nothing to do with him at all—but said she thought he was the only one who could shake Salla out of her 'slump'. She'd also said, to his incredulity, that she'd appreciate it if he'd just leave Salla alone once he'd succeeded in the aforementioned.

"My conversation with your grandmother is why I came here, actually. She insisted I ignore what you said about being left alone and just push my way on in. And I'm glad I listened. Look at you!"

"Look at me. That's presumptuous, coming from you, Aubrey." Salla's voice was muffled in the back of the couch. "Let's not forget the condition you were in, the first time we met."

Aubrey was honestly puzzled. She'd mentioned this before, but they'd never discussed it in any detail. He remembered being lost, and on her doorstep, and that Ian had gotten him there somehow. He must have been in the midst of the biggest blackout of his life, because he couldn't remember much more; only that he'd been intrigued enough by Salla herself to return again and again.

"You don't remember, do you? You were absolutely wasted, covered in your own vomit, curled up on the steps like some homeless man."

Aubrey nodded. This image of himself was not foreign.

"When I saw who you were," she continued quietly, "all I could think was how you were so wasteful. Of things that others pray for every day. Health, wealth. Beauty. Talent. At first, I was disgusted with you, to be honest. You had all these gifts, just handed to you on a platter, and this was how you gave thanks. By squandering them."

Salla rolled to her back, nudging Aubrey further to the edge of the couch, and spoke to the ceiling.

"Then, I looked at it from a Talmudic perspective. The *Midrash HaGadol* says that G-d prefers a broken vessel." She paused, remembering. "And I realized that's exactly what you were. A broken vessel. So I just... forgave you. I mean, I guess if G-d prefers you, I have to, too, right?" She looked at Aubrey for the first time since he'd walked in the door.

"I don't know Salla," he said, reaching to stroke her cheek. "I don't believe in God, remember?"

She smiled wanly at this. "I remember. I think it's what I admire most about you."

"Really? That I'm *not* a believer?"

"No, it's that you don't try to apologize for it, not to anyone, not even me. You never try to be anyone but exactly who you are. It's a rare trait, Aubrey. Admirable."

Together, they stared at the blank screen of her television. Aubrey noted the cord had been pulled from the wall.

"Well, I admire you for the same thing, actually," he said.

"Oh, I don't know. I've been so many people lately, I don't seem to remember who I am, really."

"Salla?" Aubrey's voice had an edge that bordered on pleading. "I can't see you like this. My proud friend. To do this to yourself—"

"I didn't do anything, though. There's absolutely nothing I could have done. Nothing." Aubrey had never heard Salla cry. He picked up a hand lying wanly on her chest and gave it a squeeze.

"I know, I know, I know," he said, soothing her as if she were a child. "Bad things happened, didn't they, and that's a terrible thing to bear. But it's happened, already, hasn't it? It cannot be changed. So let it go."

Salla closed her eyes, allowing herself to be soothed. "I know. I keep telling myself that I'm not helping by lying here in a pool of my own self pity. But then I just curl up on the couch and fall back to sleep."

"That's because you're depressed, my friend. Salla. I miss you. I hate to see you this way. Please let me help."

"No. Aubrey. I miss you, too. Terribly. But I absolutely cannot compromise my future. Really. You have to go. Come back, perhaps, when we're over each other."

Privately, Aubrey couldn't envision this, but he acquiesced to mollify her.

"Okay. If it's truly what you want, I'll go. But not until I'm sure you're okay."

He stood, grabbed her hands and pulled into a sitting position. She looked up at him from the couch, her eyes dull.

"I'm okay. Really." Her eyes didn't meet his, but his wouldn't look away.

"You're okay, are you? Come on, then, show me." He pulled her to her feet, gave her shoulders a squeeze.

"Prove it. Take a shower. Change into clean clothes. Tidy up. Say your prayers. Eat a decent meal."

Salla sighed, but nodded. Aubrey took her chin in his hand, gently tilting her face toward him.

"I won't leave until you've done all of these things. Okay?"

As she did his bidding, Salla felt herself gradually rejoining the world. When she finished the kosher meal he'd picked up at their favorite deli, he sat across for her at the kitchen table, put his hands on her shoulders and looked, a final time, into her sad green eyes. He kissed her cheek, hugged her and left, without a word.

"Hi and welcome back to *Dini in the Evening!* We've had a last-minute change in the program today. Dr. Salla Kahn, a Jewish Studies professor from U of T, is here to talk with us about what the press has dubbed the 'Destruction of the Temple'. Dr. Kahn's father, the late Rabbi Yosef Avi Kahn, founded the Toronto synagogue that was defiled by vandals last week."

Dini swiveled to Salla, took in her limp hair and dull eyes, and sighed inaudibly. She forced a gentle smile.

"Salla, welcome, and thanks for talking with us today." Salla nodded. "Please accept my condolences. You must be terribly upset. I'm sure you spent a great deal of time at Or Hadash."

"Yes, most of my life." Salla was subdued. Her voice cracked. But her back was straight, her face poised. "My father founded the temple when I was 18 months old."

"I see. So you must be very upset by the horrific vandalism of such a sacred place."

Salla tried not to see Dini's arched brow as barely suppressed avarice. She cleared her throat.

"It's difficult for me to describe the sorrow I feel, Dini. I grew up at Or Hadash. It was the setting of my happiest childhood moments. But I don't believe places can, or should, be considered sacred—remember 'thou shalt have no other G-d before me'?"

"One of the Ten Commandments?"

"Yes, it's the one regarding idol worship. There's a fine line between the love of an object and idolatry. As my father used to say. But Or Hadash is a very special place—to me, and to the entire congregation. We're all extremely saddened by this vicious attack on our lovely temple."

"It is a very sad state of affairs, indeed." Dini was grave. "No one has stepped forward to claim responsibility for the destruction, although the police are reputed to be focusing their investigation on area mosques. Do you have your own suspicions?"

"Well, some of the graffiti *was* written in Arabic. Bad Arabic, I've heard—these people are not Islamic scholars, that much is obvious. But the police know their job better than I, and they've said it's probably the work of a fringe group."

"But whomever it was *did* seem to have a point to make," Dini prompted.

"I can't imagine what point they were trying to make other than they have filthy habits and destructive natures." Suddenly, Salla was fighting to rein in her anger.

"So, what do you say to those who assume the vandalism was the work of Islamists from the local mosque?"

"I say it was done by people who are little better than animals. Muslim or otherwise." Salla's voice was rising. She took a deep breath. "Anyway, that isn't my area of expertise. I can't speculate on the motivations of anyone who could do such a vile thing. It's for the police to say."

Dini, sensing the potential for another headline-grabbing sound bite, pressed in Salla.

"No one's stepped forward, of course, but many in the local Islamic community have been speculating that this was retaliation for Israel's latest attack on the Gaza strip." She offered this information in a helpful tone.

"Well, I certainly hope they're condemning the act, at least." Salla pursed her lips, her voice bitter. "I can't imagine anyone wanting to be affiliated with such vile actions."

"And yet a local Imam has been quoted as saying 'when people feel attacked, they attack in return'."

"That's ridiculous, Dini." Salla's breath was audible. Her eyes were hard. "Those events are happening in a neighborhood thousands of kilometers away, in a country the size of Vancouver Island. No one here is under attack. You'd have to be an idiot not to realize that."

"So perhaps it was done out of a misreading of the Qur'an?"

"I don't know. I'm not an expert on the Qur'an." Salla paused. "But I doubt very much it was an act of any religious community. I certainly don't believe there's anything in the Qur'an that advocates leaving excrement in a place of worship, whatever your secular politics." She took a deep breath and stood.

"I refuse to accept that devout Muslims would do a thing like this. Anyway Dini, I told you I would not participate in a provocation of Toronto's Muslim community and I meant it. Goodbye." Pulling the microphone from her lapel and placing it with the accompanying body pack on the table, Salla walked off the set, never to return.

Although Dini in the Evening was live, it was played on a twenty second delay. Luckily for Dini, less so for Salla, her parting words would not make it on the air.

The phones began to ring.

Chapter 24

And if you are in doubt about what
We have sent down upon Our Servant
[Muhammad], then produce a
surah the like thereof and call upon
your witnesses other than Allah,
if you should be truthful.
But if you do not - and you will never be able to
- then fear the Fire,
whose fuel is men and stones,
prepared for the disbelievers.

Surat Al-Baqarah 2:23
The Holy Qur'an

    The cat watched through the window as the Lady gathered up Her Blanket, Her matching hat, and Her little black boxes, pressing each item to her lips before placing it in a clear pouch. The Lady took up the tool with which she groomed Her head and pulled it through and through her sweeping mane, while she stared at Herself in the reflecting window. She'd been doing this a lot lately. Sometimes, while She did, water came from Her eyes. Often, when the water came, the Blanket Lady would return to bed and lie down for a time before rising and moving through the next step. This time, happily, the water stayed in her eyes.

    She nodded at Herself in the reflective window, and walked to the stove. The cat, a creature who loved routine when he could wrest some from his hardscrabble existence, jumped from his vantage point at the window and scrambled to hide by the front steps, happy to know what came next. The door opened, and, in keeping with custom, a dish of delicious, crushed animal was placed on the step, followed by a bowl of fresh, clear water.

The cat watched—ever wary—for the door to close. Still not ready to leap, he listened for the clicking sound that indicated the door was fully shut. At the click, he zipped to the porch to enjoy his meal, twitching his tail as he kept an educated eye, ever suspicious, on the door.

Ten minutes later, the cat had returned to the windowsill for his morning ablutions—the satisfying weight of food in his belly making him take extra care. He watched the front door as his benefactress left Her den, just as the light was slanting over the tree across the street. She was a creature of habit. It was one of the many reasons he'd made Her his own.

Today, noting the Blanket Lady's attention was elsewhere, the cat decided to stalk Her. He followed at a safe distance, ducking into alleys if another human passed, rubbing himself casually against the corner of a building if She happened to turn toward him. As they traversed a dark valley between tall buildings, the cat noticed he was not the only one following the Blanket Lady. A large rolling Beast, the color of dried blood, had joined the procession, creeping along at a distance behind. The cat could smell that the Beast held several humans at once, although only one peered out the dark window. The Beast tracked the Lady, taking all the same turns as She and the cat. The Lady appeared not to notice.

The cat hid and watched as She opened a small green door, and a smaller, much older lady—whose scent identified her as litter-kin—greeted his benefactress happily. The enfolding of arms, stroking of backs, rubbing of cheeks ensued. Humans had such oddly endearing ways of interacting. The cat purred as he watched from under a neighboring porch.

He glanced down the street and noted that the rolling stalker had disappeared, then turned his eyes to watch the Blanket Lady pushing up a large, groaning door beside the house. Moments later she emerged from the darkness in a small rolling Beast of her own. After pulling down the big door, she re-entered the Beast and left, as the cat and the old lady watched.

In the upstairs window the Angry Man watched as well. Seeing this, the cat leapt away from the house and headed back the way he'd come.

The cat knew the Blanket Lady would return when the shadows were longer. And when she did, she might leave another dish of partially-eaten human food for the cat to enjoy. The cat meandered back to the Blanket Lady's warren to wait. Life was good.

Salla walked through the great hall at Ahavas Sholom for the last time, committing the details of the place to memory. Its imposing architecture had always seemed to obstruct her view of the divine; its soaring spaces and magnificent detail bordering, she thought, on the profane. As she entered the prayer hall and ascended the stairs for the women's section, she swept her eyes across the double bank of windows designed to allow G-d's light to stream in. The richly grained wood of the ark and the *bimah* glowed in the sunlight, lending a gravity and quietude appropriate to the setting, but also elevating the hall to something, it seemed, disconcertingly beyond human purpose. The giant *Ner Tamid* above the ark, its perpetual light a symbol of G-d's eternal presence, was fueled by a gas line that was most likely brought into the temple for this reason alone. It reminded Salla of her father's decision to acquire one that was powered by the sun. Or Hadash had been the first synagogue in North America to have a solar powered Eternal Flame. Considered mildly heretic at first, the solar *Ner Tamid* was, over time, adopted by many synagogues with an environmental bent.

Arriving at her customary seat, Salla found she had the women's balcony to herself. This was a relief. She'd tired of the oblique scrutiny of which she'd been the subject every time she performed her weekday prayers at this synagogue. From behind their prayer books, out of the corners of their eyes, the other women stared at Salla—defiantly sporting both phylactery *and* prayer shawl—as though her adherence to the morning prayer made her a object of abhorrence. She knew these women deemed her a lesbian. They'd made it clear that, although they considered women who acted like men to be an aberration, they considered lesbians an abomination in the eyes of G-d.

After her prayers were said and her vestments put away, Salla made for the synagogue's office to her appointment with Rebbe Efron. He was a very busy man—she'd had to book his time several weeks in advance.

"Salla, hello." Although Rebbe Efron was perpetually grave, his demeanor was, today, especially so. He gestured her into the chair opposite his oversized, intricately carved desk. She sat, rolling her chair to a spot where they could see one another between the stacks of paper rising from its surface.

"Rebbe Efron," she began, and then halted, suddenly unsure how to proceed. She'd meant to tell him that she planned to quit Ahavas Sholom, for reasons of her own, deeply held beliefs. She wanted to lecture him about women's role in Judaism generally, and in the future of the Orthodox branch specifically. She wanted to quote to him, of all people, the Torah passage that said "there is no *mitzvah* greater than the *mitzvah* of *tefillin*"; to explain that her observance of this commandment sprang from her devout wish to live the life prescribed by all the teachings she'd absorbed—and that all women should be encouraged to do so. But as she looked into the rabbi's solemn blue eyes, she knew none of it mattered.

"You, young lady, have not heeded my advice." Rebbe Eron's stern voice issued from somewhere within his lush white beard. "This business of marching around, pretending to be a man. It's unseemly. Disruptive."

"I'm sorry?" Salla shouldn't have been surprised.

"The thing is, I'm a very busy man—this is a very busy temple. And, I'm sorry to say, my office has been a revolving door ever since you became a member."

She was only half listening as the Rabbi went on; something about not having time for the affairs of women. As he spoke, she imagined herself rabbi of a busy temple, raising money, sitting on seven or eight different committees, fielding pointless disputes. She shook her head, then, self-conscious, looked into Rebbe Efron's face.

Unheeding, he went on.

"—So I've instructed my secretary to refund your dues. I have decided it is better you should join a *shul* more suited to your...ways. Please." Rebbe Efron stood. He gestured to the door.

Salla had wanted to ask about his two daughters, whether he believed their femaleness prevented the depth of introspection required for effective Torah study. She wanted to discuss the many places in Talmudic literature that supported the education of women. In the end, she said nothing other than goodbye.

What was the point of making a stand that would change nothing?

Rebbe Efron saw her out the door, politely refusing to shake her hand—touching persons of the opposite sex being yet another proscription of the Orthodox branch which Salla had forgotten. In parting, he said goodbye in a kindly tone, and sent her off with the words: "I knew your father well. He was a very good man, may he rest in peace. I'm sure he was very...happy with you."

Salla sighed, nodded, and left the office. As she descended the temple's steps for the last time, she felt free. She wished she hadn't waited so long. She headed to Or Hadash, to aid in the cleanup, with new purpose.

When his Lady still hadn't arrived and the dark had fully settled, the cat returned to the old one's den to wait. After three fitful naps, he heard her Beast back carefully into the yawning maw of the big door. He stretched, arching his back, and sat to wait for her to emerge. She pulled the big door closed, and, as was Her custom, stopped by the old lady's door for a moment of grooming. This done, the Blanket Lady proceeded in the direction of her own den. The cat, pleased to see the usual protocol resumed, trailed behind.

The cat and his Lady travelled the quiet streets, the cat trotting behind in happy anticipation of the meal that awaited. He glanced back when he noted that, once again, the blood-red Beast had joined them. The three continued on together, the cat, the Lady, and the Beast in an orderly procession.

As the Lady entered the long valley between tall buildings, the Beast pounced.

The cat shrank against a wall as the side of the Beast opened and two lunging males leapt out and snatched up his Lady. One held Her mouth to stop the sound as the other grabbed and pulled Her in. The blood red Beast closed around them and roared off down the valley. The cat followed, tracking it for as long as he could until his legs dropped him to the ground. He lay there, panting, as the scent of the Beast disappeared. When he was sure it would not return, the cat crept wearily to the Lady's den, to sit vigil on the porch for Her return. For the next day and a half, he meowed in compulsive fits outside his Lady's door, leaving only to lap water from the puddles collecting in the fresh spring rain, then returning to call for Her again.

"Shooo—off you go, then." The Lady's Man had returned to the Blanket Lady's empty den. Pounding at her door, in a manner that ordinarily would summon her immediately, the Man waited for a moment, then called and pounded some more. The door remained closed. When the Blanket Lady still did not appear, the Man sat on his haunches on the steps. He dug in his coverings and took out a flat white square, which he gazed upon for a long while, turning it over and over, examining both sides carefully. He made a sound of frustration, crumpled the square, and shoved it back in his pelt.

The Man then took up the cat's vigil, banging and yowling at the door every few minutes or so, then sitting back on His haunches, His face in His hands, to wait. This went on until the shadows had grown another length; the Man on the step, the cat watching, hopeful, from the ground beside the porch; both longing in vain for the Lady's return.

After a time, the Man stood, rearing into the air. He snatched the white square from his pelt again and smoothed it, examined it again, then yowled, crumpled the square and threw it to the ground. Then the Man returned to His little rolling Beast to wait some more, His forehead head against its interior wheel. The cat could smell the crumpled square from where he crouched; it hinted of the Lady, and cigarettes, and mold from the underground of a human house.

Sudden movement down the street caught the cat's eye, and he stared at something he had never seen before. A man, the Angry man, was running toward the rolling beast, with Fire! in his hands. The hair stood up on the cat's arched back as the Angry man paused to hurl his Fire! through the running beast's window.

There was a pause, then a roaring heat burst the air. The sky quavered and Fire! billowed from the rolling Beast, flew up around the man's face. Fire! with conflicting scents of cooked flesh and burning garbage, held the cat in thrall.

As stupefied as a mouse staring at its own entrails, the cat watched the Angry one run, then glance behind to see what he'd wrought. Fierce, yet awkward, the Angry man stumbled and fell, his eyes clenching at the Fire! billowing from the rolling beast. He lay there a moment, then yowled, and leapt to his two feet, and was running back *toward* the burning, his forearms waving in the hot air. When he reached the fiery Beast, he held an arm over his face and reached in for the Lady's Man, who screamed at His touch. Throwing the Lady's Man to the ground, the Angry one rolled Him until the Fire! was squeezed from his body. Then, shaking, forearms in the air in front of Him, the Angry Man ran off in the direction he'd come.

Freed from his paralysis, the cat ran too. He would never return.

Chapter 25

*"Hear Oh Israel, here I come
Got this hate strapped to my chest
I'm a loaded gun*

*I'm aiming at myself
A martyr for the cause
Divine retribution for
the suffering you caused*

*Kill the Jew, Kill the Jew
We're killing ourselves,
as we're killing you*

*Kill the Jew, Kill the Jew
We're all fucking terrorists
it's what we fucking do..."*

~Aubrey Bishop
Kill the Jew

Ian sat in a tiny waiting room in the busy triage area of Toronto General's Emergency Room, jumping at every whisper of a curtain. They'd given him no report on Aubrey's condition in well over three hours, an eternity he'd lived as though in a nightmare. He half-heartedly waited to wake up, but was, for once, too sober to deceive himself.

The police had interviewed Ian for hours, refusing to tell him anything about their investigation. They'd made it clear that the attack on Aubrey was to be kept secret, the better to determine who was responsible. Ian feared that suspects with a motive numbered in the tens of thousands.

Finally, a nurse appeared to tell him that Aubrey had been admitted to intensive care, and where he would not be allowed visitors. In his current state, she told Ian gently, it was unlikely that Aubrey would know anyone was there—he was far too drugged to communicate meaningfully. Better to just go home and wait for the hospital's call. Yes, they had Ian's number. No, there was nothing at all he could do at this time. Yes, she promised, they would call him immediately, the moment the doctor had something concrete to tell him. At this point, all the doctor could report was that Aubrey had severe burns to most of his body, and he was alive but his condition was critical.

Ian wept, openly, loudly—his sorrow absorbed by the chaos of the setting—for half an hour before he stood, caught his last sob in his throat, wiped his face on his sleeve, and left. He was convinced that his—as always, foolish—efforts had triggered this tragedy.

The half hour subway ride to Akil's house was excruciating in its mundanity. The doors opened and closed at each stop, the lights flickered on and off, people entered and left, all as if this wasn't the worst day that had ever occurred.

Akil met Ian at his door, surveying his red eyes, his tear streaked face. "Come in. We're expecting you."

"What have you sick fuckers done now!" Ian's voice was just below a shriek.

"What are you doing, man? Screaming shit at my house! Keep it down!" Ian didn't resist as Akil pulled him in the door.

"You know what I fucking mean, Akil! You could have fucking killed him!"

"*Killed him*? What are you talking about?"

"Fuck you," Ian said, quietly. Pushing Akil into the wall, he ran toward the basement steps.

"Hey! Where the fuck do you think you're going?" Akil threw himself at Ian, and took him down, his arms wrapped around Ian's calves. Ian kicked at Akil to free himself, and leapt for the basement.

"Get back here!" Akil's voice cracked as Ian threw open the door and headed down the steps. "Hey—you guys—Ian's here! Hey!"

Ian made it halfway down the basement stairs and then stopped, stunned. The Activists for Allah stared up at him, arranged in a semicircle around the hostage on the floor at their feet.

Tied in oversized knots to a beam in Akil's basement was the unmistakable form of Salla Kahn. Her eyes rolled languidly at the ceiling. Rope cinched her filthy white shawl around her thin arms, bound together her delicate wrists and ankles. Her small, bare feet peered from the hem of her sodden skirt.

"What the fuck is this, now?" Ian shrieked, incredulous and horrified in equal measure. He walked slowly down the remaining steps and knelt beside Salla. She was pale, her face reflecting the fluorescent light.

"This? This here is our funding-raising drive, Ian," Roger D said coldly. "Did you think we was going to organize a bake sale?" At the chuckles of the other Activists, Ian glanced around. Akil fixed his eyes on the ground. The others returned his stare, quietly confident.

"No fucking way! Have you arseholes completely lost your bleeding minds?" Ian could still not accept this as reality, still could not shake the feeling that he was trapped in a bad dream within a worse dream.

"Look, Ian," Akil started, then stopped. Roger D stepped forward, pushing Akil aside.

"Organization like this needs flow, man." Ian's mind reeled at Roger D's reasonable tone. "We can't keep up the good work without cash for supplies."

Ian gaped at him, unable to speak.

"Yeah, Ian. We can barely afford gas, eh?" Akil's tone was reasonable, too. "You know that. Bishop will give us the money, and we'll give her back, no harm, no foul."

"No harm!—Is that a black eye she's got? What kind of bleeding psychos are you? You think you'll get away with this? The cops will hunt you the ends of the earth!"

"Not if you help us out, Ian." Akil's voice was still quiet.

"You didn't really think I was going to fucking co-operate with this insanity, did you?"

"I think you'll co-operate without even trying, man." As though it had been rehearsed, three Activists grabbed him from behind and held him fast. Roger D's deep voice, the musky dank of the basement and a pinprick on his neck were the last sensations Ian would experience for the next eight hours.

Salla awoke in the twilight, at first confused, then gradually remembering why her arms were trapped at her sides, why her clothes were soaked, and why she must, at all costs, remain silent. She was freezing. She ached. Intense thirst took her mind off these other complaints.

As Salla shifted, trying vainly to move her weight to a less sore spot on her aching buttocks, she felt the warmth of another form. Someone leaned at her right, bound to the same beam in the darkened basement. A man, who smelled of cigarette smoke and stale beer and sweat. In the dark she couldn't tell why he seemed familiar. She was able to squirm close enough to touch his left arm with her right, his body chilled, like hers, from hours of contact with the cold concrete floor. Their captors must be upstairs, she thought. They watched CNN incessantly, the volume loud enough that she could differentiate between news and sports and commercial. As she tried to nudge this new captive awake, she heard footsteps on the stairs, and slumped against him. Two of their captors, whom, in silent defiance she'd named Idiot Boy and Tiny Head, were on the landing.

"Hey—what the fuck? Did she move, or what?" Tiny's voice was startlingly deep.

"Yeah man. She was laying that way, before."

"She must be waking up. Remember, wear your mask when you come down here from now on."

"Oh, come *on*, Rog. We look so stupid in those things. Where'd he get them, Walmart?"

"Hey—don't punk out on me. And we don't use names, got it?"

"Sorry, man. She's still down for the count, though."

"Look at her, rubbing up against him like that. Don't he work for her fuck buddy?"

"Yeah. Sick, eh?"

"Stupid Hebrew bitch. Probably just likes him 'cause he's rich. Bishop hates Jews as much as he hates us. She better hope he coughs up the cream, though."

"Yeah, man, that money will go far in the cause, eh?"

"Yeah, the cause." They laughed.

"Man, I hope Ishmael can come through with the drugs. I can't believe we ran out of the Calmpose so soon. It was so much easier."

"Yeah, you're pretty good at the injections, too," Tiny said. "Maybe you should be a doctor."

"Huh. Thanks man. Well, it's easy, but I guess I am good at it, eh?"

"Yeah. Well, they better hope Mister Rock and Roll comes through before Akil's parents get home. Or we'll have to go with Plan B."

"Plan B?"

"Need to know basis, homes. Need to know. Just check and make sure they're tied up nice and tight, dig?"

Salla let herself go limp as Idiot Boy grabbed her in the dark, ostensibly to determine if her bonds were secure, finding several opportunities to pass his hands over her breasts. She forced her revulsion down and willed herself inanimate. As she slumped, she tried not to think about the promising loose spot she'd created around her left wrist.

The terrorists left once they'd deemed her securely tied—and probably, Salla thought, her lip curled in disgust, with a good idea of her bra size.

Five minutes later they reappeared, wearing masks over balaclavas. The masks were child sized, the cheap, plastic variety with holes for the eyes, and a slit for the mouth. Tiny Head's was a poorly-drawn tiger, while Idiot Boy wore a girl bear with a pink bow. Salla pictured herself giving this description to the police and almost laughed through her gag. Until Tiny noticed her eyes flickering between them.

"What the fuck you looking at, bitch?" Salla lolled her head back and closed her eyes, hoping they would think her moment of wakefulness was temporary. At least they gave her water when they forced four pills down her throat.

Then they released her fellow captive from the beam, untied one of his hands, and handed him an empty bottle.

"Here you go, Ian—can't have you pissing all over yourself like she does. Just don't get anything outside of this and we won't have to kill you." They laughed as Salla turned her head away.

He did as he was told, presumably, and they retied him. *Ian?* Salla now remembered meeting him at the wrap party. She couldn't imagine why he was here. Had he come with Aubrey to try to rescue her?

Their captors' next actions so shocked her that she was unable to contain a gasp of dismay.

Ian wore thimbles in his ears; the holes in his earlobes had been stretched to accommodate them. Salla watched as Idiot Boy ripped out a thimble and cut off the loop of Ian's earlobe with a pair of scissors. Ian's scream was so muffled by his gag that their laughter easily drowned him out.

"Man, I have always wanted to do that."

"I know, eh? Next thing you know, he'd be stretching his neck like those black ladies in Africa."

"Yeah, he'll be trying out for National Geographic, eh?"

Nauseous and still confused, Salla was only certain of one thing: she now had someone besides herself to worry about. She had about twenty minutes to work on a new plan for escape before the drugs would take effect, before she fell asleep where she sat.

Five hours later, a repetitive nudging woke Salla from her latest stupor. As she slowly regained control of her body, she saw that Ian was wide awake. Tears were leaking from his eyes, and drops of crusted blood embellished the cherry blossom tattoos on his neck. It seemed he was more resistant to the drugs than she was, but their captors had miscalculated the dosage for both of them.

The dark circles under Ian's eyes stood out against his pale skin, the olive tones in his face green in the faded light. The fuchsia paisley fabric over his mouth—like Salla, he'd been gagged with a pair of socks and a lady's scarf—made him look like a frightened bandit in a children's cartoon. As that thought occurred, Salla smiled around her gag. She pictured the two of them robbing an old-timey bank, mumbling their demands around the socks in their mouths, drool running down their fancy kerchiefs as they waved their guns and pantomimed at the confused teller. The look in Ian's eyes said he thought she was terrified, and this made her laugh even harder. He kept shaking his head, his forehead deeply furrowed—plainly begging her to stop—but the look on his face only resulted in renewed bouts of merriment. In the end, she had to waste precious minutes turned away from him—shaking, the tears leaving her eyes to roll down her cheeks, her face bearing the brunt of her suppressed hilarity—and just ride it out.

Once recovered—to Ian's obvious relief—she showed him that she'd managed to loosen the bonds around her wrists. She'd noticed that one of his fingers was free and she hoped to put it to use. Try as they might, though, they were unable to get their hands close enough together at the proper angle. Discouraged, Salla went back to working on her bonds alone, her arms numb from the hours of effort.

The ever-present mutter from the upstairs television was louder than usual—it seemed to have the captors transfixed. Usually they were laughing and yelling over it. Salla pondered the meaning of this. Could it be that the cops were close? She'd confirmed—by listening carefully when her captors thought she was asleep—that the kidnapping hadn't been reported in the news. Tiny, in particular, seemed disappointed by this slight. Now, though, the captors sounded angry, even panic-stricken.

"What the fuck?" and "What now?" and "Why didn't you think of it yourself?" were shouted over the melee as panic turned outward to blame. The commotion hit a crescendo, and the sound of a scuffle was clear.

She glanced at Ian, and saw his eyes were wide with understanding. He nodded his head at her and then toward her tied hands and then toward the stairs, repeating the motion with increasing urgency. *Hurry*, he was saying, as though something had changed to make their situation dire. What he knew, she couldn't guess, but she redoubled her efforts to free her raw, bruised hands.

Adira hadn't heard from Salla in two days, and she was beside herself with worry. She'd filed a missing persons report with the police, but they hadn't seemed terribly concerned. A young woman who hadn't called her grandmother wasn't exactly breaking news. They told Adira to go home, and leave it to them. They'd keep her posted if the search yielded any information.

Adira waited impatiently, trying Salla's cell phone every ten minutes or so while she watched her stories on the TV. She stood there, clutching her hands together, when 'The Young and the Restless' was interrupted with a news bulletin saying that Aubrey Bishop had been taken to the hospital for reasons the report did not disclose. Despite the reporter's insistence that "no more information is available at this time", Bubbie knew it had something to do with her Salla.

Without telling Yigal, who, thankfully, hadn't bothered to emerge from his room that day, Bubbie went straight to the hospital to see Aubrey. Fighting past the crowd of fans, protesters, police—and a phalanx of reporters and camera men from across the globe—was nothing compared to the obstacle of the duty nurse in the Intensive Care Unit.

"I'm sorry, you say you're not family?"

"No, certainly not, but he's been spending a lot of time with people *in* my family."

"I'm sorry, Mrs. Stein, you said? I really can't let you in to see him. Only family at this time."

"But he was dating my granddaughter, Salla."

The duty nurse hid her smile as she took Bubbie's arm and propelled her gently toward the door. "Yes, we've been hearing from quite a few people who have dated Mr. Bishop. I'm sorry, we're really allowing only family and close associates."

"No, you listen, young lady!" Bubbie used the tone she found most effective when dealing with uncooperative people. "They weren't just dating." Her voice tightened. "Salla loved him. She said he loved her."

The nurse, who had thrown back her shoulders in preparation for battle, paused for a moment. The determined expression on her face faded to concern. "Wait, did you say 'Salla'? Your granddaughter? Would her name be Salla Kahn?"

"Yes. That's her. Is she here? Oh my God." Bubbie's voice rose. "Oh my God! Is she here? Is she here!"

"Uh, no, Mrs. Stein, she's not at the hospital. Could you wait a moment, please? Please. Just sit down, right here, I'll be back in just a moment." The nurse led Adira to a chair and set off at a brisk pace.

Minutes later, an RCMP officer appeared at the doors of the ward and went directly to Adira. "Mrs. Stein? I understand you're Salla Kahn's grandmother?"

"Yes. Where is she? What is going on?"

"Mrs. Stein, I'm afraid we have reason to believe that your granddaughter's been taken hostage," he said, his voice gentle.

"What? Oh my God! But, why? Who?"

"Mrs. Stein. I need you to come with me to look at something, if you could."

After a short walk through the maze-like halls of the hospital, the policeman led her to what appeared to be a temporary office in a supplies cabinet. He had Adira sit in a plastic chair, pulled another close to hers, then, donning translucent plastic gloves, retrieved an envelope from a drawer. From the envelope he removed a letter and a tattered piece of cloth.

"Now, this may seem strange, but I need to know if this has any significance to you." He held out the small piece of cloth for her to see. The dirt on the fine wool did not conceal the thin blue lines running through the fabric. On one edge, a fringe of long knotted threads drooped over the detective's finger. A ragged corner showed it had been ripped from a larger piece.

Adira stared at the scrap for a moment, her mouth opened to reveal yellowed dentures. She closed her mouth, and reached for it, slowly, as though entranced. Then, as though the sound had been pushed out of her, she shrieked, and snatched it from his hand. Standing so abruptly she knocked over her chair, she clutched the piece to her bosom.

"No!" Her voice was authoritative, but her expression was bleak. The detective reached for the piece, but she turned away, clutching the piece with both hands now.

"No! No, no, no, no," she keened.

"Mrs. Stein, please!" The officer's alarm belied his training. He stood, reaching toward her, uncertain.

"No! No, no, no, no. No, no, no, no, no." Adira rocked her body forward and back to the rhythm of her denials.

"Please, what is it? You have to tell us—we need every piece of information available."

"No! Oh dear God! It's Salla's. Her Tallit—her, her, her, her prayer shawl. It belonged to her father!"

As she uttered the words, Bubbie dropped the piece of cloth. Then she gathered the front of her dress in both hands and ripped it wide, exposing an aging gray slip to the officer's formerly jaded eyes.

"My God in heaven!" she screamed. Slowly, deliberately, she reached her hands to her head, and before the officer could stop her, pulled out handfuls of her own hair to the backdrop of her frenzied keening. "No, no, no, no, no! No, no, no, no, no!"

When Adira had finally stopped shrieking—the officer holding her arms to prevent her exposing more flesh or scalp—she went directly into something he'd heard deemed 'acute stress disorder'. From that point on, she was unable to form complete sentences, or understand the words of others. The hospital staff assumed that she suffered from dementia. And this wasn't inaccurate; Salla's kidnapping had driven Adira mad. Her worst fears were true: The world was exactly as terrible a place as she'd suspected. She'd been right all along. This revelation was simply too much for her to bear, and it continued to be so over the events of the next three days. A blessing, for Adira.

She gaped, uncomprehending—the bald patches on her scalp making her look both more sturdy and more frail—as the officer tried to show her the ransom note that had blown, undamaged, from the wreckage of Aubrey's car. It demanded ten million dollars for the safe return of Salla Kahn.

When the officer tried to question her about Salla's friends and acquaintances, Salla's comings and goings, Adira simply drew a blank. She tried to help the nice man, but, she apologized, she simply couldn't concentrate. She seemed to have forgotten why she was here, although she really preferred to stay.

When the hospital tried to locate someone to fetch Adira home, they found that her only listed relative was Salla. So they let her stay, as a sort of guest of Audrey Bishop, until they found some better way to deal with her.

The police never questioned the premise that Aubrey's immolation and Salla's kidnapping were related, which sent them off on several wrong tangents as the days wore on.

That evening, a police search uncovered a second ransom note at Aubrey's hotel, this one containing a thimble, a small piece of human flesh that had yet to be identified, and a demand for a total of twenty million dollars.

Chapter 26

He has sent me to bind up the brokenhearted,
to proclaim freedom
for the captives and release from darkness
for the prisoners, to proclaim
the year of the Lord's favor and
the day of vengeance of our God,
to comfort all who mourn, and provide
for those who grieve in Zion—
to bestow on them a crown of beauty
instead of ashes,
the oil of joy
instead of mourning,
and a garment of praise
instead of a spirit of despair

Isaiah 61:1 - 61:3
The Holy Bible

An eternity of thirst and pain and cold sidled by as Salla picked at her knots. The skin at her wrists was raw, her fingertips were blistered, but she was now able to move her restraints almost to the first knuckle of her right thumb. Ian breathed raggedly beside her. They'd both been unconscious for progressively shorter intervals, but he seemed to find solace in sleep.

With hours to do nothing but work on her bonds, Salla's mind took her places she now lacked the energy to avoid. Was she really suited to the rabbinate? Emily was right—Salla was an unlikely extrovert. She cringed every time her phone rang. If she spied an acquaintance coming toward her on the street she would cross, simply to avoid idle conversation. She thought of her father, and how he spent his days; how she, as Rabbi Kahn, would spend every single day. Committees and meetings and community outreach. Every day in the presence of people—hundreds of people, each of them demanding, and deserving, of her time. Her position as an assistant professor made her limitations clear: Salla preferred email.

Was there another way to fulfill her commitment to G-d? Was there another way to fight the shadow that, despite her scholarship, despite Emily and Bubbie, despite her students and her faith, still dimmed the light within her?

She pictured Aubrey on stage. Aubrey, pontificating. Aubrey naked. Aubrey, finishing a novel he found irritating. She smiled. It was so like him to read every page of a book just because he'd started it; complaining aloud at every contrived plot twist and laughing dryly at every poorly conceived character. Pushing through regardless. It was emblematic of his dogged need to see a thing through—whatever the thing, whatever the outcome. She pictured him draining his fifth martini and ordering another.

She pictured Aubrey singing, Aubrey playing, Aubrey brushing his lips against her belly, heading down. She thought of the way his jaw felt against hers, the way he held her hand in a movie theatre. The way his straight, smooth cock warmed her hand.

She thought of Matalin and Carville—American political consultants working on different sides of the isle—saying they never talked politics at home. They'd been married for over 20 years. Opposite sides of the same coin.

As she followed these thoughts, a voice she hadn't heard before jolted her back to the cold basement floor. A young man followed Idiot Boy down the stairs; Idiot Boy's nasal whine more patient than she'd heard it before.

"Okay, Fareed, so all you got to do is make sure they take the medicine. Okay? I'll show you how this time, and then you can do it yourself when the timer goes off. Do you think you can do that? Yes?"

Through slitted eyes, Salla could see Idiot Boy patting the back of the much smaller man. Fareed had an odd gait, a certain way of cocking his head.

"I bet Roger D would be really proud of you," Idiot Boy said. "Now, remember, they're very bad guys, so if you don't give them the medicine, they'll go do very bad things, eh? Dangerous things. So we can't let them go. Got it?"

"I got it." Fareed's voice was hushed, reverential. "Too dangerish, eh?"

"Right, you got it, man. So, if they try to get away, use the gun, okay? Use the gun to stop the bad guys, because if you don't, they'll kill you."

"The gun," Fareed said, tentative.

"Yes, the gun. I mean it Fareed, these two are from Satan. They may seem quiet and nice, but that's just to trick us. That's how Satan works. Right?"

"Right."

"So you shoot that gun if you have to. Got it?"

"I got it, Ishmael."

"And don't use my name!"

"Oh, no!" Fareed wrapped his arms over his head.

"It's okay. Just don't do it again. Promise?"

"I promise!" Fareed dropped his arms to his side.

The two proceeded down the stairs, Idiot Boy lowering his voice so Salla had to strain to hear. "This is important, too, so listen up. From now on you have to be real quiet, eh? You let me do the talking. I hear you're a good man, so you listen and do as you're told. You be a good man and stay quiet. Okay?"

From the periphery of her vision, Salla watched Fareed nod solemnly. He seemed proud to be given this responsibility.

"And another thing: Don't go outside! No matter what, don't leave this house, even for a second. Stay inside at all times. Got it?"

"Yes, stay inside. I got it."

"Good. Now repeat it."

Fareed looked confused.

"Replead it?"

"No man, I mean, tell me you're not going to go outside, ever."

Salla watched Fareed nod, then allowed her eyes to close all the way.

"No going outside. Never, ever," Fareed said gravely.

"Good man. You're a good man, Fareed."

Idiot Boy, his bear mask askew, untied Salla from the beam, removed her gag, and laid her on her back. She stayed limp, allowing her head to bump the floor. Methodically, with no malice, Idiot Boy held her nose until she opened her mouth. He dropped in four pills, and poured half a cup of water in her mouth, holding her nose until she swallowed. He replaced her gag carefully, then performed the identical ritual on Ian.

The two climbed the stairs without a word—Fareed doing an excited little dance—and as she watched, Salla gave an internal yell of triumph. She'd managed to push the bitter-tasting pills out of her mouth and into her gag. And it seemed Idiot Boy's "good man" was going to be left in charge of things for a while. Perhaps G-d hadn't forsaken her, after all. Enjoying the feeling of the pills against her chin, Salla got back to work freeing her hands.

Hours later, Ian awoke, freezing. His arms ached, his ear was sore, most of his skin, it seemed, was chafed. Worse yet, he couldn't sleep. The hard cold bed kept shaking him, shaking him, shaking him by the arms and by the legs and the head. He fought it, flailing, about to yell out, when two soft hands fell over his mouth, holding his jaw tight. He considered biting, then noticed his head was clutched to a soft breast. As his eyes adjusted to the dim light, his surroundings began to make sense.

"I should have left your gag till last," her lilting voice whispered in his ear.

It was daytime, but it seemed a watery twilight from the small windows of the basement allowed the weak spring sun to leak in. Salla held Ian's head in her lap, waiting for him to shake off his grogginess. He could smell her sweaty hands, unwashed body, urine- and mildew-tainted clothes. Somehow, it comforted him.

"You okay?" Her voice was so sweet and rich. Raspy, yet lilting. No wonder Aubrey'd fallen in love with this woman.

He nodded his head.

"Fully awake?"

He nodded, twice, quickly.

"You going to make any more noise?"

He shook his head and she released his head, then untied the tangled knots around his arms and legs with a hurried precision that evidenced hours of study.

"So," she whispered. "Are you awake enough to run?" Gingerly, favoring her aching side, she kneeled in front of him and searched his face.

Ian took in her black eye and bloodied nose. Her hair stuck out from her face in wild tangles. Her dress was filthy—with God knew what, it didn't bear thinking about. The shawl around her shoulders was ripped and wet. He tried to imagine himself in her eyes. Looking down, he noticed the dried blood that crusted the front of his vintage Ramones t-shirt. He reached for his ear, feeling the wound. Salla's eyes watched, sympathetic and patient. He thought of Giddo's thimble. He frowned.

"Bastards! Salla," he whispered, "we have to escape, right now, yeah? I think they're going to kill us. Today."

"Why today?" Salla looked at him, waited a moment for his response, but he was wordless.

"Never mind," she said, her voice quiet, her eyes intense. "Listen—Ian, right? Everything depends on aggression and speed. We can't afford any stumbles. Can you run?"

"I think so. It's now or never, Yeah?"

"Yeah."

She held out two of the bottles of urine his captors had given him for a toilet. Rags were tied around them—scraps of cloth torn from her skirt. She picked up a can of lighter fluid, which must have been scavenged in a furtive foray through the basement—and soaked the rags. She handed him one of the bottles, held his eyes with hers.

"Prepare for some burns, okay? I'm sorry. It shouldn't be more than superficial."

"Oh God. I don't care."

"Okay—we don't have much time. Just follow me and don't look back. Ready?"

"No," he breathed. "Uh...wait." He bent his head, closed his eyes and wiped his hand over his head, slicking back his hair.

"*Bismillah ir-Rahman ir-Rahim*[49]." He paused, his head bowed, then nodded. "Ready."

Salla looked at him a moment. "*Amein*," she said, nodding, then arranged her shawl around her shoulders.

"*Shema Yisrael, Hashem Elokanyu, Hashem Echad*[50]," she said.

"*Inshallah*[51]," Ian said quietly.

They paused a moment to take simultaneous, deep breaths.

Picking up a disposable lighter from the table, Salla nodded at Ian. "Okay," she said, her voice hard, "let's go."

Salla in front, Ian close behind, they crept up the steps to the closed

---

[49] *Bismillah ir-Rahman ir-Rahim*. Prayer. *Arabic*. Lit. "In the name of God, most Gracious, most Merciful".

[50] *Shema Yisrael, Hashem Elokanyu, Hashem Echad* Prayer. *Hebrew*. Lit., "Hear O Israel, the Lord is our G-d; the Lord is One."

[51] *Inshallah* / in-shah'-lah / Phrase / *Arabic*. Lit., "God willing."

door. The house was still, except for their breathing, their careful creaking.

At the top of the stairs, she lit their rags. Ian held his breath, not considering until now that the door might be locked. Salla gave him a glance, took a deep breath, and threw open the basement door. Brandishing her flaming bottle of piss, she charged headlong into the living room.

"*Lakek et hatahat sheli yah zayin lo arel!*"[52] she shrieked, terror pushing her voice to a supernatural realm. Her hair wild, blood on her face and in her eye, Salla thundered into the living room. The little terrorist sat in front of the television, a small gun laying on the couch beside him, and gawked as she ran past, her trajectory as ragged as the prayer shawl around her shoulders. Ian followed, waving his bottle about in as menacing a manner as possible. Salla screamed a final "*Zayin b'ayin yah pin noteph ziva!*"[53], threw the front door wide open to the world and stepped outside.

"Yeah! Fuck you!" With a dramatic gesture, Ian slammed his bottle on the wooden floor behind him. The flames were instantly quenched as the urine splashed out the mouth of the plastic bottle. He leapt out the door after Salla, into a world transformed by five inches of spring snow.

Across the street, a middle-aged man stared at them, shovel held limply in his hands, his half-cleared sidewalk forgotten. In the picture window behind them, their captor stared too, his face pressed to the glass.

"Well, that was anticlimactic." Having made it as far as her plan had taken them, Salla sat abruptly on the snow-covered steps as though her legs had become unhinged. She scooped up some snow and put it in her mouth.

"You know, I really have to thank Yigal," she said, musing. "Arabic has to be the most effective language on the planet for cursing. It just sounds so angry." Ian lifted her over his shoulder and, barefoot, ran across the street toward the neighbor's house. The man had run inside and was peering out an upstairs window.

Salla continued her one-sided conversation, as though chatting idly to a stranger at a bus stop. "Did you know that in Israel expletives are the same in both Hebrew and Arabic?" she mused. "Israelis and Palestinians

---

[52] *Lakek et hatahat sheli yah zayin lo arel* Phrase. *Arabic*. Vulgar. Lit., "Lick my ass, uncircumcised dick."

[53] *Zayin b'ayin yah pin noteph ziva* Phrase. *Arabic*. Vulgar. Lit. "Dick in your eye, you gonorrhea dripping penis."

swear in the same language. Interesting, don't you think?"

She babbled on in this vein, Ian holding her in his arms to keep them both warm as they quenched their thirst with the snow on the frightened neighbor's porch. The man was refusing to allow them in.

Ian looked at Salla gently, holding her shoulders in his hands, shaking her gently, to get her to meet his gaze. "Listen, Salla. You have to listen to me. Something terrible has happened to Aubrey. He's in hospital, and we have to go to him."

"What. What? What's happened? Was he taken too? Those bastards!" She threw herself from his side and whirled around, as though the threat was everywhere in the cold air.

"No. Salla, please, you must listen. Look at me." Ian waited until her uncertain gaze fixed on his again. "I hate to tell you this now, but Aubrey's car was set on fire. He has very bad burns. He's in hospital, all bandaged up. It's bad. The doctors have knocked him out while they try…" Ian cleared his throat and his voice scratched out the words, "…while they try to save his life."

Salla was silent for a long while, her eyes, unseeing, on his face. "What? I don't understand. Why didn't you tell me this before? Where is he? What hospital?"

"I'm sorry. It's not as if I had a chance before now? He's at Toronto General. Listen, the subway's right around the corner. Let's just go."

Salla stared at him a moment longer, then her eyes focusing, she turned to the neighbor's door. As she slapped it with her open hand Ian noticed her bleeding wrists, her oozing fingertips. He joined her at the door, banging insistently.

"Help! We need help! Please! We need help now!"

"I call police!" They looked upward to the sound and saw the man with the shovel, his head stuck out an upstairs window.

"You go away or I call police! Now!"

"Yes! Call them, please! But we need money for the subway. The subway. That's all. Give me enough for two subway tokens and we'll go away."

"Token? You need token?" The man seemed puzzled that this unlikely pair of home invaders would demand such a sum. He slammed the window closed. Less than a minute later, the window re-opened and a handful of tokens fell into the soft sheet of snow.

"You take. And go away!"

Snatching up two, Salla grabbed Ian's hand and yelled up at their reluctant hero, "Gladly! Now call the police, already. Please! Call them now!"

With that she headed off, dragging Ian in the wrong direction. He pulled her to change course, and, barefoot in the snow, they ran.

Chapter 27

*"Blessed are You, LORD, our God, King of the universe, Who
has sanctified us with His commandments and commanded us
concerning the washing of hands."*
~Berakhah for the Washing of Hands

Yigal lay in Adira's uncomfortable guest bed for three days, reeling
from what he had done. The surge of triumph he'd felt when Aubrey's
Ferrari burst into flames—exactly according to his carefully designed
and executed plan—dissolved the moment the stench of Aubrey's
burning flesh filled the air. When Yigal realized what he'd done, he
simply couldn't follow through. His hands were blistered raw from
pulling Bishop out of the burning car, but he didn't mind. The pain
countered the agony of his other emotions.

As the odor in the air informed Yigal that Aubrey himself was
cooking—his own car an oven—he could not shake the image of his
breathing Aubrey in; inhaling the distilled essence of another human
being. Yigal imagined his own lungs, inside his body, coated on every
surface with the molecules lifting from Aubrey's burning flesh; imagined
his entire body covered in an ointment made of Aubrey's melting fat,
tarred black by the charcoal rising from Aubrey's bones. The longer he
pictured this, the less able he was to not picture it. He felt, as he ran from
Aubrey's inferno toward the end of his own life, that he was bathing in
Aubrey, swimming in him, gorging himself on the life that he'd stolen.

As he'd run toward his Doda's house, he thought of Bishop as he'd been just before the burning—his head resting on the steering wheel of the antique car. It occurred to him that Aubrey might love Salla, too. Might be just as confused and angry and sad, in turns, as Yigal himself was.

Upon reaching his Doda's house, he'd let himself in and retrieved her little snub-nosed gun from the unlocked safe under her bed. He knew it would be there. More than once Adira had asked him, indignantly, "What will the robbers do? Sit politely and wait for me to unlock it? Isn't it better to have it in your hand when you need to use it?"

Clutching Adira's .38 special, Yigal climbed into his lumpy bed in Adira's guest bedroom . Lying there, fully clothed, his shoes still on his feet, he held the gun with both hands and clutched it to his cheek as a child would a security blanket. He rocked, and cried, and hummed a tuneless song.

Chapter 28

May the One who was a source of blessing
for our ancestors, bring blessings of healing upon Aubrey Lionel
Bishop, a healing of body and a healing of spirit.
May those in whose care he is entrusted be
gifted with wisdom and skill,
and those who surround him be gifted with love
and trust, openness and support in their care.
And may he be healed along with all those who are in need.
Blessed are You, Source of healing.

~Mi Shebeirach
Prayer for the Sick

Salla and Ian and Bubbie and Emily sat together in the ICU waiting room, an unlikely group united for an improbable purpose. The arrival of Salla—black eye, tattered hair, filthy clothes and all—had helped to lift Bubbie from her fugue state. They now waited together, and, with the possible exception of Bubbie, hoped for good news about Aubrey.

Every time she looked up, Salla was startled by her reflection, shimmering in the window of the darkened intensive care room across from her. In the greenish light of the ICU, her face looked like a skull. Her cheeks were hollow; her green eyes glowed against the purple bruise around her eye socket. Her filthy hair clung to her cheeks, stood up from her forehead; ran in streaks down her back.

Ian, too, was pale and bruised, his neck tattoos stark against his white skin, his modest Mohawk flat against his skull. His earlobe bled because he couldn't stop touching it; blood trickling down his neck onto the collar of a borrowed jacket. He'd been crying since they arrived. Salla's eyes were dry.

Bubbie wore a hospital gown over her torn housedress, modesty being the first sign of her return to awareness. Salla, holding her hand as they sat together on a hard waiting room couch had not, could not, ask about her torn hair.

Emily was dressed in a motley collection of clothes that suggested she'd dressed in the dark.

The police had come and gone, their questions answered; if not satisfactorily, at least completely. The RCMP had been to Akil's house and questioned his parents, just returned from a visit to relatives in Sudbury. His father, yelling, and his mother, wailing, were informed that their son and his associates were wanted for kidnapping, extortion, and attempted first-degree homicide. If Aubrey died, the word "attempted" would be dropped from the charges.

After the three had been there for several hours, the intensive care nurses, happy to have a conscious patient to work on, forced Salla into a shower and made her put on the clean, warm clothes Emily had brought for her. One insisted on brushing the knots out of Salla's hair, it being a slow night in a generally busy ICU. Salla tolerated these attentions, then impatiently allowed a doctor to examine the bruises she hadn't noticed she was covered in. Once the MD had pronounced her injuries superficial, Salla refused to cooperate further—insisting they all be satisfied with that until good news about Aubrey arrived.

Good news, with the extent of Aubrey's injuries, would be relative. The information thus far had been bleak. He had sustained fourth degree burns over most of his body. His toes were gone; his legs would likely be amputated at the knee. This was if he survived—which, at this point, the doctor told them—was far from guaranteed. He wasn't the healthiest specimen to begin with, and he'd breathed some fire into his lungs. The less severe burns, on his back and his arms, were bad enough by themselves to be life threatening. He was unlikely, the doctor said gently, to ever regain consciousness.

With every word, Salla's dread increased. And then the doctor said something that changed her posture in a subtle way that Bubbie would not detect until it was too late.

"I don't know what was in those bottles, but it wasn't just flammable. Even though Mr. Bishop was able to get out of the car and roll, the stuff kept burning. It was sticky, like…burning honey. The police aren't saying and we can't figure it out."

As the first day dimmed into the second night, an intern with a clipboard approached, asking for a Mrs. Bishop. When Salla stepped forward, he gave her an odd look, then, with gentle urgency, he suggested she hurry to Mr. Bishop's side, to say goodbye. At these words, instead of following the clipboard to Aubrey's bedside, Salla spun around and ran into the night, glass doors of the waiting room swinging shut behind her.

Chapter 29

If you gaze long enough into an abyss,
the abyss will gaze back into you.
~ Friedrich Nietzsche
Beyond Good and Evil

Ten minutes later Salla arrived at Bubbie's house, breathless, her mind ringing. She stopped and looked around, confused, having run the eleven blocks from the hospital, never conscious of what she might do when she arrived.

Standing on the walkway, she noticed the lights in Bubbie's house were off. She searched but the key Bubbie kept under a loose board was missing. Salla hesitated, resting her hand on the front door, jumping when it creaked open at her touch. Bubbie had never, to Salla's knowledge, left her door unlocked.

Salla threw her weight at the door. It flew open and bounced off the wall behind it with a crack.

"Yigal!" she yelled. "Yigal!"

Relentless and methodical, she moved through every room, throwing open every door, looking under the beds, pushing clothes around in their closets as though playing a game of hide and seek.

She stopped in the doorway of the room where Yigal lay, blankets over his head.

"I know you're there. Get up." Her voice was weak, but her tone was deadly.

"I don't want to." Yigal's voice, muffled by the pillow over his head, was both petulant and fearful.

"I said get up." Not waiting, she grabbed the faded quilt he was wrapped in and in one swift movement rolled him off the bed. In the middle of the bed, where his head had been, lay a small gun. She reached over Yigal's cocooned form and picked it up. Her back toward the door, the gun loose in her hand, Salla stared at Yigal's prone figure. She prodded him with her foot.

"Get up, I said. Now."

Yigal struggled to untangle himself and sat up on the floor, facing her.

"What? What do you want from me?" His deep voice cracked at the word "me."

"What have you done? I want to know what you have done." She was still dead calm, but something was rising.

"Nothing! I've done nothing!" Panic creaked through Yigal's deep voice.

"You've killed Aubrey." For the first time since her escape, tears burst from Salla's eyes, from her nose, from her chest. "My Aubrey!" Her voice rose to a shriek. "He's dead!" Even as she said this, she shook her head as if to deny it. She pointed the gun at him and cocked the hammer. Yigal jumped up and moved toward her.

"No! I did what I had to do. I saved you from him. You were being brainwashed and I had to stop him!" He sounded uncertain, but his fists were clenched.

Salla stood staring at Yigal, the gun still pointing at him, her vision awash in tears. She began to shake.

"He's a good man. He was my love." She spoke softly, as though to herself. "He is good."

Yigal's breath caught in his throat, and he held out his raw, bleeding hands to Salla. He stood. "I'm sorry. I didn't mean to. I tried to stop it." His voice broke. "I wish it hadn't happened."

She took a step backward. Yigal advanced.

"You're lying!" Salla said.

"No Salla! Stop!" he cried, his voice echoing that of the difficult boy of her memory.

She squeezed the trigger. The little gun clicked. The quiet sound filled the room. She dropped the gun, staring at her own hands in horror. Yigal stepped toward her, staring at the doorway, where Bubbie stood, panting.

Bubbie reached down and picked up the gun. She thumbed the cylinder release, cocked the hammer twice, and pointed the gun at Yigal.

"No Doda." His voice was now quiet, commanding.

Bubbie spread her legs, breathed in, and squeezed the trigger. Her steady hands put a bullet into the exact center of his face. It exited his brain three inches above the nape of his neck, killing him instantly. His body joined the crumpled bedclothes on the floor.

Bubbie tucked the gun into her bosom, wiped her hands on her skirt, and went to the front porch, to wait.

Epilogue

Making a scene
of his renegade days
Taking the wrong kind of converts
Confusing the crazies
all the wrong ways
I was always
an improbable stalwart

~Aubrey Bishop
Where it all Went

In a sickly haze, the latest hit pop song playing in constant rotation, the cold-pack bandages moving skin-searing agony to bone-deep ache— the images flitting through Aubrey's mind were more vivid than usual.

A year in Israel, not lived, and yet remembered: Sipping freshly squeezed pomegranate juice in a Tel Aviv market. Contradictory Salla, now sleek in a black bikini, trolling for shells along the Red Sea; now haggling in perfect Hebrew over an antique coffee grinder; now covered and wrapped and *davening*[54] at the front of a synagogue that had been there for over a thousand years.

Flames springing; sharp, piercing pain—receding, then returning, like a series of quick roundtrips to hell. His car, his beautiful car, paint curling from her body like scales escaping a fish.

A scruffy orange tom cat curling in his lap, kneading his thighs, purring and rubbing the side of its cheek on Aubrey's blackened fingers.

Salla's lovely profile, her face tilted at the movie screen, tears on her cheeks. Her whispered celebratory blessing. The way she stroked his belly and thighs before touching him there, and then there. His ever-faithful erection surging, then screaming?—was that *his* voice? No.

Salla's guitar, burning, then not, in the fire bursting from his car. Ian's face, too close, his voice, too far away, his eyes afloat in tears:

---

[54] *davening* / da'-vin-ing / v. *Hebrew*. Reciting prayers in the Jewish liturgy, sometimes with a forward rocking motion.

"I love you, man. I love you. Always have, old son. I wanted to make sure I told you that. I love you. You know that, yeah?"

Salla's ordination ceremony, her yarmulke slipping from its clasp to the side of her silky head, his pride in her inhibiting his ability to swallow.

Salla, leading the congregation on her first day in her new synagogue.

Now gray, in a different yarmulke on a much later day, Salla opening the gates of heaven with music from a ram's horn, blown expertly from her rightful place at the ark.

His first child, a girl named Aviva after Salla's father, waving tiny, fat hands like anemones in the sea of her cradle. He watches her hands catch her attention, then, fluttering to her sides, letting it go. Aviva's first smile. Her first steps, her first day of school, her only wedding day.

Another child, a boy who looks like Salla, sporting her long bones, cocking her crooked grin: an entire life lived within the confines of Aubrey's burning, swollen head.

Aubrey's first Oscar, gathering dust on their mantle, flickering in the firelight. Wearing a temporary yarmulke of its own, fashioned from a walnut shell placed there by his irreverent son.

His son's skepticism never slaked, his natural curiosity perpetually beckoning, they spend this momentary lifetime investigating the smallest insects and the greatest mysteries; never once arriving at an answer that satisfies the boy, but enjoying the search all the while.

The boy, now a man; an evenly matched games of chess. The daughter, his eyes, Salla's length, a face alight with daughters of her own. Music-filled family evenings, music shaking the walls of an aging London brownstone. Three grandchildren, two of them blessed with Salla's crooked smile.

Salla, at seventy-five, laughing; playing a seasoned guitar; tickling a squirming grandchild. Her face etched by decades of their very good life, her hands veined and spotted, her once milk-filled breasts dry and flat. Holding one heavily knuckled old hand of his in her lap, kissing his hoary old cheek; her eyes young in her dear weathered face.

A new quiet fell around him; in his final, greatest escape from reality, Aubrey Bishop emerged, free.

The Mourner's Kaddish

יִתְגַּדַּל וְיִתְקַדַּשׁ שְׁמֵהּ רַבָּא. בְּעָלְמָא דִּי בְרָא
כִרְעוּתֵהּ. וְיַמְלִיךְ מַלְכוּתֵהּ בְּחַיֵּיכוֹן וּבְיוֹמֵיכוֹן
וּבְחַיֵּי דְכָל בֵּית יִשְׂרָאֵל בַּעֲגָלָא וּבִזְמַן קָרִיב.
וְאִמְרוּ אָמֵן:

Yit-gadal v'yit-kadash sh'may raba b'alma
dee-v'ra che-ru-tay, ve'yam-lich mal-chutay
b'chai-yay-chon uv'yo-may-chon uv-cha-
yay d'chol beit Yisrael, ba-agala u'vitze-
man ka-riv, ve'imru amen.

יְהֵא שְׁמֵהּ רַבָּא מְבָרַךְ לְעָלַם וּלְעָלְמֵי עָלְמַיָּא:

Y'hay sh'may raba me'varach le-alam uleh-
almay alma-ya.

יִתְבָּרַךְ וְיִשְׁתַּבַּח וְיִתְפָּאַר וְיִתְרוֹמַם וְיִתְנַשֵּׂא
וְיִתְהַדָּר וְיִתְעַלֶּה וְיִתְהַלָּל שְׁמֵהּ דְּקֻדְשָׁא. בְּרִיךְ
הוּא. לְעֵלָּא (וּלְעֵלָּא) מִן כָּל בִּרְכָתָא וְשִׁירָתָא
תֻּשְׁבְּחָתָא וְנֶחָמָתָא דַּאֲמִירָן בְּעָלְמָא. וְאִמְרוּ אָמֵן:
יְהֵא שְׁלָמָא רַבָּא מִן שְׁמַיָּא וְחַיִּים עָלֵינוּ וְעַל כָּל
יִשְׂרָאֵל. וְאִמְרוּ אָמֵן:

Yit-barach v'yish-tabach, v'yit-pa-ar v'yit-
romam v'yit-nasay, v'yit-hadar v'yit-aleh
v'yit-halal sh'may d'koo-d'shah, b'rich hoo.
layla (ool-ayla)* meen kol beer-chata
v'she-rata, toosh-b'chata v'nay-ch'mata, da-
a meran b'alma, ve'imru amen.

Y'hay sh'lama raba meen sh'maya v'cha-
yim aleynu v'al kol Yisrael, ve'imru amen.

עֹשֶׂה שָׁלוֹם בִּמְרוֹמָיו הוּא יַעֲשֶׂה שָׁלוֹם עָלֵינוּ
וְעַל כָּל יִשְׂרָאֵל. וְאִמְרוּ אָמֵן:

O'seh shalom beem-romav, hoo ya'ah-seh
shalom aleynu v'al kol Yisrael, ve'imru
amen.

~~~~~~~~~~~~~~~~~~~~~~~~

*Glorified and sanctified be God's great name throughout
the world which He has created according to His will.
May He establish His kingdom in your lifetime
and during your days, and within the life of the entire
House of Israel, speedily and soon; and say, Amen.*

May His great name be blessed forever and to all eternity.

*Blessed and praised, glorified and exalted, extolled and honored, adored and
lauded be the name of the Holy One, blessed be He, beyond all the blessings
and hymns, praises and consolations that are ever spoken in the world;
and say, Amen.*

*May there be abundant peace from heaven, and life,
for us and for all Israel; and say, Amen.*

*He who creates peace in His celestial heights, may
He create peace for us and for all Israel; and say, Amen.*

1 *a chorbn* / a-'khor-bin / phrase. *Yiddish.* "What a disaster!"

2 *Alayka salām* / ah-lech'-hem sah'-lam / phrase. *Arabic.* Response to a greeting, lit., "And upon you be peace."

3 *Allahu Akbar* / a'-la a-wahk'-ba / phrase, *Arabic.* Lit. "God is great."

4 *Araboushim* / ah-rab'-bU-shEm / n. *Hebrew.* A racial epithet used against Palestinians. Roughly equivalent to "Dirty Arab."

5 *As salāmu alayka* / a-sah'-lam ah-lech'-hem / phrase. *Arabic.* A greeting, lit., "May peace be upon you."

6 *Barukh atah Adonai* / ba-rUk' a-tah' a-doh-nI'... / phrase. *Hebrew.* Lit. Blessed are You, LORD our G-d, King of the universe, Who has kept us alive, sustained us, and enabled us to reach this season.

7 *bihmah* / bE'mah. / n. *Hebrew.* A raised platform in a synagogue from which the Torah is read.

8 *Bismillah ir-Rahman ir-Rahim* / bEss'-ma-la E-rahk-man' E-ruh-hEm' / phrase. *Arabic.* The first words of the Holy Qur'an, lit. "In the name of God, most gracious, most merciful."

9 *Bismillah ir-Rahman ir-Rahim.* Prayer. *Arabic.* Lit. "In the name of God, most Gracious, most Merciful".

10 *bubbeleh* / bU' beh-lah / n. *Yiddish.* Literally, "little grandmother." A term of endearment for women of any age.

11 *davening* / da'-vin-ing / v. *Hebrew.* Reciting prayers in the Jewish liturgy, sometimes with a forward rocking motion.

12 *dybbuk* / 'dEbuhk / n. *Yiddish.* A malevolent spirit from Jewish mythology, believed to be the soul of a dead person, that takes possession of another's body.

13 *fercockt* / fer-cokt' / adj. *Yiddish.* All screwed up. *Vulgar.*

14 *fershlugina* / fer-shlug'-in-er / adj. *Yiddish*: Beaten up, no good.

15 *goy* / goi / n. *Yiddish.* Non Jew. Derogatory.

16 *halaka* / ha-la'kah / n. *Hebrew.* Talmudic literature that deals with law and with the interpretation of the laws in the Hebrew Scriptures.

17 *hijab* / 'hE-jab / n. *Arabic.* Head covering worn by a Muslim woman beyond the age of puberty, in the presence of men to whom she is unrelated.

18 *Hok a chainik* / hok'a-chainik / phrase. *Yiddish*: Literally, to "hit a tea kettle." Colloquially, to make a useless noise; to talk nonsense.

19 Huh-luhk'-khuh / phrase. *Hebrew.* Lit., "the path that one walks." Jewish law; i.e. the complete body of rules and practices that Jews are bound to follow.

20 *Inshallah* / in-shah'-lah / Phrase / *Arabic.* Lit., "God willing."

21 *Kabbalah* / kah-bahl'-lah / n. *Hebrew.* The study of Jewish mysticism, traditionally taught only to those over forty years old, who were thoroughly versed in Torah and Talmud.

22 kee'pah / n. *Hebrew.* A skull cap, yarmulke. Used by Jewish men and boys (and Reform women) to cover the head in the presence of God.

23 *keffiyeh* / keff-E'-yeh / n. *Arabic.* A headdress worn by Arab men, made from a square of cotton fabric, held on with a band tied around the crown of the head.

24 *koorvah* / kUr'-vah / n. *Hebrew.* Promiscuous woman; whore.

25 *Lakek et hatahat sheli yah zayin lo arel* Phrase. *Arabic.* Vulgar. Lit., "Lick my ass, uncircumcised dick."

26 *Lo teer tsakh* / lO-tere-sach' / phrase. *Hebrew.* Lit., "Not, shalt thou murder."

27 *mensch* /mensch / n. *Yiddish.* A person, male, who is known to possess both great learning and integrity.

28 *mikvah* / mik'-vey / n. *Hebrew.* A purification ritual requiring full immersion in water obtained from natural sources.

29 *minyan* / min'yan / n. *Hebrew.* The quorum required for Jewish communal worship that consists of ten male adults in Orthodox Judaism and ten adults of either sex in Conservative and Reform Judaism.

30 *mishegoss* / mish'-ah-goss / n. *Yiddish*. Crazy or senseless activity or behavior; craziness.

31 *mishugina* / me-shug'gen-ner / adj. *Yiddish*. Crazy; senseless. n. One who is crazy.

32 *mishugina* / mish-uh-gin'-ah / adj. *Yiddish*. Crazy.

33 *mitz·vah* / noun. *Hebrew*. A good deed done from religious duty.

34 *momzer* / mom'-zer / 1. adj. *Yiddish*. Despicable, 2. n. *Hebrew*. Child born of an inappropriate sexual relationship, e.g. born fatherless.

35 *nafka* / naf'-kah / n. *Yiddish*. Whore.

36 *Nudge* / nUdj / n. *Yiddish*: Affectionate term for a nag or pest.

37 *old Blighty* / old bly-tee / *English*. British slang for the city of London.

38 *sabra* / tsa'-bar / n. *Hebrew*. Lit. A thorny desert plant, with a sweet interior. Colloquially, a native-born Israeli.

39 *seder* / sA'-duhr / n. *Hebrew*. A ritual dinner held twice during Passover, during which prayers are said and symbolic foods are eaten.

40 *semicha* / sem-E'-khah / n. *Hebrew*. Derived from "to be authorized", in reference to the ordination of a rabbi.

41 *shanda fur die goyim* / shan'-da fir die goy'-yim / phrase. *Yiddish*. Lit. "a shame before the nations"; colloquially, embarrassing behavior engaged in by a Jew, within view of non-Jews.

42 *Shema Yisrael, Hashem Elokanyu, Hashem Echad* Prayer. *Hebrew*. Lit., "Hear O Israel, the LORD is our G-d; the LORD is One."

43 *Shi-nah' tO-vah'* / phrase. *Hebrew*. Lit. "May you be inscribed (in the Book of Life) for a good year." Colloquially, "Happy New Year".

44 *shiva* / shiv'-ah / n. *Hebrew*. A ritualized grieving, observed after the death of a loved one.

45 *Sh'ma* / shmah' / n. *Hebrew*. A reference to prayer, from the Hebrew words Shema Yisrael; literally, "Hear, O Israel."

46 *shUl* / n. *Yiddish*. Synagogue.

47 *sid'ur* / n. *Hebrew*. A Jewish prayer book designed for use chiefly on days other than festivals and holy days; a daily prayer book.

48 *Surah* / sU-rah' / n. *Arabic*. Any chapter or verse of the Qur'an.

49 *ta'leeth* / n. *Hebrew*. A shawl-like garment with fringes,at the four corners, worn around the shoulders by Orthodox and Conservative (and sometimes Reform) Jews during certain prayers.

50 *tefillin* / tih-fil'-lin / *Hebrew*. Two, small, black leather boxes, containing biblical passages, worn on the left arm and on the forehead during the weekday morning prayer. Traditionally worn only by Jewish males past the age of 13, the practice is increasing amongst observant Jewish women.

51 *tichel* / tihk-'el / n. *Hebrew*. Head covering worn by a conservative Jewish woman after marriage, in the presence of anyone other than her husband.

52 *wudhû* /wu'-dU / n. *Arabic*. The Islamic practice of cleansing parts of the body in preparation for prayer or for handling and reading the Qur'an.

53 *Yahudi* / yah-hU'dE / n. *Arabic*. Jew.

54 *Zayin b'ayin yah pin noteph ziva* Phrase. *Arabic*. Vulgar. Lit. "Dick in your eye, you gonorrhea dripping penis."